SWEET NOTHINGS

Recent Titles by Trisha Ashley

EVERY WOMAN FOR HERSELF
GOOD HUSBAND MATERIAL
THE URGE TO JUMP

THE GENEROUS GARDENER *
SWEET NOTHINGS *

* *available from Severn House*

SWEET NOTHINGS

Trisha Ashley

This first world edition published in Great Britain 2007 by
SEVERN HOUSE PUBLISHERS LTD of
9–15 High Street, Sutton, Surrey SM1 1DF.
This first world edition published in the USA 2007 by
SEVERN HOUSE PUBLISHERS INC of
595 Madison Avenue, New York, N.Y. 10022.

British Library Cataloguing in Publication Data

Ashley, Trisha
Sweet nothings
1. Humorous stories
2. Love stories
I. Title
823.9'14 [F]

ISBN-13: 978-0-7278-6478-9 (cased)
ISBN-13: 978-1-84751-002-0 (paper)

Typeset by Palimpsest Book Production Ltd.,
Grangemouth, Stirlingshire, Scotland.
Printed and bound in Great Britain by
MPG Books Ltd., Bodmin, Cornwall.

This one is for Robin,
with my love

One
Totally Bananas

'Reading your love letters?' Tom said, coming into the kitchen from the yard and finding me flicking through my postcard album which, unlike most people's, has the messages facing out, rather than the pictures.

The cards are all from his cousin Nick, it's true, but there's nothing personal in them, unless you think that addressing them to 'The Queen of Puddings' is lover-like, rather than a sarcastic reference to one of my major preoccupations.

No, shoehorned into every last bit of available space on the back of the postcards, in tiny, spiky handwriting, are interesting recipes from wherever Nick happened to find himself. This is something he started doing soon after taking off around the world at eighteen, notebook and taste buds at the ready, and although there was a slight halt in their arrival after my engagement to Tom was announced, they resumed with a large panorama of Avignon bearing an interesting twist on the traditional wedding cake . . . and really, I'd never have thought of doing that with the marzipan, but I used it and it came out *very* well.

'I'm looking for a recipe for halvah actually, Tom,' I said evenly, since he was just trying to provoke me. 'The only love letters I've got are from you, and are so old the ink's faded.'

'So you say, but I don't find you poring over mine all the time, like you do over Nick's precious postcards,' he said, turning to wash his hands at the kitchen sink.

I dished out a bowl of casserole (but no starter because he hates bananas) and put it on a tray, since he now takes all his meals alone in front of his giant TV.

He picked up the bowl of stew and stared into it like a sibylline oracle, but the only message he was likely to read was *eat this or go hungry*. 'What are these black things, decayed sheep's eyeballs?'

'Prunes. It's Moroccan lamb tagine.'

From his expression you would have thought I'd offered him a dish of lightly seasoned bat entrails.

'And I suppose *Nick* gave you the recipe. What else has he given you?' he said unpleasantly. 'Or aren't I supposed to notice that your son looks more like him than me?'

'Oh, for God's sake, don't start on that again!' I snapped, adding recklessly, 'You know very well why Jasper looks like Nick, just as *you* look like Great-uncle Roly – your mother must have been having an affair with Leo Pharamond while she was still married to her first husband. Why don't you ask her?'

Tom went livid and hurled the plate of hot casserole in my direction with enormous force, but I instinctively ducked and it hit the wall with a crash, sending sharp fragments and splatters of food everywhere. My cheek stung, and when I put up a hand to my face it came away bloody.

'Never, *ever*, malign my mother's name again!' Tom hissed viciously, just like a Mafia villain in a bad film. 'Do you hear me?'

There was a silence only broken by the occasional slither and plop of a descending prune. I had heard him all right, but my eyes had fallen on the rack of kitchen knives and I was fighting a strong urge to eviscerate him. I am an earth mother of the volcanic sort.

However, despite being almost as tall as Tom and of athletic build, my strength is no match for his when he's in one of his rages, so I managed to restrain myself. In any case, were I to succeed in my aim, the effect on poor Jasper would be catastrophic.

Instead, I walked right past him and out of the door, dabbing my face with the hem of my T-shirt as I went, and headed towards the village. Luckily it was early evening and few people were about, for the Pied Piper of TV dinners had called them away, using the theme tune of the popular soap series, *Cotton Common*, as lure.

* * *

Annie Vane, my best friend, lives in a Victorian red-brick terraced cottage in the main street of Middlemoss, so I didn't have far to go for refuge.

'Lizzie – good heavens, what's happened?' she demanded, opening the door to find me stained, spattered and bleeding on her doorstep. 'Have you had an accident? Come in, quickly!'

'Sort of,' I said, wadding up my T-shirt against my cheek again to avoid messing the floor, and following her into the kitchen. She handed me a box of tissues: 'Use these, while I get a bowl and some lint.'

Lint? It all sounded very *Gone With The Wind* – but then, she has all the Girl Guide badges and I don't suppose the first aid one has changed for quite a while.

I sank down on the chair, my legs suddenly going wobbly. Trinity, Annie's three-legged mutt, regarded me lambently from her basket, tail thumping. 'Tom flew into one of his rages and lobbed his dinner at my head – a piece of the plate must have cut me.'

'At your *head*?' she echoed, dabbing away gently at my face. It stung and the water in the bowl turned pink. 'Lizzie!'

'I'm not sure he was aiming, he just totally lost it. And it wasn't as if I'd offered him the banana, ham and cheese bake starter, either – it was a lovely lamb tagine.'

She was frowning. 'This cut is deep. Look, the surgery will still be open, let me run you down and see what the nurse thinks. You don't want a scar on your face, do you?'

So, attired in one of her voluminous cardigans to hide the gore (a bilious green, with loosely attached knitted pink roses), Annie whipped me down to the doctor's, where the practice nurse examined my face and pulled the gash together with little white strips, like parcel tape. It was small but deep, hence the bleeding, but she thought it would heal cleanly.

Then we went back to Annie's and drank Remy Martin, which she keeps in stock because her father, a former vicar of Middlemoss, always swore by it in times of crisis. She is a Spinster of the Parish, and a creature of habit. Many habits – brandy is one of her better ones.

I described the argument to her and she said: 'It's gone way beyond verbal abuse now, Lizzie – he's getting violent, and you really can't put up with that kind of thing!'

'I know. I'm just glad Jasper wasn't there,' I said, topping my glass up with a slightly trembling hand. 'He's gone straight from the archaeological dig to a friend's house, and won't be back till about ten.'

'His exam results should be here any time now, shouldn't they?'

'Yes, the nineteenth – only a couple more days.' I sipped my brandy and sighed. 'He doesn't go out in the evenings much lately – I think he's trying to protect me by being around. Even though I will miss him, it will be such a relief to have him safely off to university at the end of September, because I live in dread that Tom will suddenly tell him to his face that he doesn't think he is his son. That would be even more hurtful than ignoring him, the way he does now.'

'I'm sure it's all the effect of Tom's illness, and then the operation, Lizzie,' Annie said.

'I expect it is – all these strange ideas slowly took hold just before the brain tumour was finally diagnosed. But it makes you wonder if they were already lurking in the back of his mind and all that sweet, feckless charm he used to have was a front, not the real Tom at all.'

Annie pondered the idea. 'No, he *was* very sweet as a boy . . . as long as he got his own way, which he mostly did, as far as I recall. And he was nice with Jasper for the first few years, wasn't he?'

'Oh, yes, when he remembered he existed,' I said slightly bitterly. 'Until this strange idea that I'd had a fling with Nick took hold.'

'You *did* have a fling with Nick,' she pointed out fairly.

'Oh, come on, Annie! I was only eighteen, he was twenty-two and it lasted exactly two stormy weeks before we both realized it was a mistake: we never stopped arguing! *And* he made it clear he was going off abroad again, he wasn't changing his life plan for *my* sake. I didn't see him again until the day I got married to Tom, and he turned up to that with Leila in tow.'

'Tom and Nick were never as close after that, were they? I always thought Tom felt a bit jealous of Nick, being a real Pharamond and Roly's grandson, whereas he was just a Pharamond by name because his mother had married one.'

'I suppose they grew apart – they are very different – but

Nick often dropped in during those first years when we lived in Cornwall, and he's always kept sending me the postcards, so we sort of stayed friends.'

'It's odd how things turn out,' mused Annie. 'You always had much more in common with Nick than with Tom.'

'How on earth can you say that? The only thing Nick and I have ever had in common is a love of food, even if mine is more plebeian than *cordon bleu.*'

Food has played an important part in both our families: the search for a good meal was the downfall of my parents and would be the downfall of my figure were I ever to stop moving long enough for the fat to settle. As to the Pharamonds, the gene for cooking was introduced into the family by a Victorian heir who, having married one Bessie Martin for her inheritance, died of a surfeit of home-cooked love some forty years later, with a fond smile on his lips and a biscuit empire to hand on to his offspring.

'You've both got short tempers and love Middlemoss more than anywhere else on earth,' Annie contributed, 'and while I know that Jasper *is* Tom's son, it's unfortunate that as he gets older he looks more and more like Nick.'

'Well, you know *my* theory: Tom's mother must have been having an affair with Leo Pharamond even before her first husband was killed. But Tom just flies into a complete rage if I say anything against his sainted mother. That's why he threw the plate at me.'

'Leo Pharamond and her first husband were racing drivers, weren't they? And were *both* killed in car crashes!'

'There seemed to be a lot of fatal crashes in the early days,' I agreed. 'Someone told me they called her the Black Widow after the second one died, but when she married a third one he promptly gave it up and whisked her off back to Argentina. He seemed a horribly jealous type too, and that's why poor old Tom was packed off to boarding school over here at eight, and farmed out to Pharamond Hall in the holidays.'

'It must have affected him,' Annie said kindly. 'And he's hardly seen his mother over the years, has he?'

'No, or his half-siblings. He blames it all on his stepfather – won't hear a word against his mother. Come to that, I've only met her a couple of times and we never took to each other.'

'You'd think she would at least be interested in her grandson!'

'Apparently not. I used to send his school photos, but never got any response, so I gave up. You know, with all this rejection, it's wonderful that poor Jasper isn't bitter and twisted too.'

'Yes, but *we* all love him: me, Roly, even Mimi.'

I considered Unk's unmarried sister Mimi, who is not at all maternal and whose passions are reserved for the walled garden she tends behind the hall. 'Yes, she does seem to like him, despite him not being any form of plant life.'

'And Nick – Jasper and he do get on well.'

'When he sees him, which is an occasional Sunday lunch up at the hall, these days.'

'How difficult it all is!' Annie said, which was the understatement of the year. 'The real Tom, before he got ill, wouldn't have been so nasty and violent to you, and although I've always agreed with Mum and Dad that marriage should be forever, he's not at all the man you married.'

'No, more like someone wearing the mask of Tom's face and personality, so it's disconcerting when it slips and a vicious stranger peeps out. What seemed natural before, like all that charm, good-humour and fecklessness, now appears calculating and manipulative. And *I* thought love was forever too, Annie – but with the same person you married.'

'Remember how wonderful it was after the operation, when he looked at you and said "Lizzie?" for the first time, and we knew he was going to be all right?' she reminded me sentimentally.

'Yes, and at that moment I even felt that we might recapture the love we once had for each other – but that must have been a burst of insane euphoria due to relief that he was going to live, because it was all downhill from there. It was like you'd got to the end of *Love Story* and used all the tissues, then Ali gets up and says, "Hang on, there's another reel to go and this time I'm going to play it *differently*!" and does it all over again as though she's auditioning for the mother in *Psycho*.'

'Wasn't Mother really a man in drag?' Annie said, frowning.

'And maybe Tom was really a wolf in sheep's clothing all along?' I suggested bitterly.

'What are you going to do, Lizzie? You know you and Jasper can move in here any time you like, and stay as long as you want.'

'I know, and it's very kind of you,' I said gratefully, not pointing out that her cottage isn't much bigger than a doll's house. Basically it is two tiny rooms up and down, crammed so full of bric-a-brac you can hardly expand your lungs to full capacity without nudging something over. Jasper, when he visits, tends to stand in the corner with his arms folded so as not to damage anything. He still banged his head on a hanging basket of dried lavender last time.

'I mean to try and hang on until I've got Jasper settled in at university if I can – though if Tom gets even worse I might have to take you up on that, but *very* temporarily. I will still need to make a home for Jasper to come back to, so I might have to get a job stacking supermarket shelves or something so I can rent a place. I'm not really qualified to do anything else.'

'Yes, but you could still write the Perseverance Chronicles, that will help,' she reminded me.

'Not a lot – they don't make much money and I'm running late with the next, what with one thing and another.'

I wrote my first Perseverance Cottage Chronicle in a desperate bid to make some money soon after we were married, influenced by all those lovely, cosy self-sufficiency-in-a-Cornish-cottage books. Although I missed the high tide of their popularity, I did get published on the last eddies. When we moved back to Lancashire I just renamed the new cottage and carried on, and my small but loyal band of fans did too.

'I suppose it's hard to think up funny anecdotes to go between the recipes and tips, what with all the worry about Tom,' she agreed. 'Still, there is always Posh Pet-sitters – business is expanding *hugely* since I added general pet feeding and care to the dog walking, so you may not need another job, you can just help me.'

Annie set up Posh Pet-sitters a few years ago to make some extra money, and I help her out with it when she is busy. Her father used to be the vicar here, but he and his wife are alleviating the boredom of retirement by doing VSO work in Africa. They are lovely and pretty well took me in after I was orphaned – which is how I first came to meet Tom, parked at Pharamond Hall for the school holidays when his mother married her jealous Argentinean and started a whole new life out there that seemed not to include her firstborn.

That made us both orphans, in a way.

Nick was there sometimes too, since Roly is his grandfather, but he was older and rather aloof. Still, I do have happy memories of the four of us playing tennis and utilizing the lily pond up at the hall as a swimming hole.

The posh bit in Posh Pet-sitters comes from Annie's accent which, like mine, is fairly plummy due to being incarcerated from the age of eleven at St Mattie's, a terribly progressive boarding school in Scotland. There, all the pupils were forced to take elocution lessons and came out roughly homogenized, so you can recognize an ex-pupil as soon as they open their mouths. (And we can declaim poetry like nobody's business.)

The Posh Pet-sitters business does seem to be building up nicely, especially now the actors from the long-running soap drama, *Cotton Common*, set in a turn-of-the-century Lancashire factory town, have suddenly 'discovered' the three villages that comprise the Mosses. Where they led, other minor celebrities followed, since although off the beaten track we are within commuting distance of Manchester, Leeds, Liverpool and the M6, and in pretty countryside just where the last beacon-topped hills slowly subside into the fertile farmland that runs to the coast.

Some of them live in the new walled and gated estate of swish detached houses in Mossrow, but others snap up whatever comes on the market, including the flats in the former Pharamond's Butterflake Biscuit Factory, and any of the old cottages and farms that come up for sale.

'Did you go and see Rob Rafferty yesterday?' I asked, suddenly remembering how excited Annie had been at getting a call from the singer-turned-actor who plays Seth Steele, the rugged mill owner in *Cotton Common*. (All that alliteration must have been too much for the producers of the series to resist!)

He has bought the old rectory, a large and rambling Victorian building with a brick-walled garden, in severe need of TLC and loads of cash, while the new vicar is housed in an unpretentious bungalow next to the church.

Annie's pleasantly homely face took on an unusually rapt – almost holy – expression. 'Oh, *yes*! He's . . . he's . . .'

'Sexy as dark chocolate?' I suggested. 'Toothsomely rum truffle?'

'Just – wonderful,' she said simply. 'It was as though a . . . a golden light was shining all around him, he has such charisma.'

'Bloody hell!' I stared at her, but she was lost in a trance.

'Lizzie, he is so kind, too – when I explained that I used to live at the vicarage, he took me around and showed me all the improvements he's made, and told me what else he was going to do, and then he just handed me the keys to the house so he could call me up any time to go and exercise or feed his dog.'

'Well, if your clients didn't do that, you wouldn't be able to get in,' I said dryly. 'What sort of dog does he have?'

'A white bull terrier bitch called Flo – very good-natured, though I might have to be careful around other dogs.'

'What's the new vicar like?' I asked, but she hadn't noticed, being full of Rob Rafferty to the point where her bedazzled eyes couldn't really take in another man. However, a crush on a handsome actor is not likely to get her anywhere.

Annie *was* once engaged but was jilted, if not at the actual altar, certainly with her feet practically on the carpeted aisle. Since then she has confined her affections to unsuitable – and unattainable – actors, which are much safer.

Until now.

'I've heard he is single – *and* has red hair,' I said encouragingly since, despite being sandy-haired herself, she has a weakness for redheaded men.

'He hasn't got red hair, he's blonde!' she protested indignantly, and I saw that she was still thinking of Rob. Perhaps I ought to watch an episode of *Cotton Common* and see what all the excitement is about.

Eventually Annie ran me home, since I wanted to be there when Jasper returned. She was going to stay with me until then – as my human shield – since Tom rarely reveals his new nasty side in front of others, even old friends like Annie. But there was no need: Tom, his van, and some of his clothes had vanished. He'd locked me out, but not only does Annie have our key on her ring, I have hidden one under a flowerpot, so I was not worried about that.

'Looks like he's gone away again,' I said gratefully. 'Thank goodness for that!'

Of course he hadn't thought to feed the hens (which had put themselves to bed in disgust) or the quail, so I shut everything up for the night.

As we walked back to the cottage, Caz Naylor, Uncle Roly Pharamond's gamekeeper, sidled out of a small outbuilding and, with a brief salute, flitted away through the shadows towards the woods behind the cottage.

He is a foxy looking young man, with dark auburn hair, evasive amber eyes and a tendency to address me, on the rare occasions when he speaks, as 'our Lizzie', thus acknowledging a distant relationship that all the Naylors in the area seemed to know about from the minute I set foot in the place for the first time at the age of eleven.

Annie looked startled: 'Wasn't that Caz? What's he doing here?'

'I let him have the use of the old chest freezer in there. Since I cut down on the amount of stuff I grow, I don't need it. He comes and goes as he pleases.'

She shook her head. 'All the Naylors are strange—'

'But some are stranger than others?' I finished for her. 'My mother was a Naylor too, don't forget! Descendant of some distant ancestor made good in Liverpool, in the cargo shipping line – which at least explains why I am such a daughter of the soil and so firmly rooted here.'

She smiled. 'I expect Roly told him to keep an eye on things, after that animal rights group started targeting you.'

'More likely he's keeping an eye on his freezer!' I said, though it is true that the only evidence of the activities of ARG! I have spotted around the place lately are the occasional bits of gaffer tape where a banner has been ripped off my car or barn. 'Perhaps they just aren't bothering with me that much? I mean, I can see why they might target Unks and Caz, especially since the fate of the grey squirrels he traps are shrouded in mystery, but why me? I'm not battery farming anything.'

All my fowl live long, happy and mainly useless lives, except for an excess of male quail and the occasional unwanted cockerel, which Caz dispatches for me with expert efficiency.

'I expect they just include you in with the Pharamond estate, since your cottage is part of it,' she concluded. 'It's not personal.'

We cleaned up the mess in the kitchen as well as we could and then she left before Jasper came home, since it was clear enough that Tom wasn't coming back that night, at least – and thank heaven for small mercies.

'What happened to your face, Mum?' Jasper asked, getting his first good look at me in the light of the kitchen. 'And why are you wearing one of Auntie Annie's horrible cardigans?'

'I dropped a plate and cut my face, so she loaned me the cardigan while she ran me to the surgery to get patched up – there was blood on my T-shirt.'

He looked at the new mark on the kitchen wall and said, 'Dropped a plate *horizontally*?' in that smart-lipped way teenage boys have.

'Yes, I was practising discus throwing,' I said, and we let the subject drop.

He didn't ask where his father was. But then, these days he never does.

Two

All Fudge

It was one of those delicious early summer mornings that reminded me of the first years of our marriage in Cornwall: dreamy swirls of mist with the warm sun tinting the edges golden, like pale yellow candyfloss wisps. You could easily imagine King Arthur and Queen Guinevere riding out of it in glorious Technicolor, all jingling bridles and hooded hawks, though if they had they would probably have been surprised to find themselves transported from the land of legend into a Lancashire backwater like Middlemoss.

The last remaining acres of darkly watchful ancient woodland that crowded up to the back of Perseverance Cottage would have looked normal enough to them, I suppose – apart from Caz Naylor, Uncle Roly's gamekeeper, who as usual was camouflaged from headband to boots Rambo style. I only spotted him flitting in and out of the trees by the white glint of his eyeballs and the sweat glistening between the green and brown streaks on his naked chest. A blink – and he was gone, back to wage war on the dangerous alien life form known to the uninitiated as the Grey Squirrel.

Though actually, Caz, the real Predator lives in my house, disguised as my husband and laying waste to my life.

Still, even in Arthurian times they would probably have had some kind of shamanistic Green Man and so be used to such goings-on, and the duckpond, chickens and vegetable patch out front would look reassuringly normal. But what would they make of the big and somewhat tattered poly-tunnel greenhouse, its polythene covering opaque with age? Or my battered, once-white Citroen 2CV? A 2CV, now I came to look at it, with its hood down, so the seats would be soaked with dew, and possibly lightly spattered with hen crap. Or even, which was much, much worse, duck gloop.

It was also listing drunkenly on one *seriously* flat tyre.

Tossing the last of the feed to the hens I stuck my head inside the cottage door.

'Jasper?' I called loudly up the steep stairs, expecting him to be still asleep. By nature, eighteen year olds are intended to be nocturnal, so it felt cruel to have to drag him out of his bat cave under the eaves each morning.

He loomed out of the doorway next to me, making me start. 'I'm here, Mum. What's up?'

'Flat tyre. You have your breakfast and get ready while I change it. I hope it's a mendable puncture – the spare's not that brilliant and if I have to buy a new one it'll be worth more than the rest of the car put together.'

One of the white leghorns had followed me into the flagged hallway, and I shooed it out again. There's something terribly cement-like about hen droppings when they set hard.

'I'll change it,' he offered. 'Or I can cycle over.'

'No, I'll have it done by the time you've had breakfast, and you'll be late otherwise.'

The medieval dig he was working at was only a few miles away, but the lanes between the site and us were narrow and twisty, so I worried about his safety. Annie calls it 'mother hen with one chick' syndrome, but she is just as dotty about her rescued three-legged mutt, Trinity.

Jasper wandered out again a few minutes later with a piece of toast at least an inch thick, not counting the bramble jelly and butter, removed the wheel brace from my hand, giving me the toast to hold in exchange, and unscrewed the last nut.

'Thanks, that was stiff. You'd think if I'd tightened it up in the first place, I would be able to undo it easily, wouldn't you?'

'Dad not back yet?' Jasper said, glancing across at the large, ramshackle wooden shed Tom used as his workshop, with the 'BOARD RIGID: CUSTOMIZED SURFBOARDS' sign over it.

'No.'

'Well, remember that time you asked him to go and buy a couple of pints of milk, and he didn't come back for four days?' he said, clearly with the intention of comforting me should I need it. But actually, I'm sure he shares my feeling that his father's increasing absences are a blessing, even though I am usually the one on the receiving end of Tom's sudden rages. You can't live in a cottage that size without realizing that something is going on, even with Tom's newly installed widescreen TV blaring away in the sitting room.

And although I'd explained to Jasper long ago that his father's increasingly strange manner towards him was due to the tumour and then the after-effects of the operation, it didn't make his coldness any the less hurtful.

Just as well Jasper is the quietly stoical type.

Just let me get him safely off to university in September, then I can sort my life out – somehow, I prayed silently. But could I wait that long? And was it fair to Jasper not to talk to him about what was happening? What I intended to do? He *was* eighteen, after all.

Jasper said nothing more and with a doubtful look went back into the house. Unless I burdened him with my worries, there was nothing more to say.

His father was always a mercurial type, the erratic moon orbiting my mother earth solidity, and you couldn't hold him fast any more than that beautiful Cornish mist – he just sort of slipped through your fingers and vanished.

I think the nearest edible equivalent to the old Tom would be a dark, rich chocolate soufflé, mostly air but a trifle gooey right in the middle, the part that once loved and needed me. Who had always managed to sweet-talk me into forgiving him for anything and everything, although my exasperation levels had slowly risen over the years as my son matured and my husband remained as charmingly irresponsible as ever. Have *you* ever imagined what it would be like to be married to Peter Pan once the novelty wore off?

The new post-op facsimile is ostensibly the same, but has something in the middle you could break your teeth on – or your heart – seasoned with increasingly violent mood swings.

His cousin Nick Pharamond, whose Mercedes sports car was, I now observed with surprise, carefully bumping down the rutted track towards me scattering hens, is a different kettle of fish entirely (and I *don't* mean chocolate sardines). He's certainly no soufflé of any kind – more a strong dose of brimstone and treacle, though he cooks like an angel. He's an expert on all aspects of food and cooking, terribly well known and paid – you've probably seen his page in the Sunday newspaper colour supplements, or read one of his books or articles.

He's had a volatile, semi-detached marriage with a chef for years (which is at least one too many cooks on the home front by my reckoning), but I was glad to see she wasn't with him today, because Leila is a lemon tart. Or maybe, since she is French, that should be *tarte aux citron*?

Miaou.

Must try not to be catty about her, even if she does contrive (intentionally) to make me feel like a lumbering great carthorse whenever we meet. She is an immaculately chic, petite, blue-eyed blonde, while I am tall and broad-shouldered, with hazel eyes, fine chestnut hair in a permanent tangle, and the sort of manicure you get from digging vegetable beds.

Unks, Tom's nominal Great-uncle Roly up at the hall, doesn't like her either. He says if it weren't for her refusing to stop working all hours in her restaurant in London and settle down, there would be lots of little Pharamond heirs by now, but if they were all like Nick and Leila that would be quite an alarming thought.

Leila's been married before and is fiercely independent, with her own swish apartment above her restaurant, while Nick has a small flat in Camden. And considering he spends at least half his time at Pharamond Hall, which Leila rarely visits, you wonder when they ever see each other.

I certainly hadn't seen him for ages. Oh, he still phones up for any eggs, fruit or vegetables he needs when he is here, working on a recipe, but I drop them off with Unk's cook, Mrs Gumball.

Yet today he had deigned to pay me a visit. As his Mercedes pulled up I removed the jack and then slung the punctured tyre in the back of the car, where Jasper's folding bike (one of Uncle Roly's more inspired birthday gifts) already reposed, so he could get back from the dig if I couldn't pick him up for some reason.

Nick got out, looking his usual tall, morose and slightly Neanderthal self, in dark trousers and open-necked soft white shirt with the sleeves rolled up, the glossy, thick black plumage of his hair spikily feathering his head. His strongly marked face with its impressively bumpy nose can look very attractive when he smiles, though the last time he wasted any of his charm on me was while we were waiting for Tom to regain consciousness (or not) after his operation two years ago.

Admittedly, he was such an absolute tower of strength then that I even gave him my cherished recipe for mashed potato fudge! This was a creation I discovered years ago, while trying to cook up some comfort from limited ingredients down in Cornwall in midwinter, and which was later to be christened Spudge by Jasper.

But I can only feel *profoundly* grateful that I haven't seen much of him since, and I'll tell you why: you know how something suddenly takes over your mouth during those cold, shivery, shocked and endless hospital waits, and you can hear your voice droning on, telling the nearest person your entire life history, including the personal bits? Well, one night I told everything – and I mean *everything* – to Nick.

This included stuff I'd only ever told to Annie before,

like how bad things had been between Tom and me for ages before the operation, especially after I found out he'd been having an affair. I knew Tom had played away a couple of times before that, but he'd always persuaded me they meant nothing and it was me he loved. But this time he'd told me it was *my* fault, for being so wrapped up in the cottage and the garden and especially Jasper!

Luckily I managed to stop myself blurting out to Nick just *why* Tom had suddenly taken against the poor boy, but it was a close run thing.

Of course, once the tumour was diagnosed I'd realized it must have been that that had been slowly changing his character so radically, probably for years: it may have been benign, but the effects weren't.

Well, anyway, you get the scenario: Nick got an earful, but at least it kept it in the family. And he even told me in return that he sympathized, because Leila refused to cut down her working hours to spend more time with him, and although he respected her independence they seemed to be seeing less and less of each other. This was *really* letting his guard down, for Nick is pretty tight-lipped on anything personal, so the night-watch effect must have been getting to *him*, too.

Then I asked Nick if he thought everything would be all right again if Tom didn't die, especially once Jasper went off to university and I wasn't so tied to Middlemoss and the school run, and could accompany Tom on some of his many trips down to Cornwall? And he said it wouldn't be *my* fault if it wasn't and gave me a big, wonderfully comforting hug – and then when we turned, Tom's eyes were open and I knew everything was going to be all right.

Little did I know. And what a long time ago that moment of hope seems now . . .

I became aware that Nick was waving his hands slowly in front of my face, like a baffled stage hypnotist. 'Planet Earth to Lizzie: are you receiving me?'

'Oh, hi, Nick – long time, no recipe.' I wiped my filthy hands up the sides of my jeans – they were work ones, so it wasn't going to make a lot of difference. I only hoped I hadn't run them through my hair too, though since I didn't remember brushing it this morning a bit of grease would at least hold the tangles down.

He frowned at me. 'I sent you a card from Jamaica.'

'That was ages ago. And a recipe for conch fritters isn't exactly the most useful thing to have in the middle of Lancashire – the fishmongers don't stock them. Anyway, what are you doing here at this time of the morning? Have you driven straight up from London?'

'Yes, I'm looking for Tom,' he said shortly, checking me over with eyes the dark grey-purple of wet Welsh slate, as though he wasn't sure quite what species I was or what sauce to serve me with. 'What have you done to your face?'

I flushed and touched the Steri-strips with the tips of my fingers. 'I – dropped a plate. Got cut by one of the pieces,' I said lamely, though it was *almost* the truth even if the plate wasn't so much dropped as thrown.

His brows knitted into a thick, black bar as he tried to imagine a plate that explosive.

'Dr Patel's practice nurse says it will heal without a mark – it's already healing, in fact. And Tom's away.' *Thank God*, I mentally added.

'Oh? Any idea when he'll be back?'

'No, and I don't know where he is either. But he's been gone . . .' I reckoned up. 'Four days now, I think, so I'll be surprised if he doesn't turn up today.'

'You *think* he's been gone four days?' He raised one dark eyebrow. 'Where has he gone?'

'He didn't say,' I shrugged, casually. 'You know what he's like. He might be off delivering a surfboard. I'm pretty sure he's not doing a gig with the Mummers.'

'A gig – with the what?'

'The Mummers of Invention: you know, that sort of folk-rock group he started with three local friends a few years back?'

'No,' he said shortly. 'I'm glad to say I don't.'

'You must do – one of them's that drippy female Unks rents an estate cottage to – she sells handmade smocks at historical re-enactment fairs. And if you ever came up for the Mystery Play any more you *would* have seen them – they provide the musical interludes. Tom played Lazarus as well, last year – he stepped in at the last minute. The parish magazine review said he brought a whole new meaning to the role.'

'Unsurprising, given his circumstances – and I *do* intend being here for the next performance.'

'I thought Leila couldn't leave her restaurant at the New Year?' I said, surprised.

'*She* can't: I can,' he snapped, and I wondered if their marriage was finally dragging its sorry carcass to the parting of the ways, like mine. 'So, you have no idea where Tom is, or when he will be back?'

'Probably Cornwall, that's where he mostly ends up, and, if so, he's likely to be staying with that friend of his, Tom Collinge – the weird one who runs a wife and harem in one cottage.'

'I suppose he may be by now, but he was in London on Monday night, Lizzie – I ran into him at Leila's restaurant. He left in a hurry – without paying the bill.'

'He did?' I frowned, puzzled. 'That's odd. I wonder what he was doing in London?'

'Well, it wasn't me he came to see, since he left as soon as I arrived.' He looked at me intently, as though he'd asked me a question.

'Oh?' I said slowly, trying to remember whether Tom had actually ever said which of his friends he stayed with when he was in London.

'Well, you know Tom,' I tried to laugh. 'He probably just found himself near the restaurant and dropped in to see Leila.'

'Then just took it into his head to shoot off without paying when I turned up unexpectedly? Leila said she didn't want to charge him for the meal anyway, since he is a sort of relative.'

'That's kind of her,' I said, amazed, because it wouldn't surprise me if she gives even Nick a bill when he eats there.

'Yes, *wasn't* it just?' he said dryly. 'And one of the staff let slip that he'd stayed in her apartment the previous night, too – they seemed to know him pretty well. But I told her, business is business, and she'd never let sentiment of any kind come before making money before, so I would just drop the bill in on my way up to the hall – and here it is.'

I looked at his closed, dark face again and suddenly wondered if he suspected that Tom and Leila had something going on? Surely not – it would be totally ridiculous!

I knew that Tom had resumed the affair he'd been having before his operation, but not who it was, although I thought it must be someone local. It couldn't be *Leila* . . . could it?

My mind working furiously I took the offered bill and glanced at it, then gasped, distracted by the staggering sum. 'You must be absolutely rolling in it, with these prices!'

'Not me – Leila. And the prices aren't anything out of the ordinary for a restaurant of that standard. She's just got another Michelin star.'

'Congratulations,' I said absently, staring at the bill, the total of which would have fed the average family of four for about a year. More, if they grew most of their food themselves, like me. 'Well, sorry, I don't have that kind of money on the proceeds of my produce sales – and in case you haven't noticed, I've scaled that side of things down drastically in the last year.'

'Come on, you must get good advances for your "how I tried to be self-sufficient and failed dismally" books. You can't plead poverty – ' he looked distastefully down at the mess he was standing in – 'whatever it looks like here!'

'You should have looked before you got out of the car,' I said coldly. 'The ducks have been up. And one small book every two or three years doesn't exactly rake in the cash – I get about four thousand for them. I'm lucky to still have a publisher – my agent says it's only because my faithful handful of readers can't wait to see what else goes pear-shaped every time. And they like the recipes.'

'Ah, yes, the Queen of Puddings!' He wrinkled his nose slightly.

'What? Just because it's wholesome, everyday stuff, it doesn't mean it isn't good food!' I snapped crossly. 'At least *my* recipes don't need ninety-six exotic ingredients, four servile minions and a catering-sized oven!'

He grinned, as though glad to have got a rise out of me, and I began to remember why we never got on: an interest in food is the only thing we've *ever* had in common whatever Annie says, and he never tires of reminding me that mine is not gourmet and rather focused on sweets and desserts – hence his nickname for me.

'And this is *not* my bill, so you'll have to come back and speak to Tom about it later,' I added, sincerely hoping that

that was *all* he wanted to talk to Tom about. Clearly he is harbouring suspicions . . . But no, whoever Tom is having an affair with, it can't be Leila, his own cousin's wife, however strange the circumstances look.

The grin vanished. 'If I can catch him. Jasper had his results yet?' he asked, abruptly changing the subject.

'Oh, yes!' I said, happily diverted. 'Yesterday, and they were just what he needed for Liverpool, to read archaeology and history. He's having breakfast at the moment – why don't you come in and talk to him? He hasn't thanked you for that Roman cookery book you sent him, yet.'

Jasper's keenly interested in food and drink too – only from a purely historical perspective. Delving about in medieval cesspits and middens, which is what he seems to be spending his days at the dig doing, suits him down to the ground.

Nick looked at his watch: 'I haven't time today – congratulate him for me, won't you? I'd better be off. I'm doing some articles on eating out in north-west Lancashire – out of the way restaurants and hotels – so I need to drop my stuff off up at the hall and get on with it. Breakfast awaits, then lunch and dinner . . .'

'Lucky you,' I said politely, though sitting in restaurants isn't my favourite thing. I'd rather pig out at home than eat prettily arranged little portions in public.

He was frowning down at me again. 'You know, Lizzie, four thousand is peanuts compared to what I get for my books. No wonder you are living in a hovel – especially with Tom spending his earnings as fast as he makes them.'

'We don't need a huge amount of money, and Perseverance Cottage is *not* a hovel,' I began crossly, though it is not far off, despite Tom's slightly incongruous additions of a TV aerial and satellite dish. 'Uncle Roly had all the mod cons installed before we moved in, and it's exactly how I like it. I've got everything I want.'

'Have you? Or perhaps you got more than you bargained for,' he said, and despite myself my hand went up to touch my face.

I did have everything I ever wanted, so I have to be luckier than most women are, even if I might now have to leave most of it behind me once Jasper was safely off to university and I could finally stop pretending everything was all right with Tom and me. And could I afford to wait that long?

Nick, turning round and surveying my domain, remarked suavely: 'I wouldn't say the family have come a long way from the heady days of Pharamond's Butterflake Biscuits, but they have certainly diverged in their interests.'

And then, before I could point out that *he* at least was still vaguely in the bakery line, he was climbing back into his car and reversing in a cloud of dust. A lot of gritted chickens shot out from under it.

'Wasn't that Uncle Nick?' Jasper asked, coming out ready for the off.

'Yes, but he couldn't stay, he had an urgent appointment with breakfast. Get in. I'll just wash my hands and we'll go.'

'Can I drive?' he asked hopefully. He has recently passed his test, lessons courtesy of a lucky win on the gees at Haydock by Great Uncle Roly.

'OK. Turn it round while I get ready.'

He'd left the cottage door open, and one of the hens had made a small deposit on the rag rug.

Three

Bittersweet

All the way to the dig, while the loud music chosen by Jasper drowned out even the possibility of conversation, I wondered whether Leila could be the woman Tom had been having an affair with, taunted me with – even the same one he was involved with before the operation?

Did Nick *really* suspect that or was I imagining it? Things certainly didn't sound too friendly between him and Leila, even by their semi-detached, sweet and sour standards.

And what *would* I say to Tom when he returned? I haven't seen him since the night he threw the plate at me, which is not an event that can be glossed over lightly, especially with the evidence marking my face; but going by his increasing outbursts of rage, saying *nothing* would be the most sensible option until my plans to leave are in place.

Oh, *why* couldn't he just vanish into thin air, as some people do, never to be seen again?

In need of comfort, I stopped off at Annie's cottage on the way home. It was very early, but she had already made a chicken casserole and popped it in the slow cooker for later.

She seemed to have learned a lot more practical stuff than I ever did on that French cookery course we did in London after we left school, where volatile Madame Fresnet screamed at us all day long in French, the language in which we were supposed to learn to cook, thus killing two birds with one stone. At the end of the six months we all emerged with shattered eardrums, shattered French and the ability to whip up *Tartelettes au Fromage* at the drop of a whisk.

Trinity skipped up to greet me and Susannah, Annie's deaf white cat, regarded me with self-satisfied disinterest from the top of the Rayburn.

'All right?' Annie asked anxiously, scrutinizing my face.

'Fine. Tom's not back yet and Jasper's at the dig – I just dropped him.'

'It's great he got his first choice university, isn't it?' she said, getting down another mug from the rack and pouring me some coffee. 'Do you want a chocolate croissant? They're hot from the oven and I don't think I can eat the last one, I've had two already.'

'Your eyes are bigger than your belly,' I said vulgarly, accepting the plate, and sat down at the kitchen table, keeping my eyes firmly away from Trinity's pleading dark ones: the last thing a dog with three legs needs is to be overweight.

'I saw Nick this morning,' I told her, dunking the croissant into my coffee so the chunks of bittersweet dark chocolate began to melt, which makes a change, because I usually do it the other way round and dip my food into melted chocolate, especially strawberries. It's amazing what you *can* coat in chocolate – and I'm not talking about that revolting body paint, because I prefer to keep the two greatest pleasures life can hold completely, and unmessily, separate. 'That's really what I came to tell you about. He called in early on his way up to the hall – and he said Tom was in London on Monday.'

I described my conversation with Nick. 'Don't you think that sounds like he suspects Tom and Leila might be having an affair?'

'Oh, no, surely not? Not his own cousin's wife?' she exclaimed, looking horrified. Annie is just too nice for her own good, but I suppose being a vicar's daughter didn't exactly help to squash her natural inclination to think the best of everybody if she possibly could.

'I don't know – but I hope not. And I can't *really* see him and Leila getting it together, can you? I find her quite scary in a beady-eyed and elegantly chic way. But I always thought it must be someone local, so perhaps Nick has got the wrong end of the stick.'

'Oh, I'm sure he must have,' she agreed.

Her eye fell on the kitchen clock: 'Look at the time – and I promised I'd put in a couple of hours at the RSPCA kennels, the flu's hit the staff and volunteers hard. There are no pet-sitting jobs that I can't handle myself this afternoon, but tomorrow will be busier.' She looked slightly self-conscious. 'Rob Rafferty has asked me to go in at lunchtime and walk Flo, because he will be at the studios in Manchester all day.'

'You'd better get off then, if you are sure there is nothing you want me to do. I'll see you at the Mystery Play committee meeting later – when I'll finally get to meet the new vicar at last.'

'Oh, yes, he's . . . he seems nice,' she said vaguely, and I could see that her mind was still too taken up with the delights of Rob Rafferty to bother with lesser mortals.

'Oh – before you go, can I borrow that candyfloss maker you bought for the last Cubs and Brownies Bazaar? Some lusciously lemon morning mist has given me ideas.'

'Of course,' she said. 'Now, where did I put it?' She vanished into the pantry and came back with a cardboard box. 'The instructions and everything are still in there. Do you need anything else? Sugar?'

'No, I'm OK for sugar,' I assured her.

Lemons I already had in abundance.

I left her putting Trinny in the back of her car, and drove down to the other end of the village to drop the punctured tyre off with Dave Naylor at the local garage, Deals on Wheels. And I know it seems confusing at first that most of the indigent Mosses population who are not Pharamonds are either Naylors or Gumballs, but you quickly get used to it.

Then I headed for home, passing the entire contingent of the Mosses Senior Citizens' Club waiting to board a coach for the annual trip to Southport Flower Show . . . including Unk's alarmingly spry octogenarian sister, Mimi Pharamond. I slowed down, staring, and she waved at me gaily, the rainbow-coloured Rastafarian knitted hat Nick brought her back from Jamaica flapping over one eye.

Since Juno Carter, her long-suffering companion, was currently laid up after an accident, letting Mimi loose alone on the Flower Show seemed a recipe for disaster. I only hoped someone had been delegated to keep an eye on her. *And* a firm grip.

Four
Mushrooming

There was still no sign of Tom's van outside the cottage and you can't miss it because it has BOARD RIGID in big fluorescent orange letters up the side and the logo of a stickman surfing. The workshop door was closed, too, but in the bedroom I found his dirty clothes scattered on the rug as though washed up there by a high tide, so he'd either gone out again, or come back without his van.

Still, clearly he had returned from wherever it was he had been, and at some point I would have to make up my mind what, if anything, I was going to say to him. His outbursts of temper are unpredictable and things are escalating even if, so far, apart from hurling the plate, he hasn't done much more than push me about a bit.

But the man I fell in love with and married isn't ever coming back, I'm living with an increasingly violent stranger, and so bailing out of the situation is the only option left. Maybe I should have done it a year ago, even if it did mean disrupting Jasper's schooling at an important stage? The situation has certainly been affecting him – he seems to have practically given up going out with his friends in the evening when Tom is home. Instead, he lurks in his room (with the computer Unks gave him for his last birthday), only suddenly looming silently up between us whenever voices are raised. Trying to prevent his parents coming to blows is *not* a responsibility I want my son to have.

So, perhaps I should finally tell Tom straight that I'm not prepared to put up with his behaviour any more and, once Jasper's gone to university, I'm leaving him. I am sure this is what he has been aiming for, so he can play the hurt innocent party to everyone.

Perseverance Cottage is a grace and favour one belonging to his Uncle Roly, so obviously, if anyone is moving out, it will have to be me. And I simply *won't* ask Roly to help me, for not only do I not want to disillusion him about Tom, whom he has treated like another grandson, but he has already been so kind and generous to us all these years, letting us have the cottage rent-free.

I've been scaling down on the fruit and vegetable production ready for such an eventuality, and I expect I can find new homes for the hens and quail, but where *I* am to live will be a major problem. I'd like to stay in the area and now, due to the influx of newcomers, especially the *Cotton Common* crowd, buying up property, it appears that Posh Pet-sitters is likely to expand enough to employ me pretty well full time as well as Annie before too long. However, in a Catch-22 twist, that very influx of newcomers has sent property prices and rentals soaring out of my reach.

It was all depressingly difficult. Sighing, I gathered up Tom's clothes, added some of Jasper's and mine, then went down to stuff them in the machine. There was no beating them on a rock for me even in the first flush of self-sufficiency in Cornwall, though before I bought the washing machine out of my first Perseverance Cottage Chronicle sale, I used to do the laundry by trampling up and down on it in the bath. Then I would pass it through an old mangle in the yard, which was not fun in winter.

It hadn't taken me long to realize that most books on self-sufficiency were written by men in warm, comfortable rooms, while their wives were out there dealing with the raw realities of life. Or that Tom, while initially enthusiastic, had soon lost interest and succumbed to the burgeoning surfing culture instead. Once you added a tiny baby into the equation, the offer of a cottage on the Pharamond estate up in Lancashire was one I had been determined we wouldn't refuse.

As I pointed out to Tom at the time, if you have the contacts, you can customize surfboards *anywhere*, and besides, Middlemoss was as close to a home as I had ever got, and I longed to go back there.

Tom's jeans crackled when I picked them up to stuff into the washer, but I always have to empty his pockets of the strange assortment that gathered in them, from board wax to sherbet lemons – and, lately, less savoury items.

This time the haul was a dark blue paper napkin tastefully printed in the corner with the word 'Leila's' in gold, a teaspoon that probably came from the same place, since it was definitely classier than any of our mismatched assortment, a stub of billiard chalk, a red jelly baby with the head bitten off and a piece of pink paper folded tightly into the shape of a very small rose. Tom has doodled in origami roses as long as I have known him, which can be very irritating when it's my shopping list or the top page of a stack of manuscript; but equally, it used to be rather endearing when it was an apology for forgetting to tell me he was going off somewhere. At least, it was until the novelty wore off along with my patience.

I flattened this one out and found it was the last part of a letter, abjuring my husband to 'Tell old Charlie Dimmock you've found someone else and given her the push' and promising, if he did, to tie him up – and maybe even *down* – if he really *begged* her to. It was signed 'your Dark Heart'.

Well, that didn't sound like Leila, did it? I could imagine she'd give anyone a good basting, but would she have time in her busy schedule for *bondage*?

A horrible image of a naked Tom, trussed and oven-ready,

flashed before my eyes, and I found I was sitting on the quarry tiles feeling sick and recalling the first (and last) time we made love after his recovery from the operation, when he said I was so responsive he felt like he was practising necrophilia. And I said to him that, strangely enough, I felt much the same, since he might *look* like my husband, but the part of him I loved seemed to be quite dead.

This had thrown him into the first of his really, *really* frighteningly violent rages during which he had said I should try dying sometime, and I had thought for a minute he had been about to follow the suggestion up with some action, only we had heard Jasper moving about in his room overhead. So then he'd said that living with permanent headaches and a cold bitch of a wife who thought food could cure *anything* was enough to piss anyone off, and had stormed out.

Anyway, after this things between us went downhill rapidly, especially once he had started doing all the things the doctors had told him not to, and *not* doing all the things they recommended, like leading a quiet life, eating good, regular meals, cutting down on alcohol and taking his pills. And he'd made no attempt to conceal that he was still having an affair; the only puzzle was who with.

Feeling suddenly dizzy, I put my head on my knees and closed my eyes, wishing our old lurcher, Harriet, was still around to snuffle sympathetically in my ear.

When the feeling passed I resolutely got up and washed my face in the kitchen sink with cold water, ate an entire packet of those chocolate mini-flake cake decorations, then went out to the workshop, from where faint strains of Metallica now wafted through the Judas door.

Tom had his back to me when I went in, spray-stencilling some intricate, hand-cut Celtic design on to a surfboard. He was wearing a mask and baggy dungarees over his T-shirt and jeans, and his dark hair curled on to the nape of his neck in a familiar ducktail.

Where his cousin Nick is built on a large and rather rugged scale, Tom is a slight, wiry man and every slender bone of his body is beautiful. But despite (allegedly) not being a Pharamond other than in name, he does have the look of one.

I stood there for a minute, thrown by that familiar curl of hair, shaken by an old tenderness. Then he must have felt my presence, for he turned beautiful cold grey stranger's eyes on me, pushing down the mask. The CD came to an end and there was silence.

His eyes flicked to the half-healed cut on my cheek and away again. 'You're still here then? Thought you might have cleared off.'

'Like where?' I demanded. 'And Jasper? The animals? Did you think I had an ark ready and waiting somewhere?'

'Ah, yes – I forgot: *my* great uncle, *my* cottage. Poor little orphan Lizzie has nowhere to go, has she?'

'Don't think I'm staying with you any longer than I have to,' I told him coldly. 'Once Jasper's off to university, that's it. And, if you are interested, his results came and he got into Liverpool.'

'It's always *Jasper,* isn't it?' he said pettishly.

'Well, he is your son too, whatever mad ideas you've got in your head!'

'Oh, come on, he's the spitting image of Nick, my dear old no-blood-relation cousin. And the very first thing I saw when I opened my eyes in hospital after the operation was the two of you in each other's arms. Then I got better and spoiled things, didn't I?'

'I've told you repeatedly that he was just comforting me. And yes, he *did* visit us once or twice in Cornwall around the time I conceived Jasper – but you were there, too! No, there's another obvious reason why both you and Jasper look like the Pharamonds, only you'd rather believe ill of me than your mother!'

'We'll leave my mother out of this,' he said, that ugly look in his eyes. Then, turning back towards his board, he said dismissively: 'Fetch me a beer out, will you? There's some in the fridge.'

'Fetch it yourself – I didn't come out here to wait on you. Oh, and here's a restaurant bill from Leila – I hope the meal was worth it.'

'What?' He swung round and snatched it from me, glanced at it and then looked up suspiciously. 'Where did you get this?'

'Nick came early this morning – you left Leila's without paying the bill, and she wants her money.'

'I thought you said you never saw Nick alone?' he taunted

me. 'And I don't think this is Leila's idea,' he added, crumpling the bill into a ball and tossing it into a corner. 'I've already paid her – in kind. Bed and board. So now you know – and presumably Nick knows.'

'Suspects, perhaps . . . But – but Leila can't possibly be Dark Heart!' I blurted rashly.

He took a menacing step towards me. 'What do you know about Dark Heart?'

'I found a bit of a note in your pocket when I was sorting the washing, but it didn't sound like Leila,' I said, standing my ground.

'It isn't,' he said shortly. 'It's someone else . . . someone more conveniently local, who's prepared to please me in ways you wouldn't have, even if I'd *asked*, dearest wife.'

'The woman tempted me?' I said, bitterly quoting the Mystery Play in which, ironically enough, I was playing Eve. Perhaps Dark Heart would get the part next year? 'Is it someone I know, Tom? A friend, even? And Leila – was that a one-off? She isn't the woman you were having an affair with before your operation, is she?'

He didn't reply, just smiled rather unpleasantly. I hoped he hadn't been running two of them in tandem even then. But someone local . . . who could it be?

Oh God, he hadn't got drunk and started an affair with that drippy girl who played the electric violin and sang in the Mummers, had he? I'd noticed she hadn't been able to look me in the eye for months, but I thought he'd maybe succumbed to one of his quick, one-night flings.

Evidently, he wasn't going to tell me anyway. I thought of something else. 'Where is your van?'

'It broke down in a lay-by about twenty miles away. I had to get the garage to bring it in – think the gearbox's had it. Now, any more questions? Only I need to finish this board – I'm off down to Cornwall at the weekend to deliver it. Assuming the van's fixed by then.'

I stared at him, thinking how normal a monster could look.

'If you aren't leaving immediately, you could make yourself useful and fetch that beer,' he suggested.

'Fetch it yourself, I'm going for a walk in the woods to think all this over, and then I've got a Mystery committee meeting,' I said, and saw a flash of anger in his eyes.

You can't ever depend on a soufflé turning out right.

As I left I heard the music restart, and the hissing of the spray.

Outside I practically fell over Polly Darke, our local purveyor of stirring romantic sagas, who never lets historical facts come between her and a good story.

Come to that, she never lets facts come between her and a *modern* story either, since she's always snooping about under one pretext or another, and is such a gossip that behind her back everyone calls her the Village Voice. Divorced, she has lived in her hacienda-style bungalow between Middlemoss and Mossedge for several years, and I am sure is convinced that she is accepted everywhere as a local.

While I don't suppose she could hear anything much through a wooden door, that won't prevent her spreading lurid rumours around the three villages by sundown.

She was looking her usual strange self, in a severely truncated purple, Regency-style dress, and with her hair cropped and dyed a dense, dead black. She clutched a small blue plastic basket of field mushrooms to her artificially inflated bosom, which might or might not be a fashion statement – are plastic baskets currently a must-have accessory?

Apart from the kohl-edged eyes and puffy, fuchsia pink lips (which reminded me, strikingly, of a baboon's bottom), her face was pale as death. Paler.

'Oh – Polly! Are you all right?' I said a bit sharply, since I suspected she'd been trying to eavesdrop. 'You haven't been eating your own home-bottled tomatoes or anything like that, have you?'

From time to time she fancies herself as the earth mother type and tries her hand at jams, chutneys and bottled goods, which she then gives to all and sundry along with, in my case, a generous dose of botulism or something equally foul. Just my luck to get *that* one!

'Oh, no, I haven't had time for any of that, Lizzie – I've got a book to finish.'

'Yes, Sally does like you to keep them coming, doesn't she?'

Having fallen out with two agents and three publishers, Polly had now been taken on by my own agent, Sally McDonald – and may the best woman win.

Her dark eyes slid curiously to the closed workshop door and back to my face. 'Is – I mean, I thought I heard raised voices. Is everything OK with you and Tom? Only I've thought sometimes lately that you weren't entirely happy, and you *know* you can always depend on me if you need a shoulder to cry on.'

Yes, but only if I knelt down first.

'I'm fine,' I said shortly. 'Just discussing . . . business. Were you looking for me?'

She gave a sudden start. 'Oh – yes. I picked loads of mushrooms in the paddock this morning early and I thought you might like to swap them for some quail eggs? But if it's inconvenient, it doesn't matter.'

'No, not at all. I'm just off for a walk, but you know where they are in the small barn? Help yourself and leave the mushrooms there,' I told her and walked off, not caring whether she thought me rude or not. When she first moved to Middlemoss she went all out to be my best friend – but we have absolutely nothing in common (apart from Sally). Anyway, I already have a best friend: Annie is enough.

Nor, come to think of it, was she the type to skip about the fields at dawn gathering mushrooms, which in any case looked suspiciously like shop-bought ones: small, clean and perfectly formed. I make marzipan mushrooms that look earthier than those.

I headed for the woods, for I find their dark, cool depths wonderfully soothing. They restore a sense of my unimportance in the great scale of things, shrinking my problems down to a more manageable size. Less than an acorn, even.

Luckily I was wearing a pinky-red T-shirt today, so Caz would spot me if I strayed on to the smaller paths he stalked so relentlessly; but if he did, he didn't make himself known. He is not much of a talker in any case; but then, most of his dealings are with squirrels, so he doesn't need to be.

I sang the theme tune to *Love Story* very softly and sadly, wondering what would have happened if the doomed duo had had over twenty years together, like Tom and me. *And* we knew each other long before that, too, from the days when he had been farmed out in the school holidays up at Pharamond Hall with Unks and Mimi and I had spent mine at the Middlemoss vicarage with Annie's family.

After my parents were killed I had been naturally absorbed into the Vane household and the vicarage had become my home, much to the relief of the elderly bachelor cousin of my father's who had found himself suddenly my guardian. He had elected to use what money was left to me on finishing my education, including the French cookery course, which had finally exhausted the funds.

Nick often stayed at the hall, too, with his grandfather, and the boys got on well enough, despite being very different: on the whole Nick seemed to prefer the company of Eva Gumball, the cook at Pharamond Hall, to ours. Nick inherited the Pharamond cooking gene in spades, and so gravitated naturally to any kitchen within reach, until he took off suddenly around the world at eighteen with a rucksack, as many do. Though most do not generally spend all their time at markets and in other people's kitchens with a notebook.

His staid, stockbroker father may have washed his hands of him at this point, but look at him now – chief cookery writer for a leading London newspaper, author of numerous books and articles, and capable of taking ingredients from around the world and blending them into some amazing new twist on a dish.

He got where he wanted to go, but Tom dropped out of university and gravitated down to Cornwall, where many of his more useless friends had also ended up, and never seemed to have any sense of purpose until he temporarily adopted my dream of a self-sufficient existence in the country.

I hadn't seen Tom for a year or two after leaving school, and then we re-met across the buffet table at a large party in London. I was helping with the catering, he and Annie were invited. I'd forgotten his good looks and his overwhelming charm – *and* his quirky sense of humour. He swept me off my feet, into a registry office and down to the hovel he was renting in Cornwall, before I had had time to think.

Of course, there was *lots* of time to think later, especially during those freezing cold first two winters in a dank cottage when Tom, quickly bored with the idea of self-sufficiency and love in a hovel, resumed his usual and rather peripatetic ways. It was like living with a handsome, affectionate but wandering tomcat.

Perhaps that is why Annie, although fond of Tom, has always preferred Nick, for despite having a cat as well as Trinny, she is most definitely a dog lover and sees people as cats or dogs, just as I see them as kinds of food. To her, Nick is probably a big, rather bad-tempered dog, who has the potential to make a good family pet with the right, *very* understanding owner.

Eventually, reluctantly, I had to turn for home, even though I dreaded seeing Catman again. But there was no need: he wasn't there – and more to the point, neither was my car.

Come to that, even the punnet of mushrooms Polly Darke had presumably left had vanished into thin air, though possibly Caz had been around and fancied them. He knows he can help himself to anything edible he can find, though it seemed a bit greedy to take them all.

He keeps the freezer I gave him locked, so goodness knows what is in there. Better not to know, perhaps?

I searched for a note saying where Tom and my car had gone to, but there was nothing; unless he came back by the time I returned from the Mystery Play committee meeting, Jasper was going to have to cycle home tonight and I would be *extremely* annoyed.

I fed, watered and generally cared for everything that needed my attention, then changed and set off for the village hall – on foot.

Five
Sweet Mysteries

This year's Middlemoss Mystery committee was gathered together round a trestle table in the village hall, which exhibited reminders of its many functions: the playgroup's brightly coloured toys poked out from behind a curtained alcove and their finger-painting decorated one wall, while the other bore posters of footprints illustrating the various new steps the Senior Citizens' Tuesday Tea Dance Club were trying to master.

Personally, I thought salsa might give one or two of them

a bit of trouble, but I was sure they would all give it a go. Their line dancing ensemble at the last Christmas concert had been a big hit and Mrs Gumball, the cook up at Pharamond Hall, had got so excited she fell off the end of the stage on to the foam playmats that were always providentially stacked there after the incident a few years back, when one of Santa's little elves fell over causing a domino effect along the line until the last one dropped off and broke a leg.

'I think we might as well start, Clive,' I suggested to the verger, opening the plastic box of Coconut Consolations I'd brought with me and setting it in the middle, so everyone could help themselves. 'I don't know where Annie's got to, but Uncle Roly's gone to the races. He said after all these years he could do the Voice of God in his sleep, and he thought you could sort it all out without him.'

Round the table were grouped the usual suspects: the new vicar, untried and untested, who was looking more than a little nervous; Clive Potter and his wife Marianne, who ran the post office, the parish magazine, and pretty well everything else that happened round Middlemoss including directing the annual Mysteries. Then there was also Dr Patel, Miss Pym, the infants' schoolteacher, and my humble self, for Clive liked to have a token Pharamond on tap, since Uncle Roly was inclined to give his duties the go-by if something more interesting came along. Annie Vane was presumably held up somewhere.

'I've convened this meeting earlier than usual for two reasons,' announced Clive importantly. The verger was a busy little ant of a man, always running to and fro, and his wife was the same: my theory is they never slept, just hung by the heels for the odd ten minutes to refresh themselves, like bats. Come to that, they are so in tune with one another they have probably leapt up the next rung of the evolutionary ladder and communicate in high-pitched squeaks us mere bog-standard humans can't hear.

'First-off, I thought the vicar might need a bit more time to get to grips with the Mysteries, he having not known about them until he got here and it coming as a bit of a surprise to him, like.'

The vicar, a red-haired, blue-eyed man with a naturally startled expression, nodded earnestly: 'But I'm delighted, of course – absolutely delighted.'

I wondered if anyone had told him that the last vicar was currently having a genteel nervous breakdown in a church nursing home near Morecambe. An elderly man, I fear he had been hoping for a quiet country living where he could jog along towards his retirement, not the whirl of activity that is the Mosses parish. But at least the new one was younger – and unmarried, I recalled, watching with interest the way he suddenly went the same scarlet as his hair when Annie, breathless and dishevelled, rushed into the room.

'Sorry I'm late,' she said, subsiding into the seat next to me. 'One of the dogs slipped its lead and was practically in Mossrow before I caught it.'

She smiled apologetically around at everyone and apart from the vicar, who was still looking pole-axed, we all smiled back, since Annie is Goodwill to all Mankind personified. Even though I am her friend, I have to say that she is a plump, billowy person the approximate shape of a cottage loaf, with an amiable round face and a mass of fuzzy hair the colour of wet sand, and doesn't generally cause men to go red and all self-conscious. Interesting . . .

'We were only just starting,' I assured her. 'Clive's called the meeting to familiarize the vicar—'

'Do call me George,' he interrupted eagerly, finding his voice again.

I expect most of them will just carry on calling him Vicar. We are nothing if not traditionalists in Middlemoss, operating on the 'if it ain't broke, why fix it?' principle.

'And you must call me KP,' said Dr Patel agreeably, 'like the nuts.'

'And I'm Lizzie,' I put in hastily, seeing George's puzzled expression. 'You've already met Annie, haven't you?'

'Oh, yes.' He swallowed, his Adam's apple bobbing. 'At church.'

He was *just* Annie's type and clearly smitten – but she didn't seem to notice!

'Perhaps we'd better get on?' suggested Clive. 'Only the youth club will be in here tonight for snooker, and I'll need to set the tables up. Could you all please read this quote from a recently published book.' He passed round a bundle of photocopies and we all took one.

> Although called the Middlemoss Mysteries, this surviving vestige of the medieval mystery play, annually performed in an obscure Lancashire village, is in reality a much debased form, having been reduced at some distant point in its history to a mere series of tableaux.
>
> These illustrate several of the key biblical scenes from surviving mystery plays, such as the *Fall of Lucifer*, *Adam and Eve* and the *Nativity*, but what spoken lines remain are constantly reinterpreted by the next generation of actors, and also received a major new direction at the hands of Joe Wheelright, the Weaver Poet, mainly into sometimes near-impenetrable local dialect.
>
> The head of the leading local family, the Pharamonds, traditionally speaks the Voice of God.
>
> *The Last Mysteries of England* by Ronald Revesy-Blore

We all read it in silence, then Annie said: 'Well, it's not so bad, is it, Clive? We can't hope to keep the Mysteries a secret, and we always do get some strangers coming along, especially since the Mosses have suddenly become so terribly trendy to live in.'

'No, we just want to discourage the *folksy* visitors,' I said. 'We don't want to find ourselves on some sort of mystery play trail, being written up and taken over and the whole thing fixed like a fly in amber. I mean, the best thing about our Mysteries is that each new generation of actors adds a little something of their own to their parts, even if we do now stick more or less to the Wheelright version.'

And while the acting is done very seriously, I often suspect the Weaver Poet of having had a somewhat unholy sense of humour.

'I don't think *debased* is a very polite description,' Marianne said, bristling slightly right down to the ends of her spiky, grey, cropped hair. 'And what does he mean by *impenetrable* dialect? If everyone doesn't know the Bible stories before they see it, then they should, and then they'd know what was going on!'

'Er . . . yes,' said the vicar, with a gingerly glance at Dr Patel, who was sitting with his hands clasped over his immaculately suited round stomach, listening benignly.

'Oh, don't mind me,' the doctor said. 'I went to infant school right here – my father was the senior partner at the practice – so

I know all the Bible stories. So did all the Lees from the Mysteries of the East Chinese takeaway in Mossedge, and there's usually at least one of them taking part in the play, too.'

'We have many mysteries,' I said helpfully. 'Even the pub is called the New Mystery.'

'Little Ethan Lee made such a sweet baby Jesus last year,' Miss Pym said sentimentally. 'He simply couldn't take his eyes off the angel's halo.'

'None of us could,' Annie said. 'We've never had ones that light up before.'

'Oh?' said George, clearly groping to make sense of all this. 'Well, Clive has kindly loaned me the videos of last year's performance, which I have watched with . . . with interest.' He cleared his throat. 'While I have seen the Chester mystery plays and er . . . although the format of scenes from the Old and New Testament have similarities, otherwise they don't seem much alike.'

'They're not, Vicar,' Clive said. 'They might have been at one time – you'd have to ask Mr Pharamond, he's got all the records. But when the Puritans took over and tried to ban it, the squire – another Roland, he was – he told the players to cut it right down, so it could be performed in one day.'

'Yes,' agreed his wife. 'A short day, the first of January, instead of Midsummer Day, and up at the Pharamond Hall instead of on the green right here, so lookouts could stop strangers coming in. And then, when it was safe to perform the Mysteries in public again – well, we'd got used to doing things *our* way.'

'So it is still performed up at the hall?' George asked.

Miss Pym nodded. 'In the coach house. The doors are opened wide and the audience stands in the courtyard. The stables on either side are used as dressing rooms. It last about five hours, with breaks for refreshments, of course, and musical interludes.'

'Musical interludes? Indeed?' George brightened. 'Hymns, perhaps?'

'No, actually a local group perform – the Mummers of Invention,' I told him. 'My husband sings with them – they're quite good. Sort of electric folk style.'

'Mummers of Invention?' he murmured, looking bemused.

'The last vicar had the strange idea that the play was blasphemous in some way,' Clive said. 'But you could see yourself that it's the exact opposite, couldn't you? It's all Bible stories, and the entire parish is involved right down to the infant's school – the children always play the procession of animals into the ark.'

'And they made the virgin's bower last year with wire and tissue paper flowers,' Miss Pym said, 'though since it kept falling on Annie's head – your fifth and last appearance as virgin, wasn't it, dear? – it could not have been called an unqualified success.'

Annie caught the vicar's eye, went pink, and looked hastily away – but at least she *had* noticed him.

'And you run the Mysteries committee, Clive, and direct the play?' George said.

'Yes, that's right, and generally we start in September giving out the parts and rehearsing. No one can play the same part for more than five years, so things change, and different people volunteer or drop out.'

'Some of the new actors that have moved into the area lately have volunteered,' I informed him.

'Yes, like Rob Rafferty,' Annie murmured dreamily, and I gave her a look. I hope she is not going to get a *serious* crush on the man, since it is unlikely to lead anywhere.

'But most of them don't live here all the time, Annie, and you need people who do, especially when there are more rehearsals just before Christmas.'

'Yes, so the parts are usually played by local people, unless there's an emergency, like last year,' Clive said. 'Only, of course, a local man played that in the end, too.'

'Lazarus broke both ankles falling off his tractor,' Dr Patel explained. 'He could have laid down, but there was no way short of a real miracle he was ever going to rise up and walk. So Lizzie's husband, Tom, stepped in at the last minute.'

'He made a very good Lazarus, I gave him top billing in the parish magazine,' Clive broke in.

George turned to me. 'So, your husband is Tom Pharamond, and he also plays in a band called the Mummers? I don't think I've met him yet, have I?'

'I shouldn't think so, he's not much of a churchgoer, though he used to come to the carol service with Jasper and me every year until the operation.'

'The operation?'

'He had a brain tumour removed a couple of years back,

a benign one. He died briefly on the operating table and he hasn't been the same man since.'

'*Physically* he has made a good recovery, though he should take things easier. He is in danger of seizures if he does not,' Dr Patel said severely.

Annie said sadly, 'He used to be so sweet and laid back, even if he was exasperatingly unreliable; but now, one minute he's the old Tom, the next, he can turn really nasty.'

'Yes, and what is worse, he's entirely lost his sense of humour. I even had to stop calling him Lazarus, it made him so angry,' I agreed. 'I think that was the worst thing.'

'Well . . . I suppose that might annoy anyone after a while?' the vicar suggested gently.

Clive coughed and shuffled his papers together. 'So, we'll ask for nominations for the parts and rehearsals will start the first week in September on Tuesdays and Thursdays. As usual, I'll need a director's assistant for each scene. Lizzie, will you take on the *Fall of Lucifer*, the *Creation* and *Adam and Eve*? You *are* still doing Eve this year, I hope?'

'Yes, my fifth and final go, thank goodness – even a knitted body stocking is perishing cold in January. I had to keep warming myself over a chestnut brazier last year and a couple of my fig leaves got singed.'

'You could try thermal underwear underneath?' suggested Miss Pym. 'Those silk ones for under ski suits.'

'That's an idea,' I agreed. 'Not so bulky.'

'Miss Pym will do *Noah's Flood*, of course, and Marianne will oversee *Moses* – one of the tablets broke last time, someone will need to make a new one.' He made a note, and ticked off *Moses*.

'Vicar, if you could be in charge of the *Nativity*, the *Annunciation*, *Magi*, *Birth of Christ*, *Flight into Egypt*?'

'Yes, of course,' George agreed, but rather numbly, I thought. At least, unlike the last vicar, he had not started gibbering and foaming lightly at the mouth by this stage.

'Dr Patel has offered to do the *Temptation of Christ*, the *Curing of the Lame Man*, the *Blind Man*, and the *Raising of Lazarus*, all short scenes.'

'Seems appropriate,' agreed the doctor. 'And the *Water into Wine* and *Feeding of the Five Thousand* too, if you like.'

'I'll see to the *Last Supper*, *Judas*, the *Trial and Crucifixion* myself this year – the crucifixion's always tricky, but you might want to take that on next year, Vicar – and then that leaves just the *Resurrection*, the *Ascension* and the *Last Judgement*.'

'I'll do those again,' offered Annie.

'We do the final dress rehearsals for the whole thing up at the hall in three sessions over Christmas week,' Marianne helpfully explained to the vicar. 'But really, more than half the players have done their parts before and so it's just a question of making sure the new ones know their lines and where to stand, that's all.'

'Oh, good,' said poor George weakly. He looked at his watch. 'I'd better get back – I've got a funeral to prepare.'

'Yes, our Moses – such a sad loss,' Miss Pym said. 'We will have to recast.'

Clive stuffed his papers and clipboard into a scuffed leather briefcase and then he and Marianne started transforming the hall into a snooker parlour, turning down my offer of help.

When I went out the vicar was already halfway across the green – and so was Annie, heading off in the direction of the church. I bet they are talking about something totally mundane like Sunday School, though, and she hasn't noticed at all that he fancies her.

Miss Pym climbed into her little red Smart car and vanished with a *vroom*, and Dr Patel wished me goodnight and got into his BMW.

I winded my way home to Perseverance Cottage, where I did not find my husband or, more importantly, my car, but did find a telephone message on the machine from Unks, asking me to ring him back. When I did he told me that Mimi had been arrested by the police at the Southport Flower Show, having temporarily got away from Mrs Gumball, who had volunteered to keep an eye on her. You can't blame her, though, since Mimi is very spry for an octogenarian while Mrs Gumball is the human equivalent of a mastodon.

Mimi is also a plant kleptomaniac: no one's garden is safe from her little knife and plastic bags, and she really just can't understand why anyone should take exception to her habits. Still, the police had merely cautioned and released her this time and, since the coach had by then set out on the return journey, had driven her and Mrs Gumball home in a police car.

Roly said she was under the impression they had done it

to give her a treat, and was hoping next year's flower show would be as much fun.

Then he added, rather puzzlingly, 'And I hope Tom told you that you can stop worrying about ever losing Perseverance Cottage – after I'm gone, it's yours and Tom's. I would have said before, if I'd known it was on your mind.'

'But I wasn't worried, Unks! In fact, the thought never entered my head,' I assured him, which it hadn't, despite Unks being the shady side of ninety. Besides, since I would have to leave soon it was immaterial to me. Obviously Tom had used me as an excuse to find out how things had been left. How Machiavellian he is becoming!

After this, I unpacked Annie's candyfloss machine to distract myself from worrying until Jasper arrived safely home. The instructions absolutely forbade me to use any natural essences or colouring other than special granulated ones designed for the purpose, which was disappointing from the point of view of making Cornish Mist until I discovered one of the tubs in the box was lemon.

Fascinating how the floss forms inside the bowl like ectoplasm, and you have to wind the near invisible threads on to wooden sticks. Fine sugary filaments drifted everywhere, and the kitchen took on the hot, sweet smell of funfairs.

It was really messy but fun, which Jasper said was a good description of *me*, too, when he got home and saw what I was up to.

Maybe I'll have 'She was messy, but fun' as my epitaph.

Six

Angel Cake

There was still no sign of my car next morning, by which time I had, in a furious temper, phoned all of Tom's friends that I knew about, though trying to contact his surfing buddies down in Cornwall was like waking the dead, and I got little sense out of them even when they did answer the phone.

The first time or two he went missing for a few days I also phoned the local hospitals and the police, too, but after that I had learnt my lesson.

I woke Jasper early and he went off by bike to the dig, then called Annie to tell her I was without transport; but luckily she only wanted me to exercise the two Pekes and a Shitzu belonging to one of the more elderly members of the *Cotton Common* cast, Delphine Lake. She bought one of the expensive flats in part of the former Pharamond's Butterflake Biscuit Factory in the village and I have walked her dogs several times before.

Uncle Roly sold the Pharamond brand name out to a big conglomerate years ago for cash, shares and a seat on the board, which was both a smart and lucrative deal, so now the factory is part apartments, part café-art gallery and a museum of Mosses history.

Delphine's dogs might be little, but they loved their walks, so it was late morning before I got back to the cottage to find a female police officer waiting for me on the doorstep, and an adolescent colleague biting his fingernails behind the wheel of a Panda car.

I rammed the brakes on and leapt out, immediately thinking the worst, as you do.

'Jasper? Has something happened to Jasper?' I cried, panicking.

'Mrs Elizabeth Pharamond?' she queried solemnly.

'Yes!'

'I'm Constable Perkins, and I'm afraid I have some bad news for you.' She paused, and I was about to take her by the throat and shake her when she added: 'About your husband.'

'Oh – thank God!' I gasped devoutly, and burst into tears.

Wresting the keys from my nerveless fingers she ushered me into my own home, where she broke the news that Tom had had a fatal accident. He'd driven over the edge of the road into a disused quarry, which was odd in itself, since there's only one place within a radius of about fifty miles where he could have managed that feat, and it's up a little-used back lane.

She made me tea and spoke to me with skilful sympathy, though my reactions clearly puzzled her: all I was feeling was an overpowering relief that it wasn't Jasper. I can't say I really believed her about Tom. And then I got to thinking that this was all so blatantly unreal anyway that it couldn't be true: it was just some dreadful nightmare.

This was very calming, since I knew I would wake up *sometime,* so I agreed quite readily to go and identify Tom's body. My head seemed to be this helium-filled thing bobbing about on a string – or that's what it felt like, anyway, but there is no accounting for dreams.

Lying there, apart from his thin, handsome face being a whiter shade of pale, Tom looked absolutely fine. He was always one to land butter side up . . .

'Is this your husband?' the policewoman asked formally.

'Yes – Thomas Pharamond. Are you *sure* he's dead? Only he's got a habit of coming back, and I don't think I could bear endless resurrections.'

She gave me a strange look, but assured me that Tom had broken his neck in a very final manner. Then she offered me yet another cup of tea, which I didn't want, and took me home again, sitting beside me in the back seat while the adolescent officer did the driving. He feasted on his fingernails at every red light. I don't know why, but it suddenly reminded me of the stewed apple with little sharp crescents of core snippings that they used to give us at school.

The policewoman whiled away the journey by telling me that they thought the car (*my* car, which was now a write-off) had been at the bottom of the quarry for a few hours before it was found, and he must have died instantly – but I expect they say that every time. How can they know? There would have to be a post-mortem examination, and probably an inquest . . . I *think* she said there would be an inquest. I wasn't really taking it all in.

When we got to Perseverance Cottage, she asked if there was someone who could stay with me.

'Oh, yes – I'll phone the family right now,' I agreed, suddenly desperate to get rid of her. 'Thank you for – for – well, thank you, officer. I'll be fine.'

She looked a bit dubious, but drove off leaving me to it, and I thankfully closed the front door and leaned against it:

it seemed solid enough. So did the cold quarry tiles beneath my feet when I kicked my sandals off.

It had begun to dawn on me that all this really *was* happening: Tom was, indeed, finally dead. I could only be glad that Jasper was at his dig, since I'm sure he would have insisted on coming with me to identify Tom, though actually his face had looked peaceful enough, if vaguely surprised by the turn of events.

But now I would have to break the news to him . . . and to Unks and Mimi, who had been the closest things to parents he had had; and to his mother, in Argentina . . .

Stiffening my trembling legs I tottered into the sitting room and dialled the hall, getting Uncle Roly.

I don't think I was the mistress of either tact or coherence by this stage, but he took the news well, if quietly, and offered to phone Tom's mother and stepfather in Argentina himself, which I was grateful for, and then try and contact Nick, still off touring the eating places of rural north-west Lancashire.

'And Jasper?' he asked. 'I take it he is still at the dig, and doesn't know?'

'No, and I think I will just wait for him to come home before I tell him,' I decided. Why rush to give him the bad news? 'And anyway, Tom was driving my car – his van's off the road – so I haven't got any transport.'

When I phoned Annie, she was out. My message was, I fear, probably unintelligible.

Roly thoughtfully called in later in the Daimler to say Joe Gumball was driving him over to the dig to collect Jasper and he would break the news to him, if I wanted.

'Oh, Unks, you are kind!' I said, gratefully. 'But it must be just as hard for you – you don't have to do it.'

'My dear, having lived through the war years, I'm inured to breaking bad news.'

I offered him some of the sloe gin I had been drinking to try and dispel that feeling of being underwater with my eardrums straining, but which had just seemed to make everything more unbelievably bizarre, and said anxiously: 'Don't you think we should wait a bit, Unks, and see if Tom wakes up again, before we tell him?'

He patted my hand. 'There, there, my dear. Leave everything to me. I'll be back with Jasper in no time.'

Mimi phoned me just after he had left, but halfway through offering me her condolences in a graciously formal manner she completely lost the thread and said she was too busy to talk to me just now. Then she put the phone down.

But at least her call had jarred me into remembering to shut the poultry up for the night, and check on the quail.

Round the back of the polytunnel greenhouse I came unexpectedly nose to bare (except for the camouflage paint) chest of Caz Naylor, who indicated with a nod of his head and a raised eyebrow that he would like to know what was happening.

'Tom's driven off the quarry road,' I said, 'in *my* car.'

'Dead?'

'So they say.'

'Car?'

'That's a write-off, too.'

He grunted non-committally, then handed me a small blue plastic basket containing one slightly decayed mushroom. 'Poison,' he said, prodding it with a grimy finger.

'I know,' I began, recognizing it, but he turned and flitted off back through the shadows until he had completely vanished into the woods.

That was the longest conversation I'd had with him for ages . . . and what was the significance of the poisonous fungi in a punnet that looked suspiciously like the one Polly Darke had brought me full of field mushrooms . . . was that only yesterday? Perhaps she had inadvertently picked a poisonous one? After previous experiences of Polly's way with foodstuffs, I should have been more cautious in accepting them anyway!

Or perhaps Caz had simply taken to giving brief nature lessons in his spare time?

Jasper was very quiet and pale when he came in, and soon vanished up to his room, but I thought it best to leave him to talk in his own time.

He did reappear when Annie came over, and seemed pretty composed by then, though being the quiet stoical type it is hard to tell, even for me.

I thought I was quite composed too, but as soon as Annie walked in I burst into tears as though her arrival was a kind of sign that it all wasn't some ghastly nightmare. I fear I may have left a full set of grubby fingerprints up the back of her lavender Liberty cotton shirt.

She hugged Jasper too, something which he would normally go out of his way to avoid even though he is fond of her. Then we all just sat around in a fuzzy cloud of disbelief and sloe gin.

It was the sheer unreality: Tom had gone missing so many times, it was hard to believe he wouldn't just walk through that door at any minute with the TV remote control in his hand (he secreted it away somewhere in his workshop), and sit watching endless films on the Sky channel he'd had installed soon after he got the TV.

A TV of any kind was not something I'd wanted – it hardly fit in with the self-sufficiency ideals we'd once nurtured together. The acquisition of that and other consumer items had formed rather a bitter chapter in book five of my Perseverance Chronicles. Jasper used to watch history programmes on it sometimes, though, if Tom was away – he knows how to turn it on and change channels without the remote. I prefer the radio in the kitchen: you can't watch a TV and do things at the same time.

Strangely, although the present still seemed unreal, the past suddenly became quite clear to me and I could see that Tom had always been supremely selfish. Yes, even the Tom I fell in love with, charming though he had been, really only thought about himself for at least ninety-five per cent of the time, which is why he always did exactly what he wanted and apologized afterwards. He never considered how it might affect anyone else.

'Yes, I know,' Annie agreed when I shared this gem with her, together with the rest of the bottle of sloe gin, after Jasper had gone up to bed. Or at least, back to the bat cave. 'But when he was around he seemed to cast a spell of charm on you, so that you didn't realize it until later. Or if you realized it, you didn't mind, because he wasn't doing it intentionally, it was just how he was.'

She might not be the brightest bunny in the hutch, but she usually cuts straight to the heart of something with solid common sense.

The gin wasn't such a good idea after all, for my past life seemed to suddenly take on a darkly ominous pattern. 'Why?' I demanded. 'Why, Annie?'

'Why what?'

'Why *everything,* that's what I want to know. For a start, just look at me – anyone can see I'm meant to be the earth mother type, goddess of the organic compost heap, yet my effect on those I love is more Angel of Death.'

'We all have to die,' Annie said soothingly, passing me the plate of angel cake she'd found in the fridge while looking for something to blot up the alcohol. I must have sliced and buttered it earlier, under automatic pilot.

'Yes, but why don't *my* loved ones die naturally of old age? Look at my parents, for a start! OK, Daddy was a diplomat, but of all the British Consulates in all the world, why did they have to be sent to *that* one? And having got there, why did they have to immediately sit in the wrong restaurant and get blown up? Couldn't they have settled for baked beans on bagels at home, and then lived nice, peaceful lives and been more than a few faded snapshots and some stored furniture to their only daughter?'

'But you had nothing to do with it – you'd just arrived for your first term at St Mattie's,' she pointed out. 'You weren't even in the same country. Of course you're not the Angel of Death! What would Daddy say if he could hear you?'

From past experience I could confidently predict that he would go wandering off into a scholarly monologue on angels of death, angels the existence of, and the symbolism of their dancing on pins. Then he'd probably end by pointing out, with gentle humour, that angels of any kind, including death, were not generally depicted as sturdy women of athletic build, with unruly chestnut hair and hazel eyes, and so far my influence seemed to preclude any world-scale death dealing proclivities.

'OK then,' I continued stubbornly. 'Why did my husband have to die – and to add insult to injury, *twice*? Wasn't once enough?'

'He only died for a minute or two, the first time,' she reminded me. 'They got him back quickly, and he made a good recovery in the end – or he would have done,' she added honestly, 'if he'd done what they told him and taken the pills, and led a quiet lifestyle.'

'I wish he'd stayed dead the first time,' I said bitterly. 'When he came back – he wasn't the same. He wasn't Tom any more.'

Annie gave me a hug. 'I know – I know what it's been like and you are a saint to have stayed with him.'

'For better, for worse – for a total stranger? And I'm not a saint – what choice did I have?' A tear rolled down my cheek and landed on the half-eaten slice of angel cake I seemed to be holding. Funny, I didn't remember taking a piece.

'He did love you in his way, Lizzie, for years and years – remember all those paper roses with little messages on? *And* he needed you; you and Jasper were the fixed point of his life. He wandered off, but he always came back again, until the illness.'

'But I knew there were always other women, when he was away in Cornwall or on a gig with the Mummers. I tried to shut my eyes to it, but it hurt, Annie. And I'm not sorry he's dead now . . . .' I swallowed hard. 'I'm just – just grieving for the Tom I married, that's all. And he may never have existed!'

Annie comforted me as well as she could, and I have a vague recollection of her helping me up to bed, where I must have passed out.

When I staggered down next morning feeling like Lady Lazarus, everything had been cleared and tidied and washed up.

There's probably a Girl Guide badge for that, too, together with the Advanced Award for staying in control of your faculties while under the influence of sloe gin.

Seven

Loose Nuts

'Even the old Tom, the one I loved, was selfish,' I said to PC Perkins, when she came back to lightly grill me next day, fortunately just as I'd finished quick-candying the orange peel from yesterday's breakfast juice.

Even the sitting room, when I led the way into it, still smelled enticingly of citrus and hot sugar. 'It's funny, but I can see that quite clearly now. People thought he was endearingly absent-minded and eccentric, but really he was just too wrapped up in himself to bother doing anything he didn't want to or that wasn't to his advantage.'

I was keen to share the illuminations engendered by last night's over-application of strong sloe gin, in the hope that it would help her to understand my possibly strange behaviour when she broke the news to me. I tried to explain to her how Tom's illness and operation had changed him. 'But of course, I can see now that the illness only emphasized some aspects of his character that had always been there. He always did exactly what he pleased, like a cat.'

'But you can still love a cat,' Jasper pointed out thoughtfully. After last night's hair-down, sloe-gin-fuelled wake with Annie, I have pretty well stopped trying to hide anything from him, since obviously it had never worked in the first place.

Having phoned up the dig to explain his absence, he was now looming about protectively. 'Most cat owners seem to think their cats love them back . . . and Dad certainly loved you, Mum,' he said kindly. 'Right up until he got sick.'

'He loved you too, Jasper, when you were small,' I said, wiping a runny tear away, 'even if he never thought of actually doing anything with you that he didn't want to do himself, or taking you anywhere . . .'

'Well, I expect it would have been OK if I surfed, or was interested in weird folk rock music and stuff – if I'd fitted into his interests,' Jasper agreed. 'History and archaeology bored him.'

'Yes, he wasn't even interested in food, was he, except from the eating it point of view?'

The police officer, who had been listening in a sort of fascinated silence, now broke in, notebook at the ready. She seemed to have an agenda of her own. 'Just a few more questions, Mrs Pharamond – and I'm sure you have a few you would like to ask me.'

She gave me a reassuring smile, though it contained no warmth today . . . and yesterday she had seemed so kind and sympathetic, too. Maybe she could switch a façade on and off at will, like Tom. She had coral pink lipstick on her front teeth and it was *so* not her colour.

'Perhaps your son – Jasper, isn't it? – could make tea,' she suggested.

'I think I'll stay here,' Jasper said thoughtfully, settling down on the sofa next to me.

'Can you tell me what time your husband left here on the Wednesday – you said you last saw him then?'

'I don't know. I went for a walk in the late morning – a long walk in the woods – and when I got back, my car had gone.'

'Did he often borrow your car?'

'No, practically never, because I usually make sure he can't find the keys. His van had broken down, that's why he took mine.'

'So you were surprised to find your car gone?'

'Yes, and annoyed when he didn't come back in time for me to go and collect Jasper from the dig . . . or at all. I *needed* my car.'

'He would probably have come back in time, if he . . . if the accident hadn't happened, Mum. His mobile was in the workshop and he would have taken it with him if he hadn't just popped out for something,' Jasper said. 'Wonder where he was going? He'd wiped his messages, so that was no help.'

'I don't know,' I said dubiously. 'He probably just forgot it.'

'Where do *you* think he might have been going, Mrs Pharamond?'

'I've no idea. But he told me earlier he had to finish a surfboard for the weekend, so I was surprised when he didn't come back.'

'Finish a *surfboard*?'

'Yes, he customized surfboards. You know – spray-painted designs on them? He was a keen surfer, too . . .' I stopped, having a sudden vision of Tom freewheeling into space off the quarry road and wondering if he found the sensation exhilarating? I wouldn't put it past him, and of course he would never expect anything he did, however dangerous, to actually kill him.

'And you were here all evening?'

'Yes, after I got back from the Mystery Play committee

meeting in the village hall I was experimenting with candyfloss. And I had quail eggs to boil and jam to make. I was pretty busy.'

She gave me a strange look but didn't follow that one up. Instead she turned her attention to Jasper.

'And you were at this archaeological site all that day?'

'Yes. Sometimes I cycle there in the mornings, but Mum usually picks me up in the evening. She took me too, that day – she thinks the roads are dangerous. When I got home she'd got back from the Mystery Play committee meeting and was making lemon candyfloss. Yummy.'

'Right,' she said, scribbling away. I nearly asked her if she would like me to whip her up some Cornish Mist, but I could see she had no sense of humour.

'So, Mrs Pharamond, weren't you a bit cross with your husband for taking the car without telling you?'

'Yes, and even more so when he didn't come back. But I knew if I didn't turn up, Jasper would cycle back, he really didn't mind.' I was starting to feel strangely worried, despite knowing I had nothing on my conscience other than guilt for that profound moment of relief when I heard that it was Tom who had had the accident and not Jasper.

'Jasper, perhaps tea *would* be a good idea? Or coffee. Would you mind?'

He gave me a look, but rose to a gangling six-foot and, stooping under the low beam, went to the kitchen, though he left the door ajar. This is not a cottage where you can have private conversations . . . or indeed, private much of anything.

'Can you tell me how the accident happened yet? I thought he must have had some kind of seizure, perhaps – the doctors warned him that if he didn't live a quieter lifestyle and take care of himself, he might get them, and his behaviour was getting increasingly erratic and . . . well, *odd*.'

'It looks as though one of the Citroen's wheels came off, while your husband was driving down the quarry road.' Her eyes were fixed on my face to gauge the full effect of this pronouncement.

'A *wheel* came off? But – would that have caused him to veer off the road?'

'Not necessarily. It's usually possible to drive on three wheels to a safe halt.'

A sudden rather nasty thought struck me. 'Do you know *which* wheel came off?'

'The front driver's side.' She looked at me intently again, and I realized I must've turned pale. 'Why?'

'I – I had a flat tyre . . . it must have been that same morning,' I said slowly, and 'I – we – changed the wheel for the spare and took that one to be mended.'

'We?'

'Jasper undid the last nut – it was stiff – but I changed the wheel and put the nuts on again,' I said firmly. 'Jasper had gone back in the house. And what's more, it was absolutely fine on the drive there and back!'

'Mrs Pharamond, I'm not accusing you of anything.' *Wasn't she? It began to sound amazingly like it!* 'It's just possible you didn't tighten them up quite enough and they slowly worked loose, isn't it? Accidents do happen.'

'You mean – I might have *accidentally* killed him?'

And, now I saw which way they were heading with this, I thanked God it was me who tightened the nuts and not Jasper!

'They might have worked loose slowly – and then the tight bends of the quarry road could have completed the job,' she said. 'It's a possibility. We haven't found any of them yet.'

'But I am *sure* they were tight because I used a wheel br—' I stopped as Jasper came back in with a battered tin tray of mugs and an open carton of milk.

'Yes, they were,' he said, putting the tray down on the coffee table with a thump. 'I could hear what you were saying from the kitchen,' he added to the policewoman. 'Mum put the wheel back on and tightened the nuts – and then when she went in to wash her hands, I tightened them up even more.'

We gazed at him, though possibly not both with the same mixed sharp feeling of affection and exasperation as I was feeling.

'Oh, Jasper,' I said. 'I'm not being accused of anything except carelessness, so you really don't have to try and protect me!'

'I'm not, Mum. It's true – I left you putting the wheel back on, but I went down and just checked it was tight enough later, when you weren't about.'

How often does he feel he needs to check up on me, I wondered?

From my expression he deduced that he ought to add something: 'It was fine – I thought it would be.'

'Of course,' I said, 'any idiot can change a wheel.'

PC Perkins had lost interest in the ins and outs of our dispute, and turned to Jasper. 'So you are quite sure that the wheel was in a safe condition?'

'Absolutely, and I often check them and the tyre pressure, especially since I passed my test,' he said, 'for practice.'

'So, how do you account for the same wheel coming off?'

'I don't – that's your job, isn't it? But we don't know how long he'd been out – he could have left it standing about somewhere and loosening the wheel nuts might have been someone's idea of a joke. The wheel brace was on the back seat last time I saw it, so the means was at hand, and even if it was in the boot, the car doesn't lock any more, it broke ages ago.' He shrugged. 'Mum's car was ancient, so who knows? Maybe the threads had gone or something, even?'

I stared at him, thinking that he certainly didn't get his coolness and sangfroid from me or Tom – but of course, my father *was* a diplomat.

She closed her notebook. 'Once the post-mortem has been completed, if everything is in order, an inquest will be opened and adjourned and an interim death certificate issued,' she said briskly, by which I presume she meant unless they found I'd been feeding him Cyanide Chutney for months. Or Polly Darke's poisonous tomatoes – pity I hadn't thought of that one. He'd been away at the time, but I could have saved some. 'The funeral can then take place, and the inquest proper will take place at a later date.'

'Must there be an inquest?'

'Yes, it's standard procedure in cases of this kind.'

'Which kind?' I had just demanded, when the cottage front door suddenly burst open and crashed back against the wall, making everything on the dresser jingle. I leapt up just in time to catch a prized Worcester plate that had belonged to my mother.

Polly Darke stumbled over the threshold like a dishevelled, shrink-wrapped Bacchae, all billowing green chiffon sleeves, stick-thin legs and enormous boobs.

Well, stay me with flagons, I thought. (Sloe gin for preference.)

Her slightly prominent eyes passed over the policewoman and

fixed on me. 'Is it *true*?' she demanded, in rising tones. 'Is Tom really dead? They're saying he had an accident – in *your* car!'

Presumably this was rhetorical, for with an anguished cry of 'Tom! Tom!' she threw herself into the nearest chair and burst into hysterical sobs.

Jasper and I exchanged a look. Attention seeking taken to extremes was, I am sure, our first thought, combined with a raging desire to know what was happening.

'This is Polly Darke, Officer,' I explained resignedly. 'She's a novelist, and lives near Mossrow—'

Polly looked up, her face like a drowned flower. A slightly withered pansy. 'I can't believe it! Only last night Tom was with me, and now he's gone. *Gone!*'

'*Why* was he with you?' asked Jasper, puzzled. 'I thought he'd finally finished those Celtic murals you asked him to do ages ago?'

'Because he loved me!' she exclaimed tragically and began to sob again.

I stared at her, my mind whirling faster than a tumble-dryer. 'He was with you last night? Good heavens – don't tell me that *you*, of all people, are Dark Heart? No, it can't possibly be you!'

'Yes it is! Why not?' she demanded belligerently, straightening from her pose of utter despondency. 'I could give him what he needed—'

'*Tie him up, tie him down?*' I said numbly. You know, I'd never even considered her as a possible suspect? To me she was a rather pathetic and ludicrous creature – but maybe men see her differently? But not *young* men, apparently, for Jasper seemed even more incredulous than I was.

'Dark Heart?' he queried.

'Yes, I knew your father was having an affair with someone, and then I found a note the morning of the day he vanished, signed "Dark Heart", but I didn't know who it was.'

'You mean Dad was having an affair with *her*?'

'Evidently, but I certainly thought it would be someone younger.'

I am quite sure Polly is older than I am, even if she does try and hold back the years with every ancient and modern art known to woman – or every woman except Annie and me.

'What do you mean?' she demanded indignantly, glaring at me. 'I'm only thirty-five!'

'*And* the rest,' Jasper said dryly.

I'd entirely forgotten the policewoman was there until she interjected into the sudden lull in the proceedings: 'So you knew your husband was having an affair, Mrs Pharamond?'

Her notebook was open again, pen poised.

I glanced uneasily at Jasper. 'He . . . well, he *had* had lapses occasionally in the past, but they didn't mean anything. I found out about a more serious affair a couple of years back, just before his operation, but I realized after the diagnosis that the tumour had caused character changes he couldn't help. I'm so sorry, Jasper, I didn't want you to find out about your father's affairs, especially like this.'

'Oh, I knew all about the women, Mum,' he said calmly. 'I even caught him at it with that girl out of the Mummers once, when I walked in on them in the workshop.'

'You – you did?'

'That's a lie!' Polly yelled furiously, but Jasper just glanced coolly at her, one eyebrow raised, as though she were a failed soufflé. He looked terribly like Nick.

I don't think Polly is any kind of soufflé, though, more of a synthetic Black Forest gateau with poisonous cherries.

'So you were not on good terms with your husband,' the policewoman suggested to me, 'although he'd had affairs in the past to which you hadn't objected?'

'Of course I objected!' I exclaimed. 'What do you take me for? And they were usually more in the nature of one-night stands the first few years after we were married, when he was often away in Cornwall for weeks at a time on his own. But he was . . . well, he was the kind of man who drifted, who couldn't say no, and I'm sure he never pursued anyone. They were just a passing thing.'

'Yes, but that was the old dad, not the model we've had to live with lately,' Jasper pointed out. 'Even I've overheard him, taunting you about some woman he's been seeing. He's not coming across as a very admirable sounding character, is he?' he added thoughtfully. 'And yet, he was very popular.'

The police officer said patiently, 'So this time he was having a serious affair, Mrs Pharamond? He would have left you?'

'No – this cottage belongs to his great uncle, Roly Pharamond, so I would have had to leave him. Which I was going to do, once Jasper was at university and I'd found new homes for the livestock and sorted out somewhere to go, some sort of job . . .' I trailed off.

'That's not true – I heard you arguing in his workshop that very morning and, when I asked him about it later, he said he'd asked you to leave and you refused!' Polly cried. 'He was afraid Roly Pharamond would take your side and he'd lose the cottage and everything he'd worked for.'

I stared at her. 'Obviously you didn't hear much: what I *actually* told him was that I'd had enough and was going to leave him as soon as I could. And if anyone worked around here and stood to lose everything, it was me!' I added incautiously, and the policewoman's pen skidded quickly across the page.

'Well, at least you don't have to do that now, Mum,' Jasper remarked, and a small silence fell.

I sighed. 'But we might still have to move, Jasper – it depends on Uncle Roly.'

'Uncle Roly won't put you out, Ma. He's really fond of you.'

'So,' said the officer to Polly, 'you overheard an argument, and what then?'

'*She* came out,' Polly said, with a venomous look at me. 'So I said I'd brought her some field mushrooms to exchange for eggs, and she said, "Help yourself, I'm going for a walk." She was really odd – she looked furious. When she'd gone I spoke to Tom briefly and he said he would come over later, after he'd finished the board he was painting – which he did. And that's the last time I saw him – when I woke up early next morning he had gone. He parks around the back of the house, out of sight, so I had no idea he hadn't come in his own van,' she added. 'I just assumed he had.'

'No, it had broken down and been taken to the garage,' I said. 'But if he hadn't taken my car, when he knew very well I wanted it later, it might have been me – and Jasper – who had the accident.'

'It should have been you!' she said venomously. Her reddened eyes and sharp nose made her look like a particularly unsavoury rodent.

Jasper stood up slowly and said, with a tone of menace I'd never heard from him before, 'I think you've said – and done – quite enough. Why don't you clear off?'

She floundered hastily and inelegantly out of the chair and backed towards the door. PC Perkins closed her notebook with a snap and stood between them.

'If I could have your name and address, Ms Darke? I'll follow you over and just ask you a few questions in your own home, if I may?' She turned to me with a thin smile. 'Thank you for your assistance, Mrs Pharamond.'

I had a horrible feeling she suspected me of loosening the wheel nuts on my own car on purpose, and then leaving the keys out where Tom was sure to find them. And goodness knows what Polly will tell her.

'Jasper,' I said when she'd gone, 'you were wonderful!'

'Don't worry, Mum – that cop may have a suspicious mind, but we know there's nothing to find, so they can't pin anything on you.'

'Thank you, darling,' I said weakly. I had a thought. 'I wonder if Tom had anything to eat at Polly's? Only if he had had an attack of food poisoning, it might account for why he lost control of the car.'

'I don't think he went there to *eat*, Mum,' Jasper said.

When I went into the kitchen half of the candied peel had vanished, presumably eaten by Jasper while waiting for the kettle to boil – but then, it is very more-ish. But it didn't matter, I was only going to dip it in dark chocolate as a treat for later.

Meanwhile, there was a whole row of lettuces getting ready to bolt, that needed turning into cream soup and freezing.

Eight
Soft Crumb

It took a couple of days before Unks tracked Nick down to give him the bad tidings, since he was still off touring the far-flung eateries of north-west Lancashire.

In the meantime I received a postcard of Morecambe Bay bearing a scribbled recipe for spiced potted shrimps on the back, which I found immensely comforting.

Being a true professional, Nick finished his assignment and sent in his copy before phoning me up – which was more than I had managed to do, for the date for sending in my newest Perseverance Chronicle was approaching at light speed.

Bringing the last one to a close on any kind of upbeat note had been difficult, but this one would be impossible – unless I brought it to an abrupt halt just before Tom's demise? Then it could just be a footnote at the start of the next Chronicle, after a decent interval.

Ending my current book with an apocryphal near-death by mushrooms instead is a possibility – it is the sort of thing my readers seem to like, and I have never let a strict adherence to the truth hold me back from a good story. Saved by Caz Naylor in the nick of time . . . assuming he *had* found the poisonous fungi in the basket of mushrooms Polly left me, which I don't think was ever clearly established. He could have been just giving me a swift nature lesson, you never know with Caz.

Or even a suggestion? I am sure he must have often been flitting about the place in the evenings like a shade, and seen and heard some of what has been going on.

But I should know better than to accept anything edible from Polly's hands, even if the mushrooms had looked suspiciously like supermarket ones used as an excuse to snoop around Perseverance Cottage – maybe, now I know about her affair with Tom, in order to see him without my suspecting anything.

A horrible thought – if I'd cooked the mushrooms and not spotted the poisonous one, Jasper might have been made ill too! But not Tom, who doesn't eat them.

I think it has put me right off mushrooms, whereas before I was all for any kind of free food.

A lovely letter came today from the Vanes – they must have posted it practically the minute Annie told them about Tom. Of course, they only really knew the old, charming Tom and not the monster I have been living with lately, but it was very kind and comforting all the same.

There was also an announcement in the Mosses parish magazine, which I found a bit poignant:

> IMPORTANT NOTICE!
>
> Everyone wanting to take part in next January's Mystery Play should put their name forward immediately to Clive or Marianne Potter at the Post Office, Middlemoss, including last year's performers intending to reprise their roles. Applicants must be resident of Middlemoss, Mossedge or Mossrow and able to devote at least one night a week to rehearsals. Sadly, due to bereavement, the important roles of Moses and Lazarus need to be recast and, as always, we need a new baby Jesus. Auditions/rehearsals will start the first week of September.

I am sure I will never be able to watch the *Raising of Lazarus* scene again without thinking of Tom, though actually when Lazarus's mother says to Jesus, 'Our Lazarus hath popped his clogs, and he were my only child,' my eyes do tend to well up anyway.

But then, of course, Jesus tells Lazarus to stop larking about, because his mother is in a proper state about him, and up he jumps with a cheery 'Hello, our ma. Is summat up?'

Tom, however, had already had his one allotted miracle. He hath well and truly popped his clogs this time.

'Hi Lizzie, I hear fate caught up with Tom before I did,' was Nick's bluntly uncompromising opening gambit when he did finally phone. 'Roly told me what happened.'

I gripped the receiver tightly. 'Oh, Nick! Did Unks tell you it was my car, and the wheel came off, and it was the one I'd just changed the tyre on, so I'm sure they think I did it on purpose?'

'Don't be so bloody stupid, of course they don't think that! Why would you tamper with the wheel on your own frigging car?' he snapped, and I stopped wilting over the receiver and glared at it, as though Nick could see me.

'That's true, I wouldn't – but his van was at the garage and I left my keys out somewhere where he could find them, which I usually take good care not to. *And* we had an argument that morning, which Polly Darke overheard – she told the police. Nick, *she* was the one Tom was having the affair with, but I don't think anyone except the police and Jasper know about that yet.'

'Well, I certainly didn't. But it doesn't surprise me – apart from you, he always did have crap taste in women.'

That was as close to a compliment as I'd ever got from Nick – and he can't include his own wife in that statement either, can he? So he mustn't *really* think Tom and Leila were having an affair. The idea of Leila as Tom's lover is even more ludicrous than Polly, so he was probably just after free bed and board in London and lied to me to spur me into leaving him.

'I had to go and identify Tom,' I said. 'It was all right until we actually went in, because I thought it was a nightmare so it didn't matter. But then there he was and . . . I kept expecting his eyes to open . . . I couldn't believe he was really dead this time, even though they said his neck was broken. Now I keep thinking about him, so white and . . . gone.'

'*Don't* think about it, then,' he said flatly. 'It's a pity I wasn't home to identify him for you. Anyway, it wasn't your fault, and I think he's given you a rough time the last year or two. I've kept my nose out, but I've heard things.'

Tears pricked behind my eyes. 'Well, it's over now. They're releasing the body – they've done the post-mortem, and adjourned the inquest,' I added, shivering. 'The inquest will reopen later, but not for ages, probably, so the funeral can go ahead on Thursday.'

'Then they *don't* suspect you of anything, you stupid bat,' he said, with what sounded suspiciously like relief. Surely even Nick didn't secretly think I'd bumped Tom off, too?

'I'm heading down to London tomorrow, but I'll be back in a couple of days if you need any help with the arrangements.'

'Thanks, but I've got Annie, and the new vicar seems very pleasant and helpful . . . everyone has been so kind. Roly offered to have the bunfight after the funeral up at the hall, but I wanted it here. I'm going to do everything just the way the old Tom would have wanted it – the fun one with a sense of humour.'

'Let's hope it's a nice day then, because you won't get more than six people standing up in your sitting room.'

'I'm going to use the polytunnel greenhouse, it's huge. I was going to get rid of it, so it's fortunate I haven't got round to it yet.'

'It'll still have to be a fine day: it leaks like a sieve,' he objected.

'Caz Naylor asked me if he could do anything, and he's out there now mending the worst bits with gaffer tape.'

That was a slight exaggeration. Caz's precise words had been a questioning, 'Do owt, our Lizzie?'

'You're honoured: whenever Roly or I ask him to do anything, he vanishes. How is Jasper taking all this?'

'Stoical and quiet. Tom's been increasingly odd with him lately, so like me, it is a relief to know he's not coming back. And then we feel guilty for feeling like that and sad at the same time and . . . and I don't suppose he could help it, really . . .' I broke off, my voice wobbling.

'Do you want me to come straight back now?' he asked abruptly.

'No, of course not – what could you do?'

'Nothing, I suppose. Where's Jasper?'

'The dig. He thought he might as well go back as mope around the house.'

'Very sensible. Has he sorted out his university accommodation yet? Or is he going to live at home?'

'I wanted him to live in the student's hall for the first year at least, because that's what university is all about, isn't it, getting away from your parents and making your own life? Only now he says he might share a house with one of his friends and some other students.'

'He's very level-headed for his age. I'd let him do whatever he wants.'

'Yes – I suppose so, and at least it is close enough for him to come home for the weekend, or for me to drive over, if he gets homesick or anything.'

'I expect he will have other distractions.'

'I should think the course will be distraction enough. I am so proud of him, getting on to it. And he should get the full student loan, too, shouldn't he, because it will be based on my earnings now as a single parent, and I actually earn hardly anything in actual money . . . ? I don't suppose barter counts. But Unks told Jasper yesterday that he was going to make him an allowance – he is so kind, and really, we have no claim on him.'

'Roly thinks of you as family. Have you heard from Tom's mother and stepfather? You'd think they would offer to help!'

'Oh, they have and it was dreadful! He phoned – says Tom's mother is too upset to speak to me, and probably won't be well enough to travel all this way for the funeral, but he would pay for it all! I told him I didn't want his money, and I haven't heard anything since.'

'Well, burn all your boats at once, why don't you?' he said sarkily.

'You're such a comfort to me!' I snapped, but beginning to feel much more like the real Lizzie Pharamond rather than the horse under water.

'Fellow feeling, darling – Leila and I are going to split, though I hope not in *quite* so final a manner as you and Tom.'

'You are? I'm so sorry!'

'Are you? Then don't be – things haven't been good between us for a long time, though she's always refused to discuss divorce.'

'Well, she is Catholic,' I said. 'That's probably it.'

'Only nominally. No, I don't know why she's so adamant, but she is going to have to get used to the idea, the sooner the better. That's why I'm going straight down there now, to tell her.'

'You mean she doesn't *know* yet?'

'She knows how I feel: our marriage is dead in the water, and it's time to call it quits. And I want to spend more time in Middlemoss than I do now: I feel much more creative there.'

'Lawrence Durrell's "spirit of place",' I said. 'Middlemoss gets your creative juices flowing. Mine too – this is my real home and I'm not sure I could write anywhere else.'

'If you can call your stream-of-conscious burblings writing, any more than you can call your recipes cookery,' he said, back to his normal sharp self. 'We can only be grateful you do your ghastly chronicles under your maiden name and disguise anything that might give away the location!'

'Well, at least *anyone* can make my recipes, you don't need a thousand pounds worth of equipment and three underlings to help you!' I shot back rather unfairly, since I know very well that he whips up his recipes in his own kitchen or the one at the hall himself: personally tried and tested before being unleashed in his Sunday newspaper cookery column, or his books. They are mostly straightforward recipes too, not *nouvelle cuisine* or anything, though some are a little fancy for my taste. But then, anything with a list of more than eight ingredients is a little fancy for my taste.

Plebeian, he once called me, when he found me devising a new recipe for strawberries and custard bread and butter pudding – but then, as I recall, he ended up eating two plates of it.

You know, I haven't made that for quite a while and it is really yummy . . . *real* comfort food.

'I think we're digressing,' he said coldly. 'I am going to London in order to tell Leila that I'm instructing my solicitor to start divorce proceedings, whether she wants it or not. After that I will be back at the hall, so I'll be around if you want me. Don't tell anyone about it yet, I'll break the news to Roly later. I'm not sure how he will take it, and I don't want to give him any more shocks.'

Actually, I thought Roly would be pleased rather than shocked, but I didn't say anything.

'No, I won't mention it to anyone,' I assured him. 'And . . . oh, I don't think Leila knows about Tom yet! How awful, I forgot to tell her!'

'I'll tell her,' he said. 'And I'll be back before the funeral.' Then he put the phone down.

I wondered, if he'd been here, if he would have given me a big, comforting hug like he had in hospital that time? And whether he would have looked at me with that same startled expression in his slatey eyes, as though surprised to find himself doing it?

He *does* have a softer side, and he may have a bad temper but he is never violent, which is why I suppose I've never found him at all frightening: I'm much the same myself, all bark and no bite.

In the event, he *wasn't* back before the funeral, having phoned me to say briefly that Leila refused to discuss anything about the divorce until after it, and insisted on being present, so he would be driving her up on the morning.

There wasn't anything for him to do, anyway – I was pretty well organized, Annie having taken over the finer details.

When you have been Leader of the Pack (Brownies) for years, these things come naturally to you.

We'd covered most angles and finished the preparations for the Feeding of the Five Thousand – or however many turned up to be fed and watered after the ceremony – late the evening before. Every surface in the kitchen and larder groaned under the weight of plates and bowls and platters. The fridge door kept trying to spring open, and plastic bags of yellow cotton candy swung from the rack above the kitchen table. The very air could have been sliced up and served with whipped cream, it was so loaded with mingled aromas.

When all was done, we sat in the tiny sitting room at Perseverance Cottage drowning our sorrows in elderberry wine, while Jasper was out the back, immolating Tom's favourite surfboard on the garden bonfire, accompanied by a strange, small dog rather like a hairy haggis with legs. Annie had brought it with her, as well as Trinny, and it had immediately attached itself to Jasper.

He came in now from his bonfire with the little dog under one arm and vanished up to his bat cave in the attic to bludgeon his emotions with loud music.

'Annie, that dog—' I began.

'Jasper has agreed to foster it until he goes to university,' she interrupted brightly. 'The kennel was full, and no one seems to want to adopt it.'

'You surprise me,' I said tartly. 'It nipped my ankles when it came in and it sheds so much hair it leaves a trail behind it across carpets.'

'I expect Jasper will give it a good brushing. You've still got all Harriet's stuff, haven't you?'

'Yes, but I don't want another dog at the moment, and what if Jasper gets attached to it? He can't take it to university with him. You'll have to take it away with you right now!'

Putting my glass down I went upstairs, determined to oust the creature before things went too far. Jasper's door was open just a crack, and through it I saw him sitting on his bed, his face buried in the hairy haggis and his shoulders shaking.

Silently I backed away and tiptoed downstairs.

'It can stay for a couple of weeks,' I conceded to Annie. 'But that's it – you'll have to keep looking for a permanent home for it.'

'OK,' she agreed. 'Unless you find you want to keep her, after all.'

'I doubt it, I've still got puncture marks in my ankle.'

She went home soon after that. She is going to come here straight after the church service tomorrow instead of attending the interment, and organize the Women's Institute volunteers who are manning the buffet at the funeral feast in the poly-tunnel.

Around three in the morning, entirely unable to sleep, I went downstairs and whipped up a batch of strawberries and custard bread and butter pudding *à la* Lizzie Pharamond, and then Mimi wandered in out of the night, dressed in wellies with a man's overcoat over her nightie.

'Hello, dear, I've come for tea,' she said brightly, sitting down at the kitchen table. 'And to tell you that Tom's dead.'

'I know,' I said, handing her a portion of bread and butter pudding and the cup of cocoa I was just going to drink myself.

She seemed very taken with the words, and was still repeating softly: 'Tom's dead, Tom's dead!' all the time I was walking her back up the dark drive to the hall, which was a little trying.

Juno had just discovered her absence and was frothing gently at the mouth, but there was no harm done, though the sooner her leg is healed and she can keep tabs on Mimi, the better.

Nine
Soul Food

I had one of those confused moments standing at the edge of the grave, where I couldn't remember where I was, or even *who* I was – let alone who was six feet below me tastefully attired in best, sustainable Norwegian pine. The coffin was crowned with a home-made wreath of dried hops, bearing the hand-written epitaph:

For the Tom we loved
from
Lizzie and Jasper

The circle of eyes fringing the grave reminded me of a stargazey pie, except that they were not blank and dead, but expectant – and fixed on me. What *could* they want?

There was the tall, broad-shouldered figure of Tom's cousin Nick, his purple-grey eyes dark and brooding, possibly because his chic French wife was hanging tightly on to his arm, as she did to all her possessions.

Next to Nick was his father, Nigel, in whom the strong Pharamond genes had surprisingly been subjugated by the more nondescript ones of his mother, his expensive suiting trying to turn a sow's ear into a silk purse.

Polly Darke had turned up uninvited and unwanted, as she did most places, wearing a short and inappropriate black chiffon garment cut low over the twin pink Zeppelins of her bosom.

Dr Patel, Marianne and Clive Potter from the post office . . . Miss Pym, the infants' schoolteacher, nodding encouragingly at me, as though I were a recalcitrant four year old. A ragbag of Tom's old surfing chums stood there looking shifty. The new vicar with his pale, interestingly knobbly face, his bright red hair blowing in the slight breeze like a fiery halo . . .

Jasper nudged me with a bony elbow. 'Mum?'

Then, as though someone had opened the sluice gate, a scummy dark tide of recollection rushed into my head: Lizzie Pharamond, forty-one; widow, mother of the willowy youth next to me, and now expected to toss earth on to my late husband's remains like a cat tidying up after itself.

My *late*, late husband, because he'd already had that brief flirtation with death a couple of years ago on the operating table when, unfortunately, the doctors hadn't managed to resuscitate his sense of humour along with the rest of him, and something dark, angry and increasingly violent had slipped in to inhabit the empty spaces.

So, this was a blessed release . . . for me, at least. And since I've been mourning the loss of the old Tom for such a long time, these last rites were just a necessary epilogue to our life together and a full stop.

'Mum?' Jasper said again, draping a sinewy arm across my shoulders. For a teenage boy this is touchingly demonstrative and, for the first time that day, I felt painful tears at the back of my eyes. Though earlier I had struggled to suppress grossly unbecoming giggles during the new vicar's eulogy, when he tried to reconcile wildly conflicting descriptions of Tom's character, while using surfing as a metaphor for his journey through life, and on into the great ocean that was death.

Something, I remembered, was expected of me. Slowly I reached into my large, gaily embroidered shoulder bag and took out Tom's mobile phone and the TV remote control, then tossed them with a clatter into the open grave on top of the coffin. Grave goods: the things lately most dear to him – apart from his favourite surfboard, which Jasper had already immolated on the garden bonfire. But even *that* was here in spirit, for as I turned and left, amid stunned silence, I stumbled over its effigy worked in wired flowers and a card that read: *Yo, dude! Catch a big one.*

From behind me came the light patter of earth as the mourners hastened to cover up the evidence of my eccentricity, though I fear Tom will be gone but not *entirely* forgotten until the battery on his mobile runs out.

He was always popular.

At the end of the gravelled path stood Tom's white van, which had done duty today as his hearse, and I had a sudden vision of the six mismatched surfers and Mummers trying to shoulder the coffin.

A hysterical bubble of laughter attempted to force its way up my throat. How Tom would once have loved that bit! Where *did* that Tom go? He imperceptibly slipped away over the years of our marriage, until only his sense of humour remained, the last smile of the Cheshire Cat. Then that, too, was gone.

I stopped the giggle escaping by clamping my lips together, but two painful tears squeezed out and ran down my cheeks, compounded of laugher and sorrow inextricably mixed with an over-heavy seasoning of the guilt that seems to be an inescapable component of death.

'Ow-do, missis,' Dave Naylor said. The proprietor of Deals on Wheels had driven Tom's van to the funeral and was now leaning against it, rolling a cigarette between scrubbed but darkly crackled fingers.

Another Naylor, you note – and also, on less official days, likely to address me as 'our Lizzie'. I really must do a bit of family research some time.

'Bear up, lass. It's all sorted now and a great send-off it were, too. Them Mummers singing *Amazing Grace*?' He shook his head in slow wonderment. 'By heck, we'll never see the likes of *that* again.'

'Oh, I do *hope* not,' I agreed fervently. 'And thanks, Dave, for driving the van. You are coming back to the cottage, aren't you?'

'Aye, but I'll let the fancy cars go first. I'll take the van back to the garage with me afterwards and drop your new car off in the morning.'

'That's fine – see you later,' I said gratefully and carried on to where Roly Pharamond awaited me in his long black Daimler on the main pathway, having sensibly eschewed the interment in favour of a sit-down and a swift nip of brandy. His sister Mimi seemed to have eschewed it altogether.

Joe Gumball, husband of Roly's cook and jack-of-all-trades up at the hall, got out of the driver's seat and opened the door for me. He was wearing the hat and jacket of a chauffeur over faded blue dungarees and wellington boots.

Jasper, who was silently following me, got in the front and I slid on to the leather back seat, where Roly patted my hand with his thin, dry one and said gently: 'All done and dusted, my dear?'

'All done and soon to *be* dust,' I agreed numbly. 'It all seems so surreal – and the way everything keeps undulating slightly isn't helping,' I added. This underwater rippling feeling has been going on ever since I got the news of the accident and nothing, not even the best elderberry wine, can entirely make it go away.

He shook his head sadly. 'Never thought to outlive Tom, especially after he made it through that operation – but there, anyone can have an accident. Well, better get the bunfight over with, I suppose? Mimi should be along later with Juno.'

Joe pulled out and headed for the cottage where, with the help of Annie and two ladies from the WI, I had turned my big, ramshackle polytunnel greenhouse into some approximation of a venue for the funereal baked meats. Trestle tables and folding chairs were borrowed from the village hall, as were the tea and coffee urns.

The plants had all been moved towards the far end, but an aroma of tomatoes and moist earth scented the air. Still, I had judged that better than holding it in Tom's wooden workshop, with its stale smell of dope and the spray paint he used to customize surfboards, several of which were propped in various stages of completion around the walls.

'You know, I still expect to open his workshop door and find him there,' I said, following this train of thought. 'Just like all the other times when he's vanished for a few days and turned up as though he'd never been away. But of course, I always somehow expected it to be the old Tom, for him to be himself again.'

Whatever that was. I'm beginning to think I invented Nice Tom.

Jasper turned around and looked anxiously at me, and I summoned a smile from somewhere. Luckily he couldn't hear us, because the sliding glass partition was shut and Joe was playing muted country and western music.

We drove over the hump-backed bridge crossing the stream, scattering the gaggle of five vicious geese that had taken up residence there among all the innocently stupid ducks.

'Must get something done about those creatures,' Roly said absently. 'The children are all too frightened to go to the playground, and you can't feed the ducks without being mugged, I'm told.'

'Well, that local animal rights group, ARG!, might have something to say about that,' I said, getting a grip on myself. 'Anonymously, of course. They seem very vociferous about it in the parish magazine. But the geese are getting more and more aggressive, and they leave such a mess behind them, too. Now they have started wandering up to the shops, someone is bound to skid on it and then there will be hell to pay. Though I don't know who you can sue, if no one owns them?'

'Perhaps I own them – or the rights to deal with them – since I own the green and the stream?' Roly said. 'I'll ask my solicitor – Smithers will know. Or perhaps I'll just get Caz Naylor to quietly round them up one night and move them somewhere else.'

'How's he doing with the squirrels?'

'Very well – constantly patrols the exclusion zone, of course – have to do, to keep the grey buggers out. Only way. Reds, that's what we have at Pharamond Hall. Always have, always will. On the coat of arms, even.'

I think this shows a touchingly Canute-like optimism, since the tide of grey squirrels seems to have swept over most of Britain. But then, the reds *have* got Caz on their side.

'I think the signs Caz has put up on the main pathways have caused some talk,' I suggested. 'RED OR DEAD! is a bit ambiguous and that new one just inside the gate that says WARNING! KEEP TO PATH!! TRESPASSERS MAY BE UNEXPECTEDLY TERMINATED!!! is a bit over the top.'

'Only to outsiders – and what are *they* doing wandering all over my estate, that's what I want to know? Locals – yes. They know the score: keep to the public footpaths, don't wear grey.'

'Are you still being targeted by ARG! too? I don't seem to be so much, but I suspect that's because Caz's keeping an eye on the place.'

'Well, family, aren't you?' he said vaguely. 'And they've eased up on the estate a bit since I put that piece in the parish magazine saying Caz uses humane live traps to catch the grey squirrels. Ingenious things – the reds can get out again, but the grey ones are too big.'

'Mmm,' I said, because of course the question *not* to ask was: what *does* Caz do with the grey squirrels after he's caught them?

We passed through the impressively pineappled gates of the hall, then turned sharp right on to the track that led down to Perseverance Cottage, which is just inside the estate boundary wall. I'd stuck a sign up earlier deflecting the mourners from the hall. The ravening and curious horde would be hard on our heels, probably expecting an abundance of finger food and alcohol in a suitably sombre setting; but instead they would find themselves eating home-made scones spread with jam and cream, strawberries-and-custard bread and butter pudding, and other perhaps even less usual comestibles, all washed down with tea or coffee, in a huge polythene greenhouse. And I hoped Annie had remembered to dot those 'No Smoking' signs around the place.

I had noticed the police presence at the funeral (PC Perkins and Little Boy Blue), but somehow their car arrived at the cottage first. As I got out, so did they, and Perkins came over and said they had come to offer their condolences. But there was an underlying implication that she thought I was a merrier widow than I let on, and she had been expecting me to cast myself on to the coffin with a last minute confession. But I fear I may be becoming paranoid.

'Do stay for refreshments in the greenhouse,' I said politely and, after a small, uncertain pause, she said they would follow us over. At least her colleague would have something to eat other than his fingernails.

'How the wheel came off is destined to be one of life's great mysteries,' I mused aloud, as we walked across the cobbled yard. 'And why he didn't stop it going over the edge? Though they think he might have had a blackout. Still, at least I know who Dark Heart is now, so that's one puzzle solved.'

'Dark Heart?' Roly said. I'd quite forgotten he didn't know about Tom's affair.

'Oh God, I didn't mean to tell you about that!' I said remorsefully.

'Dark Heart is how the woman Dad was having an affair with signed herself,' Jasper explained helpfully. Roly was leaning on his arm as he picked his way over the smooth, slightly slippery stones. 'It's that novelist woman – Polly Darke. Would you believe it? She's got to be even older than Mum, and a complete hag.'

'Thank you, darling,' I said. 'I think she is fashionably haggard, rather than a hag, really.'

'Boy must have been mad!' Unks exclaimed. He patted my arm. 'Wondered why she turned up to the funeral. Wearing a black see-through nightdress, too. Woman's got more bones than a picked chicken carcass!'

'Was she in church? I didn't actually take in most of who was and who wasn't.'

'She was there, Mum, but I thought Uncle Nick was going

to throw her out when she tried to sit in one of the front pews. And it was a black chiffon dress, Unks, but she's like fifty years too old to wear it.'

I think that might have been a *slight* exaggeration, but I didn't feel I was a winner in the sartorial stakes either. I didn't have any black, so was wearing a floaty, dark, paisley-patterned Indian dress over a long pink crinkle cotton skirt, both borrowed from Annie. I'd belted it severely in around my waist, but I still looked more Widow Twanky than that elegantly mysterious figure from the Scottish Widows commercial in her hooded velvet robe.

'Woman's got a nerve turning up at all, if she was carrying on with Tom! Well, well – it just goes to show you that the boy wasn't himself since he had that tumour, even if the operation did seem to be a success.' He shook his head. 'He was never the same.'

'No, he wasn't, though it might have helped if he'd kept his doctor's appointments and taken his pills and – oh, here they come!' I added, as the nose of Tom's white van appeared, followed by a cortege of assorted vehicles. 'Dave must have got tired of waiting and decided to lead the way instead.'

'Let's have a drink before battle commences, shall we?' Roly suggested.

'It's only tea or coffee, Unks – unless you want Jasper to fetch you a glass of elderberry wine? I've hidden a couple of bottles under the table in the corner just in case – I didn't want this to turn into some kind of drunken revel and go on for hours.'

'Quite right, but I've got some brandy in my cane,' he said. 'Ah, Annie, my dear!'

We established him on one of the chairs grouped before a veritable thicket of tomato plants and rampant bell peppers and he unscrewed the top of his cane and poured a generous slug of brandy into his tea while I went and peeped out of the entrance.

As the cars arrived, people milled about in front of the cottage, so Jasper went out to usher them in the direction of the greenhouse and I retreated back to Unks. I expect I should have stood in the doorway and accepted their condolences as they came in, but I couldn't face it.

The mourners massed in the entrance like worried sheep,

nearly balked and broke away, then came slowly in a surge towards me. At the last minute most of them sheered off and spread out to range up and down the trestle tables, probably looking for alcohol.

I accepted a slug of brandy in my teacup and sat down.

'That's it: let them come to you and do the polite,' Unks said. 'The ones with manners, anyway. Half of this lot weren't at the funeral – probably just after food and drink. Freeloaders!'

'Weren't they? The church did seem to be full, though, and I thought the new vicar did a brave job of it.'

'Not bad – bit much to expect him to do a complete stranger's funeral two seconds after he arrives. Let's hope he lasts longer than the last one. Ah, here's Nigel.'

Roly's portly, retired, stockbroker son was indeed forging towards us, though there was no sign of his wife. Still, I hadn't expected even Nigel, who didn't seem to care much for the North – or indeed Tom, for that matter, whom he considered a cuckoo in the nest – to make the effort to come today.

'My son and heir,' Roly said dryly in my ear. 'And unless Nick and that French woman get a move on, nearly the last in the line.' He nudged me with a sharp elbow. 'What do you think, Lizzie – is she past it?'

Leila, chic in a vintage Chanel suit, bold red lipstick and with her hair drawn sleekly back like a bleached Mini-me Paloma Picasso, stood poised in the doorway looking capable of anything, though the curl of her lip said exactly what she thought of her current location. Just wait till she saw the catering.

Nick, wearing his best brimstone-and-treacle expression, loomed behind her.

'I wouldn't get your hopes up, Unks,' I said while thinking that, as a recipe for a funeral feast, it was a pretty volatile mixture.

> Step 1: In a large polytunnel greenhouse, mix together approximately sixty assorted mourners, half of them uninvited, several wearing wildly inappropriate surfer garments and some hovering furtively around the edges that you are certain you have never met before in your entire life.
>
> Step 2: Add two police officers steeped in dark suspicions, a mad historical novelist dressed like the porno version of a Poldark widow and a depleted folk/rock group all wearing identical 'Gaia Rocks!' T-shirts.

Step 3: Gently fold in your best friend, trying valiantly to suppress her natural expression of cheerfulness, a mourning, lightly intoxicated nonagenarian great-uncle by marriage, a tall, dark and glowering chef and his acidulated and tangy French wife (soon to be ex, and who might, or might not, have been having a fling with your late husband), and the man from the garage who'd volunteered to drive Tom's now mended white van, with the Board Rigid logo up the side, to the funeral.
Step 4: Throw in a pompous stockbroker, the entire Mystery Play committee, including a nervous but well-meaning vicar, and a furtive-looking youngish man in a strangely mossy green suit, who has forgotten to remove his Rambo-style headband.
Step 5: Sprinkle with borrowed WI tea and coffee urns and crockery, garnish with halved scones spread with clotted cream and home-made blackcurrant jam, trays of cubed spudge on cocktail sticks, wedges of bread and butter pudding, and bowls of Cornish Mist.
Step 6: Stir well before it coagulates into clumps.
Step 7: Garnish with assorted hens, a three-legged whippet, and one yapping hairball that someone, probably Jasper, has let out of the cottage.
Step 8: Stand back, since once warm the mixture could go up like a rocket – and down like the stick.

Ten
Good Egg

The Pharamond family slowly began to converge on me from all directions, although once Nigel had kissed my cheek he wandered off, probably in search of non-existent sherry.

Great-aunt Mimi was pushing Juno in a wheelchair, though she'd told me last night she was hoping Doctor Patel (not KP, who is semi-retired now, but his daughter) was going to let her start walking again by the end of the week. The expression on her face was grimly stoical, at odds with the gaily frivolous arch of tissue paper flowers Mimi had attached to the back of the chair.

'Isn't that the bower from the Adam and Eve temptation scene that the infants school made last year – the one that kept falling on the snake?' Annie asked.

'Yes – thought it would brighten things up,' Mimi agreed. 'Damned gloomy things, funerals,' she added. 'Better if he hadn't come back last time – would have got it all over by now, and he was never the same. Nowhere near as much fun.'

I focused slightly. The shot of brandy had been generous, on an empty stomach – I hadn't been hungry first thing. 'Oh, did you notice that too, Mimi?'

She leaned over the chair towards me. 'Possessed!' she hissed. 'The devil was looking out of his eyes!'

Juno twisted her head upwards. 'Mimi, you haven't taken your pill today, have you? Where have you hidden it?'

Mimi backed off, looking guilty and slightly agitated. 'I didn't need it – why do I need it? Lizzie doesn't need one, and she's seen the devil looking out, too!'

'She's quite right, I did,' I assured Juno. 'And Mimi seems fine to me. I'll get her a glass of elderberry wine, that will do her good. I've hidden it under the end table, so the surfers and Mummers don't get drunk and silly. Sillier,' I added, for they seemed to have joined forces behind the tomato plants, together with some flagons and bottles *I* certainly hadn't supplied.

As well as the wine I also collected a tray of food, since my appetite had suddenly come back and I was ravenous. One or two people spoke to me (including one of the WI ladies, who complimented me on the dishes of golden quail eggs, an effect I achieved by boiling them wrapped in onion skins), but I was glad I had decided to dispense with the moving about doing the graciously thanking everyone for coming bit, because I wasn't at all thankful to most of them.

The Mummers of Invention – or what was left of them – were

now playing a lively tune at one end of the polytunnel. The drippy girl (my God, Tom must have been *desperate*!) stuck one finger in her ear and started to drone a song. She'd have to do her own harmonizing without Tom, but since she talks to herself worriedly all the time like Alice's white rabbit, that shouldn't cause her any great problems.

I gave Mimi her glass of wine and then sat next to Unks, eating steadily, as is my usual wont when stressed, unhappy, worried . . . *or* happy, cheerful and optimistic . . . Let's face it, I eat. This morning was simply an aberration.

Leila seemed to have the same thought. 'If you didn't do all that digging and outdoor work, you would be as fat as a pig,' she commented, coming to a halt in her stilettos in front of us, Nick right behind her like an attendant thundercloud. Then she kissed the air about an inch from Unk's cheek and said, 'Well, Roland, how are you?'

'Very well, Leila,' he said cautiously. 'Ah, Nick – there you are. Haven't heard how the two thirty at Haydock went, have you? Only I had a sure thing running – couldn't lose. Happy Wave out of Surfer's Paradise – couldn't go wrong with that pedigree, could it?'

'On a day like today, you can have no interest in horse racing!' Leila exclaimed, scandalized, and Unks looked slightly abashed.

'Joe's probably listening to it on the car radio, Unks,' I said. 'I'll go and ask him in a minute. In fact,' I added slightly worriedly, 'I ought to go and see where Jasper is.'

'It's all right, I saw him sitting on the Daimler running board talking to Joe when I came in,' Nick said. 'That's a weird-looking dog he's got – I thought you'd go for another lurcher, like Harriet.'

I pulled a face. 'It's one of Annie's strays. We are only supposed to be fostering it, so it wasn't put down, but she and Jasper have taken a shine to each other. I'm going to end up looking after it when he goes to university, I can see it coming.'

One more responsibility, when it came to leaving Perseverance Cottage and forging a new life on my own.

Leila seemed to be thinking along the same lines, for after looking me over in her usual critical way, as though she found me wanting in all aspects, which she probably did, she said:

'So, Lizzie, I expect you will be moving on, now? Those books are your only real source of income, are they not? And those you can write anywhere.'

'But they are the Perseverance Chronicles,' Juno said, 'about life here in Perseverance Cottage – that's the whole point! All Lizzie's daily struggles – that's what her readers like.'

'They'll certainly love the next volume, then, even though I'm ending on a happier note, before the tragedy. After that – ' I shrugged – 'who knows?'

'But you *must* keep writing them – and including the wonderful recipes,' Juno enthused, her square, rather weather-beaten face animated. I hadn't realized she was a fan.

'Oh God,' groaned Nick, temporarily distracted from silent thundercloud mode, 'don't remind me! Why anyone should find Lizzie's sugary, fatty recipes for nursery puddings and inedible bakes of any interest at all entirely beats me – and what's more, wasn't that yellow, lemon-flavoured stuff someone just served me in a bowl *candyfloss*?'

'Cornish Mist,' I said automatically and Leila snorted.

Roly, who had been sitting looking quietly baffled, suddenly put in: 'What did you *mean,* Leila, that Lizzie would be moving on? Moving on *where*?'

'I suppose Leila means that I will be looking for somewhere else to live, Unks.' I smiled at him affectionately. 'It has been so very kind of you to let us have Perseverance Cottage all these years, when you might have rented it out for a decent amount, but I realize you will have other plans for it now.'

'That's right,' agreed Nigel belligerently. He had suddenly reappeared behind his father and was swaying slightly, like a pot-bellied palm tree in a breeze. I couldn't imagine him hobnobbing with the Mummers and surfers, so he must have found the elderberry wine the way pigs find truffles. 'Told you it was stupid, not charging them rent all this time, Father – and Tom is not even a real Pharamond! Besides, the place is too big for Lizzie on her own. I'd do it up and sell it – get a fortune for it, the way house prices are rising round here.'

'Would you?' Unks said coldly. 'Perhaps you'd sell off the rest of the estate for housing too, while you were at it?'

'Probably wouldn't get planning permission – sodding red squirrels and trees are more important than people,' he slurred. 'But you could divide the hall up into apartments – executive ones – and keep the best for yourself. Make a huge profit!' His eyes lit up with the fire of acquisitive greed.

'So, that's what you would do to the Pharamond Estate, Nigel, is it?' Unks said. '*If* you inherited it, of course.'

'But he is the heir, is he not?' Leila said. 'And his ideas, they are eminently practical!'

'Nigel shouldn't count his chickens before they are hatched. The entail on the estate was broken long ago, don't forget, so it is mine to leave to whoever I wish.' Roly turned his head and smiled at me. 'I told Tom that I was making Perseverance Cottage over to him and Lizzie, but now it will be Lizzie's home for as long as she needs it – and Jasper's.'

'Oh, thank you, Unks! That is *so* sweet of you!' I said, tears coming to my eyes, and kissed the top of his head.

'It's been a pleasure having you living so close, my dear, and the boy's a Pharamond – he should grow up here, regard it as his home.'

'But he isn't *really* a Pharamond, Father,' Nigel pointed out, swiftly sobered by the possibility of disinheritance.

'Course he is,' Mimi said, leaning on the wheelchair and waving her empty glass emphatically, and Juno twisted her head round and gave her another anxious look. She would be getting a crick in it at this rate. 'Only have to look at him to know that – the boy's the spit of Nick.'

There was a small silence, which Unks broke by saying dryly: 'Before anyone lets their imagination run riot, Tom's mother confessed to me when she asked me to take him on, that she was having an affair with Leo Pharamond before her first husband died, and she was pretty sure Tom was his. I promised not to say anything, but I feel current circumstances absolve me from that.'

'His mother said that? Oh, I *wish* she'd told him!' I said indignantly. 'He always had a chip on his shoulder about not really being a Pharamond, but he wouldn't hear a word against *her.* Instead he pretty well accused *me* of—'

I broke off hastily, meeting Nick's eyes, and went pink. 'Well, I just wish he'd known, that's all.'

'I think you, Roland, are just saying this to cover up the

truth! Jasper is *Nick's* child – Tom told me this himself,' Leila exclaimed unguardedly. 'They had an affair when they were young, and then they picked it up again after she married Tom.'

'Rubbish!' Unks said firmly. 'Boy and girl affair one summer and fought like cat and dog – and then Nick went off on his travels again and that was that. Daresay they hardly even saw each other for years, and Lizzie was mad about Tom, anyone could see that!'

'Of course it isn't true,' I said hotly. 'Jasper is Tom's child. But I'm glad to have the truth I suspected come out at last, even if it is a bit late in the day.'

Nick glared at Leila. 'You mean, Tom told you *that* and you believed it? *When* did he tell you?'

'Oh, years ago.'

'It *can't* have been that many years ago, he only started saying that kind of stupid thing when his brain was affected by the tumour,' I said. 'He got all sorts of strange ideas then.'

'I think we all know you've been a saint to put up with him since the operation,' Unks remarked, to my surprise. 'I hear things – know more than you think.'

'Yes, but it had got to the state where I was going to *leave* him, Unks,' I confessed. 'I'm not such a saint. I was just waiting for Jasper to be settled at university.'

'Well, now you don't have to,' Mimi said brightly. 'You can stay here, and dear Jasper can come home in the holidays. Such a clever boy!' She took a bowl of Cornish Mist from a passing tray and dug in her pastry fork. 'Mmm!'

Then she looked up again, yellow-moustached, at our rather silently thoughtful tableaux. 'Where's Tom? He's missing all this lovely food and he is *so* fond of his stodgy puds.'

'He's gone, Mimi,' Juno said shortly. 'I'll explain later.'

Mimi's brain had clearly done one of its little loops and shunted Tom's death into a siding. I wish mine would.

'Oh, will you? Good,' she said, her eyes wandering around the very motley crowd. 'Look – that woman's wearing a black baby-doll nightdress! Should I have come in fancy dress too, Lizzie?'

'Good grief, it's that Polly Darke woman! As if it wasn't bad enough her coming to the funeral, without turning up in your home, Lizzie!' Annie exclaimed, scandalized, appearing beside me suddenly with her sandy bun of hair hanging dementedly over one ear and her cheeks flushed – but then, it *was* getting slightly steamy in the polytunnel in more ways than one.

Polly staggered backwards through the concealing tomato plants, where she had presumably been drowning her sorrows with the surfers and Mummers. She regained her balance with an effort, turned and fixed her dark-ringed, sunken eyes on me. 'Lizzie! Not so much the grieving widow, I see! Maybe you're even celebrating – it wouldn't surprise me if you loosened that wheel on purpose, and then *told* Tom to borrow your car!'

'Polly, that's entirely stupid – and you watched me walk off into the woods that morning, don't forget! When would I have done it?'

'You could have come back. You were probably hiding, waiting for me to leave!'

'Do you all know Polly Darke?' I said resignedly. 'You can probably spot without my telling you that she's a novelist, but she was also Tom's mistress.'

'Good grief!' Juno exclaimed incredulously. 'Was she really?'

'More, much more, than that – Tom *loved* me! He had to get Lizzie to move out so the split looked like her fault, and then Roly would leave him the cottage, but after that we were going to get married,' Polly cried, looking about her wildly as though expecting a sympathy vote and not getting it.

'You are quite mad – a fantasist!' Leila said, looking her up and down disgustedly. 'He would not have even a tiny affair with a woman such as you.'

'I'm afraid he did have a mistress, but I've only just found out that it was Polly,' I told her. 'It was a shock to me, too!'

'And me,' Unks said dryly. 'Revelations, indeed!'

Leila narrowed her eyes at Polly, like a snake. 'What could *you* possibly have to offer him?'

'You'd be surprised,' I said darkly. 'I certainly was.'

'This is fun, isn't it?' Mimi said cheerfully, but no one took any notice.

Leila drew herself up. 'She is lying. It is true that Tom had a lover, yes – but it was *me*!'

Nick's hand closed in a vice-like grip on her arm. 'But you

swore you had never been more than friends with him when I asked you! *And* you wouldn't agree to a divorce.'

She shrugged. 'He planned to move in with me eventually, but it is as this woman says: he wanted to keep in with his great-uncle, who is fond of Lizzie, and inherit the cottage, so he was forcing her out. She deserved it – she was still having an affair with you! Tom said that even in hospital, when he was so ill, you couldn't keep your hands off each other.'

'That is *so* not true,' I said hotly.

'No, Lizzie isn't like that in the least,' Annie agreed loyally.

Polly, who had been quiet, rallied again: 'Oh, I knew he had an *old* mistress who wouldn't accept that their affair was over. But it was *me* he loved – and *me* he spent his last night with!'

'I don't believe you – he was with me only a few days before he died, and he swore he loved me and soon we would be together always,' Leila declared.

'Presumably after I had obligingly died, and he had inherited the cottage?' queried Roly mildly.

'You *are* ninety-two, Roland,' Leila said defensively. 'In France we are more practical about these things.'

'Not practical enough, my dear – I was leaving the cottage to him for life only, then to Jasper after him, not outright.'

'And you were going to tell me all this *when*, exactly?' Nick demanded of his wife in a voice that reverberated through the polytunnel like thunder. 'And why refuse me a divorce?'

'I knew that you would try and take half my restaurant that I worked for so hard – half my money. Why should I give you what is mine? I thought once Lizzie was free, you might be more reasonable about it, and I would wait. And I will fight you through the courts for every penny!'

'I don't want your money – I don't want *anything* of yours, just my freedom!' Nick said furiously. 'I'll sign a statement to that effect any time you choose – would have done before, if I'd known what was worrying your mercenary little heart. You and Tom seem to have been made for each other!'

'No they weren't – she's a lying cow and it's *me* he loved and wanted to spend his life with!' Polly said, quivering with rage, then entirely lost it and lobbed her plate of food at her rival. Half a scone daubed with cream and red jam clung to the side of Leila's face like some exotic wart, before sliding slowly down her cheek and dropping off, smearing her suit on the way.

Mimi giggled, but Leila gave a scream of rage and lunged at Polly with her long, sharp red nails. I was just thinking that I'd put my money on Leila, when Nick seized her arms from behind and two of the surfers, who must have followed Polly through the tomato plants, lunged forward and grabbed her too.

'Put them out!' Unks snapped. 'You!' he said to Polly. 'Whatever the truth of the matter, you should have had the decency to stay away. If you don't go now, I'll have you removed.'

Polly went limp and started sobbing, and the two surfers let go of her arms. She stumbled towards the door on her extremely high heels and, as the crowd parted to let her through, I realized we had unwittingly been providing entertainment for everyone within ear and eyeshot – which in a greenhouse is pretty well everyone who could cram in.

The only good thing was that the police and the vicar seemed to have left before the floorshow.

Nick, still grasping Leila's arms, snapped in my direction: 'Excuse us! Back later, Roly – hope your horse won.' And he frog-marched her off. I would have liked to have been a fly in the car on the way back to London: Nick's invective can be quite inventive when he is in a rage.

Unks looked quite pleased: 'Well, she was always a bitch,' he remarked happily. 'Don't know why he took up with her, except she was beautiful, I suppose, and they had the cooking stuff in common. Well, once he's over her he can start again – with a sensible Lancashire lass this time, perhaps?'

'They're both lying old bags!' quavered the small, pathetic voice of the drippy girl from the Mummers right next to me, and it was quite lucky from her viewpoint that neither of them were there to hear that description, because it would have been tantamount to staking a kid to attract tigresses. 'He loved *me* – and what's more, I'm having his *baby*!'

White as a sheet and naturally rather pop-eyed, Ophelia Locke seemed an unlikely candidate for Tom's attentions, so I was probably the only person who believed her. Still, it was another reason to be glad the other two had gone – and that

Tom *hadn't* done the resurrection shuffle this time and come back to us, since even Solomon in all his glory would have had trouble with a three-way split.

There was a general feeling among the onlookers that this was a scene too far and we were into the farce; but then, before anyone could rally enough to say so, she fainted backwards.

Caz Naylor, stepping forward, caught her neatly and slung her over his shoulder, where she dangled limp as a shot rabbit. 'Not right in't head, Mr Pharamond,' he said tersely.

'Evidently, poor girl,' agreed Unks, looking rather taken aback.

Hanging upside down must have sent the blood rushing to Ophelia's head, for she revived enough to beat weakly on Caz's back and whimper, 'Put me down, you big bully!'

Caz ignored her and carried her off, the crowd parting to let them through.

Unks unscrewed the top of his cane. 'Anybody want a shot of brandy? I certainly do! And wasn't that the girl I let an estate cottage to – makes handicrafts, or some such stuff?'

'Barbola work?' suggested Mimi. 'And is Caz walking out with her?'

'Smocks,' I said. 'Yes, Unks, that's the girl.'

'Nobody does Barbola work these days,' Juno said. 'And I shouldn't think she's Caz's type.'

'Oh? Well, that was all just like a play!' Mimi said, clapping her hands. 'Was it a play, Juno? Is that the end?'

'Yes, time for us to go home,' she agreed. 'Come on, that gardening programme you like will be on by the time we get there.'

Mimi whirled the chair about with no more ado. 'Lovely party – thank you for having me!' she called politely over her shoulder. The remains of Polly's jam scone squidged under the wheels.

The excitement clearly over, some of the remaining guests followed them out, though the last two Mummers were still obliviously droning on in the background and I could see one of Tom's surfing chums stretched out under the trestle tables, snoring.

'Jasper,' I said, as he finally came in, closely followed, nose to heel, by the little dog, 'Unks says we can live at

Perseverance Cottage for as long as we want to. Isn't that kind?'

'Really? Thanks, Unks – I was worrying what would happen to Mum when I went off to university, but now I won't need to any more.'

'You don't have to worry about me at all!' I said indignantly. 'I'm perfectly capable of taking care of myself.'

Jasper eyed me uncertainly. 'Are you all right, Mum? Only you look a bit strange.'

'Strange? Why on earth should I look strange?' I demanded, though I could feel hysteria trying to tweak my mouth into an idiot's grin.

'I think we are all tired and a bit overwrought,' Annie said quickly. 'What an exhausting day! All these scenes and revelations.'

'What scenes and revelations?' asked Jasper, looking from one to the other of us.

'I'll tell you later,' I promised, which I would have to, even if only the edited lowlights. 'I wonder how we can get rid of the last of the guests?'

'I'll send Joe back to turf out the stragglers,' promised Unks, hoisting himself to his feet with Jasper's help. 'But most of them will go when they see me leaving.'

He advised me, as I saw him out, not to dwell on events, but instead remember Tom as he once was, at his best, then Joe drove him away. He looked frail and tired, so I hoped it all hadn't taken too much out of him.

I was fine – too numb and full of wine and brandy to feel anything except a desire for oblivion.

It was early evening before Joe Gumball loaded the last drunken surfer into the back of the taxi called to take them to their B&B in Mossedge, and finally persuaded the two Mummers to go away: they had been too drunk to notice the scene with Ophelia, or even question where she had vanished to.

And what had Caz done with her?

The urns and crockery had long been efficiently removed by the WI ladies, with my grateful thanks, and Marianne and Clive Potter had supervised the local Cubs and Brownies in carrying the trestles and chairs back to the hall, so that was that.

Annie saw to the poultry, and then cooked us a meal we none of us really felt like, except the dogs, before going home.

Finally alone with Jasper I felt almost too exhausted for the effort of explanation, but when I told him that he really *was* Unk's great-great-nephew he just said: 'Yes, I know – Unks told me ages ago, when I asked him why I looked more like Uncle Nick than Dad.'

'You did?' I stared at him. Then I sighed, tiredly, and decided to tell him about the other pretenders to the throne of love and get it all over with at once. 'Did you also know that your father was having an affair with Leila as well as Polly? They nearly came to blows this afternoon in the polytunnel.'

'Oh, so that's what she and Nick were arguing about when they left! He pushed her into his car and roared off, and then Polly came out and took off, too, though she didn't look fit to drive. And another thing,' he added thoughtfully, 'why was Caz giving that Mummer girl a fireman's lift? She didn't seem to appreciate it.'

'She fainted – right after declaring that it was really *her* your father loved, not the other two – and Jasper, she says she is pregnant!'

His eyebrows rose. 'She does?

'I hope it isn't true – things are complicated enough without that.'

'Well, look on the bright side,' Jasper said, with the breezy insouciance of youth. 'At least there's no chance the baby's mine!'

Eleven

Popped Corks

I was woken early next morning by a thirteen gun salute, which proved to be half my stock of ginger beer exploding.

Let me give you a few words of wisdom culled from many

years of making the stuff. (You can find the recipe for making a ginger beer culture in Book One of the Perseverance Chronicles.)

1) Ignore the Quatermass-experiment effect once the yeast starts working – whatever it may look like, the ginger culture will not take over the world . . . yet. And isn't it amazing that water and a bit of yeast and ginger scum can turn into something so delicious?
2) Ask everyone to save their screw top plastic pop and water bottles for you, because if you go the traditional route of glass bottles and corks, expect your house to explode at frequent intervals.
3) Even with screw top bottles, it is not a good idea to transport large quantities of ginger beer about, especially in a car. Nor should you be tempted to celebrate any special event by shaking the bottle before opening.

After cleaning the sticky mess up and loosening the rest of the caps so I wouldn't lose all of it (Jasper and I are very partial to ginger beer), I went out to see to the poultry.

There appeared to be less quail. Presumably Caz had taken the opportunity yesterday to cull the male ones again, though I am not sure how he found the time, unless he popped back after taking Ophelia to . . . well, where *was* he heading? So long as it wasn't to his giant freezer, I don't suppose it really matters. Perhaps he just put her in a Mummer's car and left her to it? Or carried her home to her estate cottage, which is not far from his, protesting all the way? Though I don't think most local girls would protest if he wanted to carry them off, the auburn-haired sheikh of the western Lancashire world.

I hadn't really thought of him in the knight-errant role before, even if he appears to have been protecting me against ARG! Perhaps he's got something going on with Ophelia? But then, that does seems a bit unlikely, since he is definitely carnivore, and I remember Tom telling me once that all the other Mummers were vegan and wouldn't even wear leather shoes.

The quail in their little pens all made identical cheeping sounds. I've never managed to tell one from the other, which is lucky since it means I don't actually get attached to them, like I do the hens and ducks. But sometimes even they are so nasty and vicious to each other that I start to feel maybe their real destiny is to be on a plate with stuffing and gravy or orange sauce. Nature is red in beak and feather as well as tooth and claw – someone should tell ARG! that.

But after wrapping dozens of quail eggs in onion skins during the sleepless night watches, I really don't care if I never eat another one, let alone a quail itself . . . so I think I will get rid of them. Find them another home.

The duck population was here before me and is pretty self-sufficient, but the hens can just naturally reduce, as they die of old age – so long as I find the eggs before they hatch. After all, it's just going to be me here at Perseverance Cottage now, and if I don't produce much more food than I can eat, then I will have time to really throw myself into helping Annie expand Posh Pet-sitters and earn money. Barter can work well up to a point, but electricity bills and the Inland Revenue are way beyond that.

Yes, even the oversized polytunnel that I bought second hand years ago, when I had delusions of market gardening on the grand scale, can go. The small, ramshackle old greenhouse behind the cottage will be enough, especially if I replace some of the glass and mend it a bit.

I'll put an advert in the parish magazine, and see if I get any local takers – buyer dismantles and removes. But what I am to do with Tom's workshop contents I can't imagine.

Back at the cottage I was surprised to find Jasper up and getting ready to go to the dig, which on the whole was probably a good idea – though possibly not in the designer jeans that had cost me a fortune. I think we both had that spaced-out, anti-climactic feeling, and the alternative was sitting about thinking unproductive thoughts.

'Do you know how many eggs I had to sell to buy those jeans?' I demanded, but he took the question as rhetorical and carried on cutting multi-layered doorstep sandwiches.

I couldn't drive him there, since even if the van hadn't been down at the garage, now it had done duty as a hearse neither of us fancied ever getting in it again. But Dave Naylor was coming this morning with the ancient but, he assured me, very genuine Morris Traveller I had in a rash moment agreed to swap it for.

So Jasper cycled off to the dig with the fur ball – and he is calling her Ginny, for short, thank goodness, for anything less like a Guinevere I never saw – in a basket strapped to the carrier, together with a bowl and a big bottle of water. He said there was plenty of shade to tie her up in and he could walk her at lunchtime, though so far as you can see of her shape beneath the fuzz, rolling her about a bit would do just as well.

Dave brought my new old car about an hour later, after I'd drafted the adverts for the polytunnel and the quail. One of his sons followed him down the track in Tom's van, to save him the quarter mile trek back. That damned van with the horribly apposite Board Rigid logo seems to be a recurring motif, and I'll be glad when it is re-sprayed and sold on, preferably away from the area.

The Morris was a green, wood-trimmed estate, and wasn't in bad condition at all. It had a full history of one owner and the sort of mileage that suggested it had spent most of its life having sedate little drives to church and market a couple of times a week max, though after so many years even that can mount up. It was also car tax exempt, being so old. Another advantage.

I'd managed to find the paperwork for the van, and Dave gave me the Morris's in exchange. I expect the van will soon reappear for sale on the garage forecourt after a quick makeover.

The old Morris looked cosy and friendly and I confidently expected I would soon grow to love it. Jasper thought the swap was a good idea too and is looking forward to driving it. It is fortunate I have a son who prefers antiquities.

I tootled it around the yard, up the track and round a bit, to get a feel for it, and it certainly felt more solid than my 2CV ever did; so later I steered it cautiously down to the post office and handed in the adverts for the parish magazine to Marianne. She said I was just in time for the next issue, which would be out at the end of the week: their publication dates are erratic, entirely depending on how Clive feels about it, and they are devoted more to village news and advertisements than parish business. There are usually a few words from the vicar, though, and a Bible quote.

In the late morning one of Tom's surfer friends, who had been a bearer at the funeral, phoned up and asked if he and his mate, Jimbo, could drop in.

'That's nice of you, Freddie,' I said, assuming they wanted to say goodbye before setting off back down to Cornwall, which was amazingly thoughtful of them and, I would have said, totally out of character.

'Well, we wanted to say goodbye, Lizzie, but we've also got a proposition.'

'A proposition?'

'Yes, we thought we might take on Tom's business and wanted to discuss it with you. If you've no other plans for it, of course.'

'No, I haven't really had time to think of it,' I said. 'But of course you can come down and we can talk about it,' I added, for it would be a relief: I had no idea what to do with all his equipment and half-finished boards and stuff. And it *would* be rather nice if his friends carried on with Board Rigid.

Freddie and Jimbo had been, so far as I could gather from the male bonding rituals, two of Tom's best friends. They had all been at Rugby together, dropped out of university and then washed up in Cornwall, bumming around on family money. But I suppose even that and the patience of your family is finite and, when a man reaches his forties, it is time to stop being the playboy of the western UK and earn your own bread and wetsuits.

I went into the workshop and opened the big front door to the sunshine for the first time since the accident, instead of the little Judas door, though as it turned out that would have been more appropriate.

Things looked dusty already and there was that familiar smell of paint, varnish and dope. His wetsuits swung from a hook like the spent chrysalises of some strange creature: which I suppose they were, when you came to think about it.

One or two boards, obviously orders, were nearly finished, and there were several of the ones he bought in and painted himself to sell on through shops. I had a rough idea what they were worth and the people who had ordered the almost finished boards had their names and phone numbers taped to the back, Tom's idea of paperwork. Mind you, the system seemed to work, which is more than could be said for his tax returns: I only hope the Inland Revenue is not now going to fall on *me* like a ton of bricks.

Tom's friends turned up so quickly they must have phoned from a mobile up the lane, and were very kind, kissing my cheek and hugging me as if they had always liked me, which they didn't. I was the wrong sort of girl: Tom should have married someone limp, acquiescent, well connected and above all, *rich.*

Jimbo has a long body, stumpy legs and a big nose, but he didn't get his name from his appearance: his name is James Bow. Freddie is tall and skinny, with grey-blond hair fuzzing over his head like a bleached coconut. They must have to get their wetsuits made specially.

They looked over the workshop as though it was a dubious garage sale, ummed and ahed a bit, then said they would take the worry of it off my hands for three hundred pounds, what did I say?

'What, for the whole lot?' I gasped, thinking I hadn't heard right.

'Well, let's say four hundred, to be fair. There's not much here, and we'd have to finish off the old orders and deliver them, of course,' Freddie pointed out, as if this would be a big favour.

'But Tom's almost finished them, and he hasn't been paid yet. And the other boards that belong to him alone are worth more than that!' I protested, stunned.

They exchanged a quick look and then I realized they hadn't expected me to know anything about the business or the value of it, and be too upset to think straight, so had come prepared to pay me a pittance under the cover of 'taking the worry of the business off my hands'.

I'd fallen among thieves.

'Oh, no – they're not top quality boards,' Jimbo said quickly, 'and several of them are half-finished – you'd never sell them like that. Besides, you don't have the contacts, do you? But *we* do.'

I looked at them: these were supposedly Tom's closest friends. He had been to school with them, hung out with them over the years, and they were well off by *my* standards, even if they did look like bums most of the time. And now they wanted to make a quick profit by cheating his widow!

They were also *cunning* beach bums, for Freddie now produced a neatly printed agreement. I read it through a couple of times, noting the words 'sale to include everything pertaining to the business of Board Rigid', but my brain wasn't really up to coping with possible pitfalls.

'Trust us – we're doing you a favour, Lizzie,' Jimbo said persuasively. 'I mean, who else would be interested?'

'Take it all off your hands – one less thing to worry about,' agreed Freddie.

Under my expression of acute disbelief they shifted and avoided my eyes. But then I looked around the workshop again and discovered I didn't have any fight left in me. I really didn't care that much – and Tom wouldn't have seen it as anything other than a smart move by his friends.

Reluctantly, I signed. They paid me cash from a wad of notes: I said they were rich. 'Do you want a pint or two of my blood as well,' I said bitterly. 'Or a kidney, perhaps?'

'Poor Lizzie,' Jimbo said sadly, 'I can see Tom's death was a huge shock to you. You're doing the best thing, putting all this behind you.'

'Yes . . .' Freddie began to look around again with more of a proprietorial air. 'Once it's gone, you'll feel much happier, you'll see.'

'Might as well load it up and take it all now,' Jimbo agreed. 'Where's the van parked, Lizzie?'

'The van?' I said blankly.

'Tom's van – the one we've just bought,' Jimbo said patiently.

'But – you didn't mention any van!'

'Well, not as such, perhaps, but you did agree to sell us *everything* pertaining to the business, lock, stock and barrel.'

'*Two* smoking barrels!' I said, woken out of apathy into indignation. 'Look, you've already screwed me over on this deal, you couldn't possibly have expected to get Tom's van for even *twice* that much!'

'Lizzie, you don't know how big a favour we're doing you. Of course we only offered you that much money because of the van – it's worth more than the stuff in the shed,' Freddie began sadly.

'I know, because I bought it myself, out of the advance for the third of the Perseverance Chronicles! And anyway, you're too late: I've already disposed of it.'

They stared at me, aghast. '*Disposed?*' they exclaimed as one.

'If you're interested, it's down at Deals on Wheels.'

'Deals on Wheels?' echoed Freddie.

'The garage in the village – I swapped it for that Morris Traveller in the courtyard this morning. The van is now the property of Dave Naylor – I suggest you go and talk to him, if you are interested in it.'

They were not happy, but the van *was* legally my property and they couldn't do anything about my having already disposed of it, which certainly made *me* feel better. Eventually they stopped trying to browbeat me into getting it back and giving it to them, and went off to talk to Dave at the garage, saying they would be back later to empty the workshop.

'Fine.'

'Perhaps you could give us the key, so we don't have to disturb you again?'

'Not until I've removed his personal things. The CD player and stuff like that.'

But there wasn't actually much in there that I cared to take, so when they came back again in Tom's van, which I'd hoped never to see again, I left them to it. I bet Dave struck a hard bargain. Serve them right.

Later, I went to collect Jasper and Ginny in the Morris and when we got back the workshop doors swung open, and it was empty of life except for some curious hens, one of whom had laid an egg on the old easy chair among the burst stuffing.

Jasper and I have decided to sell Tom's insanely huge TV and buy a small portable one with the proceeds, which he can take to university with him. I am quite happy with my radio.

When it began to get dark I went out to shut everything up for the night and, coming back, noticed that the light was on in the workshop.

My heart stopped dead for a moment or two, until reality set in and I thought it might be Freddie and Jimbo, returned in a fit of pique to make a through job of it: there was still the tattered old sofa and chairs, the ancient upright piano and the kettle, for instance. No resurrected Board Rigid van stood outside to load anything into, it was true, but I wouldn't have put it past them to have parked it on the road and sneaked in through the side gate.

Then again, it could be Caz, curiosity stirred by the unlocked door, or ARG! setting dynamite charges. Even Mimi on the loose.

I crept up to the open Judas door and, to my astonishment, found the workshop infested with Mummers. They weren't doing anything, just hanging about with a sort of aimless expectancy, but when they saw me they drew together into a defensive huddle like sheep.

Ophelia was mumbling to herself as usual and I thought her pale froggy eyes were going to pop out altogether. 'Oh God! Oh God! It's *her* – she'll kill me – she'll kill me! Oh *God*!'

I looked dispassionately at her. She was as limp and wet as seaweed and I was still finding it hard to square what Jasper had said about finding her and Tom *in flagrento*, with the reality of what she actually looked like. In fact, she has all the allure of a blancmange bunny, so it must have been simply availability allied with drink or the demon weed. After the Leila/Polly revelations it didn't seem of much moment anyway, unless she really *was* pregnant by him? Hard to tell when she dresses in her own smocked garments most of the time.

'Ophelia didn't mean what she said, yesterday,' Mick said hastily, his fingers fiddling with the blue feather in his hat. The three of them edged even closer together.

'No, no-no-no!' whimpered Ophelia, while nodding rapidly.

'She's *not* pregnant?'

'No, she meant that bit.'

'Tom loved me!' Ophelia said, but rather uncertainly.

'Nah, we keep telling you – he just wanted a quick shag,' Jojo said brutally.

'So the baby *could* be Tom's?' I asked him.

'It could be anyone's – Caz Naylor's even.' They stared accusingly at her. 'Sleeping with the enemy!'

'The enemy? Caz's your *enemy*?' I frowned over that one, but I suppose gamekeepers and rabid vegans *are* oil and water and shouldn't mix, though clearly at some point two of them, at least, had.

'Well, come to that it could be mine – or even yours,' Mick pointed out fair-mindedly to his friend.

'Ooh!' moaned Ophelia, chewing her lip frantically like a mad albino rabbit, huge pink eyelids fluttering.

'You've got around a bit,' I said to her, but it was quite a good thing in a way from my point of view, because it seriously lessened the chances of the baby being Tom's. I supposed I would just have to await the outcome, and so would she.

'Mr Pharamond's bound to put her out of her cottage, after what she said at the funeral,' Jojo suggested helpfully.

Ophelia wrung her hands and stared at me with the eyes of a mad martyr embracing her doom. 'Yes, yes – it's all my own fault and I *deserve* to be punished!'

Oh, good heavens, she wasn't *another* kinky one, was she? I sighed, resignedly: if there was any chance she was pregnant with Tom's child, I couldn't let her be turned out.

'Roly won't give you notice, Ophelia – or at least not until after the baby is born. I'll speak to him about it, but I am sure you are quite wrong.'

'Don't think he could do it anyway,' Mick said belligerently. 'She's got her rights!'

'Possibly not, but I don't think the question will arise. Anyway, what are you all doing here?'

They shifted uneasily again, looking around the near-empty workshop as though expecting something – or someone – to materialize out of the dark shadows.

'He's not coming back this time, if that's what you're all waiting for,' I said evenly. 'Tom's played his last gig and you'll have to get a new singer: not that I thought he was much good anyway.'

'Yes, but his voice harmonized with mine very well,' Ophelia blurted, then blushed as she caught my eye, like she usually did – as well she might. 'Oh God!'

'And he wrote most of the lyrics to my tunes,' said Jojo, slowly turning the gold hoop in his ear as though tuning what remained of his brain.

'No, actually, that was me,' I said incautiously and they stared. 'He used to hammer them out on the old piano and I'd try to fit words to them – just give you a base to work it up from, you know? I mean, they weren't really mine when you'd finished with them, because they evolved into something else – something better, usually.'

At their best, after a pint or two of Mossbrown Ale, the Mummers sometimes acquired a near-Pentangle unity that was quite hypnotic. 'But the last couple of years, he didn't ask me to help him with them any more.'

'*Thought* they'd gone off,' Mick, the one who looked like an escapee from *Clan of the Cave Bear*, said. 'Can you sing, too?' he asked hopefully.

'No.'

'But—'

'Absolutely not,' I said firmly. 'Look, I don't mind if you want to come and keep using the workshop to practise in, as long as you don't bother me. But you will have to find a new Mummer.' A thought struck me: 'Annie – you know Annie Vane, don't you?'

They nodded.

'She pet-sits for an ex-pop singer who bought the old vicarage. He's called Rob Rafferty, and he's an actor now, playing a Victorian mill owner in that *Cotton Common* soap.'

'Not Rob Rafferty from Climaxxx?' Miss Drippy said breathlessly. 'I thought that was just a story, that he'd bought the place. He's famous . . . but *old*,' she added belatedly.

'Nah, he can't be much more than forty-five, at most,' Jojo said, giving her a dirty look and adjusting the bandanna over his bald spot to the point where it almost became a headscarf. It'd have to be the pirate look next. 'And he might want to keep his hand in, do a couple of gigs with us – worth asking . . . Good to talk to him, you know?'

'You do that,' I agreed.

'But would the Mysteries committee let us play for them, if one of us wasn't from the Mosses?' said the girl. 'You know how stuffy they are about second-homers. I shouldn't think he lives here all the time.'

'I don't know, Ophelia, but you could ask – its not like you are performing in the plays and have to go to all the rehearsals, is it? Just incidental music and filling in between scenes.'

'Olivia,' she corrected me.

'What?'

'My name's Olivia, not Ophelia.'

'Oh?' That was a surprise, but I fear due to her water-dipped appearance she will forever remain Ophelia in my mind. It seemed to strike a chord with the other two as well.

'Suits you,' Jojo said, and Mick agreed.

'Why not change your name – new name, new start?'

'*Another* resurrection,' I said wearily, but she seemed to suddenly take to the idea.

'Yeah! Ophelia Locke – cool,' she said, brightening slightly. 'I'll do it! Ophelia . . . Ophelia . . . *Ophelia.*'

Loopy Locke, more like.

'Looks different in here, somehow, without Tom,' Jojo remarked intelligently.

'That's because I've sold the surfboard business and all the stuff's gone,' I said patiently. 'Look, Jojo, here's the key to the workshop – I've got a spare. It'll save you asking for it if it's locked, and you can leave equipment here safely if you want to.'

'Thanks,' he said and, giving my arm an earnest squeeze, added, 'and, you know, anything you want – we'll do anything we can . . .' He trailed off, made earnest eye contact and let me go.

They both seemed to have done their bit already.

'Ophelia Locke . . .' whispered Miss Drippy in an ecstatic undertone. There were brown rabbits stencilled on the pockets of her smock.

Watership Down has a lot to answer for.

Twelve

Just Desserts

The funeral was not much more than a week ago, yet with disconcerting rapidity the summer has slid into September and what passes for normal life has resumed. Even when Tom was home he never played much part in the family round, so his absence is not really missed, except insofar as you would miss a ticking time bomb.

Jasper seems to be feeling much the same, but I expect like me he has not quite accepted that Tom will not suddenly turn up again. It doesn't help that half the time Mimi forgets what has happened and we have to explain it all over again.

I have persuaded Unks not to evict Ophelia the Drip from her estate cottage. Pity it is not in his power to evict Polly Darke from *her* house, though, since she is apparently seen everywhere, dressed in weirdest widow's black, playing for the sympathy vote.

But I have much to distract me, for the garden has taken advantage of my lack of attention to burgeon forth into a burst of late flowerings and fruitings like a butterfly dancing on the edge of winter. I was out there in a Canute-like attempt to assert my authority over Nature, when the vicar came to visit me.

While George ostensibly came to offer comfort and a shoulder to cry on, should I need it, I quickly discerned that he wanted to talk about Annie. So I told him all about our long friendship, dating back to our schooldays at St Mattie's, where she was hockey captain and my best subject was Nature Studies, and the French cookery course we did afterwards in London.

Then I said what a lovely, trusting person she was, even after being jilted practically at the altar when her fiancé ran off with one of the prospective bridesmaids, and pointed out her many activities within the parish.

'Of course,' I added casually, tossing a handful of weeds into the wheelbarrow, 'the way to Annie's heart is through her love of dogs. She even puts in several hours a week as a voluntary helper at the RSPCA kennels.'

George left looking thoughtful, so I hope I have planted some ideas of how he is to go on if he wants to win her: the ball is in his court.

He is very nice in a serious and *terribly* good way, so I think they would be very well suited. I wouldn't give my best friend in marriage to just *any* old eligible bachelor, he has to be Mr Right. Or, in this case, Mr Bright.

This could be just the right moment for him to make his

move, too, for I have got the impression that Annie is finding Rob Rafferty a little disconcerting now her initial bedazzlement is wearing off. She's never had one of her fantasy men become *flesh* before.

No, if George plays his cards right, she could very well rebound quite happily into his arms.

Annie has managed all the Posh Pet-sitting stuff herself since the funeral, but I told her I could cope now if she needed help, so this morning I walked Delphine Lake's two little dogs, who were very glad to see me because Delphine's idea of a walk is from the car into the house.

Then I went to collect a cat from the vet's surgery and returned it to the owner – or rather, the owner's au pair, who did not seem very pleased to have it back. But I expect once it had got over its rage at being confined in a carrying box it would soon calm down. How weirdly vocal Siamese cats are!

On the way home I popped in at Annie's little terraced cottage to see if anything else needed doing, and found her making a chart of her Posh Pet-sitting for the next fortnight, with different coloured stars for the regular ones and fluorescent spots for the one-offs – very organized. Even the keys for houses where she lets herself in were starred and spotted to match.

'I see Rob Rafferty's bagged all the gold stars,' I commented, having made us both a cup of coffee.

'Well, he is our major celebrity so far,' she said defensively. 'And he seems to be turning into a regular customer, though he doesn't give me much notice. He's terribly casual – handed out the keys and the code to the burglar alarm to me and his new cleaning lady before he really knew us at all.'

'Who has he got cleaning for him?'

'Dora Tombs. She was a Naylor – niece or great-niece of Ted, the gardener up at the hall.'

'We Naylors get everywhere, like Mile-a-Minute.'

'I think you are more of a rambling rose,' she said kindly.

A frizzy strand of sandy hair fell into her eyes, and she pushed it back and clamped it down with a white Scottie dog slide. She has no taste: even the smock she was wearing over her cord trousers and T-shirt had dogs stencilled around the bottom and made her look like a pregnant bun loaf.

'What on earth are you wearing?' I demanded. 'Isn't that one of Ophelia Locke's little creations?'

'Yes – the big pockets are really useful, and it wasn't expensive. She sells most of them at those historical re-enactment fairs, but she printed one with dogs as a special order for me.'

'It does *nothing* for your figure,' I told her frankly.

'I haven't got a figure.'

'Yes you have, an hourglass one with a very small waist. But that thing doesn't go in at the middle at all – you look entirely globular. Take it from me, it's a mistake.'

'It's very practical – which is why I wanted it,' she said defensively. 'Anyway, no one is interested in my figure.' Then she blushed underneath all the little freckles.

'Come clean, obviously someone's interested! Tell Auntie Lizzie,' I said encouragingly. Had George actually made his move *already*?

'They're – he – he's not really, it's just that he can't seem to take his eyes off my bust when I'm wearing a T-shirt,' she confessed. 'So I feel happier covered up.'

'What, the *vicar*?' I exclaimed, astonished.

She looked at me as if I'd run mad. 'The vicar? No, of course not, Lizzie! No, I meant Rob Rafferty. I thought he was lovely at first, so charming and amazingly handsome. Only there's something in his eyes when he's talking to me – and everything he says seems to have some kind of innuendo in it . . . and . . . well, I'm simply not used to that kind of thing so it makes me feel very gauche and uncomfortable, though I'm sure he doesn't mean anything by his manner, it's just his way.'

'Oh? So he's turned out to be mad, bad and dangerous to know?'

'It's just me being silly and not knowing what to say back, I expect. For instance, when I was bending over patting Flo the other day he walked into the kitchen and stared at my chest, then said: "You don't get many of *those* to the pound!" I simply didn't know where to put myself.'

I choked. 'Oh, dear! That was *very* rude and un-PC of him.'

'Yes, but you would have known what to say to him, wouldn't you?'

'Probably. Or socked him one.'

'I find I just – just don't want to go there any more in case he is in, although Flo is a very nice dog.'

'Then don't – I'll do his pet-sitting instead. He knows you've got a partner, doesn't he?'

'Oh, yes: but Lizzie, he might be even worse with you, because you are so pretty!'

'I'm not pretty at all, you need glasses! But I can deal with him, no problem – some of Tom's friends were rather oddball too, don't forget. No, hand over his keys and pass on any requests for pet-sitting – *I'll* sort him.'

'Well, actually, Lizzie . . . he wants me to go in and walk and feed Flo tonight, because he's out at some party until late. But then George – the vicar – has asked me to dinner and I said yes without thinking, so I don't know what to do.'

'He has? There, I knew he fancied you, I could tell at the Mystery committee meeting, and he made a bee-line for you at the funeral feast!'

'No, of course he doesn't fancy me,' she protested, blushing again. 'I can't imagine how you got that idea!'

'So, why has he invited you to dinner, then?'

'We just sort of got chatting the other day – he was admiring Trinny and said he would love another dog – his last one died of old age just before he moved here. Isn't that sad? Only he's out such a lot he doesn't feel it would be fair just at the moment. And I told him about the kennels and the rescue dogs and how they always needed people to walk them, and he said he would come with me whenever he has time. So *then* he asked me if I would have dinner with him and help him understand what he is supposed to be doing with the Mystery Play and village things like that – there's a lot for him to take in, coming into somewhere like Middlemoss.'

'There certainly is,' I agreed. 'Especially pitchforked straight into a strange funeral, poor man. But he's quite right; who better than the former vicar's daughter to help him make sense of it? But *don't* wear the smock.'

'Of course not! He's very good looking, isn't he?' she added, thoughtfully.

While I was glad to see she had stopped mooning over Rob Rafferty and transferred her interest to George, I couldn't help but feel that calling him good-looking was pushing it a bit, unless you particularly fancied knobbly, red-haired, blue-eyed, lanky men who didn't seem to be fully in control of their limbs.

If something comes of this, their children will all be ginger nuts. Though I expect they will raise a family of rescue dogs instead.

'He's delightful,' I agreed, hastily banishing my mental picture of their possible progeny. 'And don't worry about Mr Rafferty: *I'm* not afraid of the big bad wolf.'

When I got home, the new parish magazine with my adverts in it had been pushed through my door, and there were two messages on the answering machine. I seem very popular, suddenly.

The first was from Nick, saying he was finally returning from London, though why he thought I would be interested in his movements I don't know. *Or* what he thought I would do with the postcard of Camden Lock, with 'Sorry!' and a recipe for jellied eels scrawled on the back, which arrived the other day. I couldn't possibly eat eels – they're too snaky. And what was *he* sorry about? Leila and the permanently absent Tom are the ones who should be sorry.

'Hi, Lizzie, I'm on my way back. Things took longer than I expected – I couldn't persuade Leila I really *didn't* want any of her precious assets if we divorced, even after her solicitor drew up an agreement for me to sign until, in the end, I stuck his ebony paperknife in my thumb and signed in blood. A bit melodramatic, perhaps, but it seemed to do the trick.'

There was a pause, then his voice resumed with just a hint of rueful laughter in it: 'OK, *very* melodramatic. And the solicitor didn't seem to want the knife back – said I could keep it as a souvenir. Anyway, the divorce is on its way, a clean split, and no claims on each other's property or earnings. We never shared anything anyway, so that makes it easier. Oh – and it's all given me an idea for a recipe. Got any raspberries, or am I too late?' The message clicked off.

Raspberries?

The second message, from my agent, Sally McDonald, was short and to the point. After drumming her fingers and humming a brief snatch of *Will ye no come back again?,* she said: 'Lizzie? Can you send me the new book pronto? Only Crange and Snicket want it right now, and your sales figures aren't so good that you can afford to miss your deadlines. You did say you'd just about finished it – slap it into the post right this minute!'

Well, don't stop the carnival on *my* account, even if I have only been widowed for five minutes!

Still, it was as finished as it would ever be and Jasper's already transferred it to his computer and printed it out for me, so really I only need to read through it and make final corrections before it goes off.

What will happen when he and the computer go off to university, I don't know. But then, when I think about writing another Chronicle, I don't know about that, either.

I said as much to Sally when she rang me back later to make sure I had got her message, and was obeying orders.

'Oh, don't worry your wee head about that one just now. I had a brainwave – and I've already sold Crange and Snicket on the idea of a collected book of your recipes and hints, with the odd anecdote thrown in. They think it's a great idea – they're going to call it *Just Desserts*. Shouldn't take you long to do, should it? Toss in some new recipes to liven it up.'

I stared at the receiver as if it had bitten me, while her voice rolled inexorably on. 'What? When? I mean, when do they want it?' I broke in urgently, when she stopped for breath.

'Oh, not until early next year – January, say. Loads of time. Now, have you put that manuscript in the post?'

'Tomorrow,' I promised. 'I'm just making final corrections – I might have to get Jasper to reprint a few pages later.'

'See you do – I'll be expecting it,' she said, and rang off. It was only then I remembered: Jasper wasn't going to be home until late tonight, because he's going to Liverpool with a friend after he finishes work at the dig.

I wandered rather aimlessly round the kitchen for a few minutes, then dolloped clotted cream and raspberry jam on to some meringue halves I made yesterday with leftover egg whites.

They were so yummy I ate six, and I think I'll put them in the new Chronicle and *Just Desserts* as an alternative to scone cream teas.

I did try and read through the manuscript, but I just couldn't concentrate and found myself staring blankly at the same page. Eventually I gave up temporarily and went to do a bit of gardening. I picked loads of late strawberries, and even a few late raspberries from the end of the polytunnel – everything was still burgeoning forth like nobody's business. I wish someone would tell my garden it's time to wind down and take it easy.

As I worked I thought about Ophelia Locke, also burgeoning forth with a baby that might just possibly be Tom's. But whoever the father proved to be, the poor little thing was trying to grow on a vegan diet . . .

With a resigned sigh I fetched a big wicker basket from the outbuilding, and began to pack it with fresh fruit and salad vegetables, a bunch of baby carrots and ripe tomatoes. Then I set off up through the woods to Ophelia's estate cottage.

Like me she lives right next to the boundary wall of the estate, so it would have been quicker to walk up the road, but not as pretty as the woodland paths. Or as cool – the sky was a brazen blue and it was hot.

Ophelia had attached a nameplate to her front door that said 'Whitesmocks', but whether she meant that as a name or a description of her way of making a living, was unclear. There was unlikely to be any passing trade interested in purchasing antique style clothing down here anyway, since her only next door neighbour was the old and very deaf gardener who was Mimi's sparring partner and occasional accomplice in plant larceny, and I couldn't see Ted taking to smocks. Caz's cottage was quite nearby, only set further back in the woods in isolation, on the other side of a small stream bridged by mossy, ancient slabs of stone.

'Oh God!' she said predictably, opening the door and staring at me, 'Oh, no, oh God!' and fell to chewing her lower lip.

Oh, my ears and whiskers!

'Hello, Ophelia,' I said bracingly. 'Can I come in? Only

I've brought you some spare fruit, veg and salad stuff, which will do you good.'

She fell back rather reluctantly and I stepped straight down the one worn step into the tiny living room. It smelled of natural cotton and herbal tea. A sewing machine was set up by the window, and white material was festooned everywhere. A clothes rack on castors crammed with the finished product swayed slightly in the breeze from the open door.

'That's kind – that's *so* kind!' she said, and for a horrible moment I thought she was going to burst into tears or embrace me or something equally embarrassing. Instead, she wrung her hands and stared at me despairingly. 'But Ted, the old gardener next door, he says that Mr Pharamond *will* give me notice to quit the cottage because I was – well, he won't want me here.'

'I've spoken to him and he has no intention of throwing you out, so you don't need to worry about that. We will see what happens after the baby arrives – which will be *when,* do you think?'

'I don't know really – January, maybe?' she said vaguely. 'I didn't know I was pregnant for ages and then I thought I'd sort of just wait and see . . . '

I frowned. 'Wait and see what? Have you seen your doctor?'

'Oh, no – I believe nature should take its course. One of my friends will come for the birthing.'

'The *birthing*? Come on, Ophelia, this isn't the dark ages! You need to see a doctor, have the baby in hospital – nature's way may turn out to be pre-eclampsia or something like that.'

She stopped chewing her lower lip and looked stubborn.

'I hope you are eating well, anyway? Couldn't you give up the vegan stuff for the duration?'

'Vegan is healthy. There are lots of vegan mothers.'

'Well, make sure you vary your diet as much as you can, then. I'll keep leaving you fresh fruit and vegetables. I'll make up a box a week, a bit like one of those organic delivery services, and leave it on your doorstep.'

'You don't have to,' she began, blinking nervously. Her big pink eyelids remind me of those festooned blinds.

'No, but I want to. Whatever you did isn't the *baby's* fault, is it?'

'Noooo . . .' she muttered, walking backwards until she was half-enveloped among the hanging smocks. 'No, no, no!'

'There you are then, that's settled,' I said soothingly, following her and thrusting the basket into her arms.

'I'll – I'll unload this, so you can have it back!' she gasped and, fighting her way out of the folds of material, escaped into the lean-to kitchen.

I looked in from the doorway: although basic, it was at least clean and tidy, though yet *more* eternal rabbits had been stencilled everywhere. On the little gate leg table lay a roll of familiar-looking recycled yellow paper, a big black felt tip pen and a coil of silvery gaffer tape: something clicked in my head.

'Ophelia, when Jojo and Mick said you'd been sleeping with the *enemy*, meaning Caz Taylor – well, did they mean because you three are all members of ARG!'

She dropped a bunch of baby carrots. 'No, no, no . . .not me. Not us. No, I—'

'You're a *terrible* liar,' I said dispassionately. 'I recognize the paper on the table from the posters you put on my barn and my car and even over my front door!'

'No, no, no!' she jabbered, backing away, her prominent eyes starting. It is a pity she didn't say 'no' more often when men were around, it would have saved her a lot of trouble.

'Yes, yes, yes,' I said firmly, quite certain now. 'So, Ophelia, let's get this straight: you are living here on the Pharamond Estate and, as a member of ARG!, targeting not only the *owner* of that estate but also his gamekeeper, with whom you have been having an affair?'

'Oh, no! He – we didn't – well, only *once* when Caz caught me putting up a banner on the hall gates and . . . and I don't know what came over me! But I said I wouldn't go with him again because he was evil and persecuted the poor woodland creatures!' she whimpered.

'Once?'

'Or . . . maybe twice . . . three times,' she conceded, which reminded me of the joke about only being unfaithful once, with the Household Cavalry. 'And Caz's not really murdering the grey squirrels, he catches them and takes them away!' she said earnestly. 'I still have to put the posters up, because the

Pharamonds are on the ARG! hit list, but Caz takes them straight down again, like he was doing with the ones I put up at your place.'

'I suppose you might have some kind of case for targeting Caz and the estate, though it's a pretty shaky one to my way of thinking, but none at all for me. I mean, there are battery hen farmers and goodness knows what else in the area! Why?'

'S-someone said that you were cruelly exploiting your hens and the poor little quail, and when I said I wouldn't do it unless ARG! told me to, this person *made* me do it . . .'

I frowned, while she stood there wringing the feathery stems of the carrots between her hands. I am not sure I would trust her with a small baby when she is overwrought. 'So someone *made* you target me? Who? And how? Do they know something about you?'

'No – yes, oh God!' Ophelia went white. 'And if ARG! find out I've been targeting someone not on the list, I'll be expelled from the organization!'

'Jolly good idea, especially in your condition. Who exactly is this person with a spite against me?'

But she pressed her lips together firmly and said nothing.

'You know,' I said to her severely, 'there are better – and legal – ways of campaigning for animal rights, aimed at the people who really *do* abuse animals . . . ' Something I'd read in the local paper suddenly came into my head: 'Ophelia, were *you* involved in that big raid at the end of last year, on the lab rat farm over near Skem?'

If possible, she went even paler. 'Nooo . . .' she moaned. 'I wasn't there – she didn't see me – there wasn't any proof!'

'Ah,' I said. 'I see. So it's a *she,* and she knows you were involved in that raid?'

She moaned again. 'I was the last into the back of the van and her headlights caught me.'

'Don't you all wear masks or something?' I asked curiously.

'I forgot my balaclava and the scarf slipped,' she said rather sulkily. 'But now Caz says I don't have to do anything she says any more, because *he's* got something on *her* and so she can't make me – and now I know the truth about her, I wouldn't anyway!'

'So Caz knows all about it, and who this person threatening

you is?' I said, trying to disentangle her sometimes cryptic and convoluted utterances. I had a growing suspicion that *I* knew who it was, too.

'He already knew most of it, he'd been watching me . . . following me! He made me tell him everything,' she said, blushing.

I didn't ask how. 'At least Caz seems willing to take some responsibility for you.'

She went pink and looked away. 'He's not so bad really – not now I know what he does with the squirrels.'

'What *does* he do with the squirrels?' I asked, then added quickly: 'No, don't tell me, I don't really want to know!'

She snivelled. 'I thought Tom loved me, I really did, but I see now it's just like Jojo and Mick said, I was a handy bonk.'

'At least you seem to have grasped the situation,' I agreed. 'I suppose it's none of my business – but Caz rescued you the other day after the funeral, so he must care about you.'

'He's furious with me,' she whispered, twisting a strand of dishwater-blonde hair around her fingers, 'for making a scene and saying that about . . . about Tom. Only I was so angry, hearing those two going on as if they meant something to him, when I was the one who was pregnant!'

'And did Tom *really* say he loved you?' I asked curiously.

'He said I knew how he felt about me, and so I thought he meant he loved me. But he wasn't any different to me afterwards – and sometimes he could be very cruel, even though he didn't mean it!'

'Yes I know.' I wondered how many times Jojo and Mick and even Caz had . . . no, even *I* couldn't ask that, though the odds on it being Tom's baby were at least three to one, it seemed. We would just have to await the birth and guess. Or do DNA tests, or something. If it is Caz's, I suspect the entire Naylor clan will instantly know it anyway, in a very Midwich cuckoo way, just like they recognized me the second they saw me.

I walked home, thoughtfully swinging the basket. Someone had been angry with me, or jealous enough of me, to force Ophelia to include me in the ARG! campaign in an act of petty spitefulness.

When it came down to it, I could only think of one likely person. I'd like to know what Caz has got on her, but I don't suppose he would tell me even if I asked.

Thirteen
Raspberries

When I got home Nick's car was there, and he was just walking out of one of the outbuildings, brushing light coloured feathers off his sleeve. When he saw me, he stopped dead and looked slightly taken-aback, though goodness knows who else he was expecting to find in the yard when it is *my* house.

'Oh, hi, Lizzie! I was just talking to Caz.'

I expect he meant that literally, since he was unlikely to get a complete sentence in exchange, let alone a conversation. Caz often makes me feel like a Shakespearean actor embarking on a long monologue, although of course he does nod, shake his head or scratch his nose from time to time.

'It was kind of you to let him have that big freezer to store stuff in,' he added, carefully closing the door behind him.

'Well, why not? I wasn't using it any more now I don't grow so much, the one in the house is quite enough.' I turned to lead the way to the cottage, since I was hot and thirsty after my walk. 'God knows what he puts in it – I have a horrible feeling it may be all those grey squirrels from the humane traps.'

'Oh, no, not squirrels,' he assured me, so I assume Caz had let him see into it. That was quite a relief, really – I expect it is just rabbits and stuff, for the pot. (And what a strange mismatch it is that vegan, animal rights Ophelia and carnivore Caz should ever have come together!)

'I've been downsizing the fruit and vegetable production

for months and months, ever since I realized I was going to have to leave Perseverance Cottage – only now, of course, I don't have to. Unks is so kind.'

He leaned against the fridge, arms folded and glowering darkly, like a slightly Neanderthal Mr Darcy in a strop. 'I hadn't realized things were so bad – you should have told me or Roly. I wondered, when you had that cut on your face and were so evasive about how you got it – and Caz says when he's been down here he's heard you arguing and Tom being pretty abusive.'

That accounts for the feeling I often got that our arguments had an audience. I should draw the downstairs curtains more, which you tend to forget when other houses do not overlook you. And who knows when Caz is flitting past on his nefarious activities?

'It was none of your business. What could you have done? And do you want some ginger beer?' The top came off and it fizzed gently into glasses. I simply love the sensation when the bubbles get up the back of your nose and ginger explodes in your head.

'I could have helped in some way, Lizzie!'

'You haven't been around to have a private conversation with, even if I'd wanted to,' I pointed out snappily. 'I could hardly have bellowed out the information while we were all sitting round the dining table up at the hall over Sunday lunch, with Tom being his usual charming self and you in and out of the kitchen, worrying over the roast beef and whether the horseradish sauce was just a trifle too *piquant*. Maybe I should have sent *you* a postcard?'

He ran a hand through his black hair so that it stood up like a cockatoo's crest and said more reasonably: 'I already knew you and Tom were going through a rough patch – he more or less accused me of having had an affair with you, just before his illness was diagnosed. But after what you said at the hospital, about hoping things would be good between you again once he had recovered, I thought it best to distance myself a bit.'

'He did? I hadn't realized . . . I mean, I know you two weren't getting on so well, and didn't see much of each other any more but . . . And did you know he suspected Jasper was yours?'

'Yes. But once we knew about the tumour, like you, I put it down to that and I hoped . . . well, I hoped for your sake and Jasper's that he would recover and be the old Tom again, and things would settle down. And that's why I've kept such a low profile around the place.'

'Well, you might have told *me* all that when we were having our true confessions chat in hospital!'

'I didn't think it was the time or place, and also I wasn't sure how much he had said to you, so I thought it better not. And of course I didn't know then that my wife was having an affair with him,' Nick added. 'But when I found him in Leila's restaurant that night it all sort of clicked into place, even though she denied it.' He looked sombrely at me. 'He probably only started it to get revenge on me for something he imagined I'd done – and I'm sorry she made that scene at the funeral, Lizzie!'

'Well, it wasn't your fault.'

'I know, but I brought her, and I knew she was still lying when she insisted there was nothing between them, although I didn't know why she wouldn't agree to the divorce.'

'And then it turns out she was sharing Tom with Polly Darke, with Ophelia Locke as the side salad! Oh – did you hear about Ophelia's revelations, too – the pregnancy?'

He nodded. 'Roly says she's deranged and invented it.'

'No, she's not mad; she just deluded herself into thinking a quickie meant something deeper,' I said, considering it. 'She seems very naive for her age.'

'So he did—?'

'Oh, yes, I already knew that. I think there's a good chance the baby isn't Tom's, though – we will have to wait and see. But at least Ophelia is just credulous and silly: with Polly and Leila it all boils down to greed and self-interest, doesn't it?' I said sadly. 'And the ironic thing is that Tom thought Unks was going to leave him the cottage outright when he died, and even I could have told him that he would never have split the estate up like that!'

'No,' he said ruefully, 'and I'm afraid my poor father scuppered his chances of inheriting by giving us his plans for turning Pharamond Hall into apartments!'

'I expect Unks will leave it to you – *you* wouldn't do that to it, would you?'

'No, of course not! I love it the way it is. And actually, Roly says he *is* leaving it to me, though keep that to yourself. Which means that I do have every right to worry about your welfare, if only because you live on the estate. And, you probably haven't thought about it, that now puts Jasper in line as next heir.'

I stared at him: 'Don't you *dare* put that idea into his head! You'll remarry, probably some young, skinny model type like that photographer who came here last year to photograph you in the hall kitchen – Lydia, was it? – and have a multitude of children.'

'I don't think so,' he said shortly.

'Famous last words. But *I'm* certainly not getting married again: the single life for me from now on. Pretty much as before, actually, only without the threat of occasional violence and verbal abuse hanging over me – Tom and I led very separate lives even before he started turning weird.'

'And I married a woman who was so territorially defensive she insisted on keeping her own flat on and pencilled me into her schedule if I wanted to see her. Now that Leila and I are divorcing, I'll be spending most of my time up here – I might even sell my London flat. Roly never uses it, he prefers his club, and I send most of my work in by email these days, so I can base myself anywhere.'

Nick picked up his glass and absently drank his ginger beer down in one go, which made his eyes water – it is good, strong, peppery stuff. 'My God, you are just *so* Enid Blyton at times, Lizzie! Aren't you going to offer me a sticky bun and an adventure, too?'

'No, but there are peanut biscuits in the tin, if you want one?'

'No thanks, you know I don't like sugary stuff much.' He finally sat down, uninvited, on a spindly old kitchen chair that groaned slightly. 'Lizzie, didn't it occur to you that Unks would have been sympathetic if you'd told him what was going on? He would certainly have helped you and Jasper to find somewhere else to live, for instance.'

'Tom generally managed to be quite charming to me whenever Unks or anyone else was around, so I wasn't sure he would believe me, and I didn't want to tell him about the affair, especially since I had no idea who it was . . . and – oh,

Nick, I'm so sorry!' I exclaimed, 'I keep forgetting it was Leila.'

'Among others, and I don't really care, except on your account,' he said shortly. 'I've been trying to get her to agree to a divorce for ages, so one good thing has come out of it.'

'Well, these last couple of years have been hell, but all's well that ends well . . . Though I suppose I shouldn't say that when it is Tom's *death* that has made everything come right, and really I feel so mixed up and guilty and relieved and sad . . .' I sniffed and took a gulp of ginger beer.

Being Nick he didn't rush to comfort me, but instead said brusquely: 'Time to move on, for both of us. And since I'm going to be around, if you want any help with anything, you only have to ask.'

'Thank you, that's very kind – but I do most of the work here myself and as I said, I've scaled things down no end. In fact, I'm putting an advert in the parish magazine to see if anyone wants the polytunnel and the quail, and I'm going to sell that enormous TV of Tom's, too. I don't want a TV at all, but Jasper says he would like a small portable to take to university, so I'll get him one with the proceeds.'

I took another sip of ginger beer and reached for the biscuit tin. 'At least I got rid of the goats years ago when they learned how to climb trees.'

He gave me a look. 'Goats can't climb trees, Lizzie!'

'You obviously don't know much about goats. And you wouldn't believe how strong they are! If a goat sets its mind on going somewhere, there's not a lot you can do to stop it. Anyway, I never did get used to goat-flavoured milk and yoghurt.'

'What are you going to do with Tom's business?'

'Oh, I've already sorted that,' I said, taking a bite of crunchy biscuit. 'The day after the funeral two of Tom's friends – Jimbo and Freddie, do you remember them? – came and made me an offer for everything, and I accepted it. I could have got more, but I wanted to – well, I wanted to just get rid of it all! And they thought they'd got a really, really good deal; but the funny thing is that they assumed Tom's van was in with everything, only I'd already swapped it with Dave Naylor for that nice old Morris Traveller in the yard, so they had to go and buy it back!'

'Really, Lizzie, you should have left all that to me – I'd have got you a good price for everything!' he said, not seeming at all amused.

'It's none of your business,' I said tartly. A few faint, plangent notes wafted across the courtyard and through the open kitchen door.

'What the hell's that?' he demanded, startled. 'It seems to be coming from the workshop!'

'It's just the Mummers, Nick. I let them carry on using the workshop to practice in – I wasn't using it.'

He stared at me. 'But Ophelia Locke is—'

'Pregnant with Tom's child? Chances are it isn't his, but I think she was more sinned against than sinning; she seems very . . . very easy and persuadable. Gullible, even. I've just been up to her cottage to take her some spare fruit and veg to build her up a bit, but if I'd known she was coming down here tonight she could have taken it back with her.'

'You're crackers!' he said.

This didn't seem to be the moment to tell him she was one of the members of ARG! who had been targeting my cottage in particular and the estate in general. Anyway, she had said that she'd stopped now and I expect Caz will see she does.

'Funnily enough, I think Ophelia's half in love with Caz, only she doesn't want to admit it,' I said, following that train of thought.

'Is she? Well, they do say that opposites attract! Maybe *we* could have made a go of it all those years ago, if you hadn't suddenly decided to marry Tom on the rebound after we split up.'

'I did *not* marry Tom on the rebound, we fell in love!' I said hotly. 'And we split up after you decided to go off on another of your world recipe-finding missions, don't forget.'

'You should have understood – and waited. I wrote to you.'

'No, you sent me recipes on postcards!'

'That's the same thing.'

His eyes, that always reminded me of the purple-grey of wet Welsh slate, looked baffled.

'Well, whatever,' I said. 'It's pointless having post-mortems at this stage, isn't it? We married other people and moved on.'

There was a tap on the door and a shadow darkened the threshold. 'Hello,' called a deep and attractive voice. 'Mrs Pharamond?'

The man, who was tall with curling blond hair and a ruggedly handsome face, stopped halfway through the door. 'Oh, sorry if I'm disturbing you,' he said, with a charmingly apologetic smile. 'I'm Rob, you know – Rob Rafferty?'

As my eyes met his incredibly blue ones, it struck me that Annie's description of his charms had been *wildly* understated. A force-field could not have held me faster at that moment and I fear I might even have been drooling – but then, he did make me think of slabs of golden brown Honeycomb Crunch.

His gaze left mine and he looked enquiringly at Nick, who was sitting there with his arms crossed like a terribly gloomy wooden Indian.

'Oh, you're not interrupting anything!' I said, managing to get my voice back. 'This is my – my late husband's cousin, Nick Pharamond.'

'Hi,' he said in a friendly manner, but the two men seemed to me to be eyeing each other in a very sizing-up-for-battle way. It reminded me of a film I once saw of bull elephants fighting, probably a territorial thing. They were both big, fit men – I wouldn't know which one to put my money on.

'I just wanted to say how kind it was of you to let the group practise here still, Mrs Pharamond, and let you know I'll be up here jamming with them sometimes, if you see a stranger around your place!'

'Do call me Lizzie,' I said. 'And actually, I'll be the stranger round at *your* place tonight, if you still want Posh Pet-sitters to come, because I'm Annie's partner and I'll be seeing to Flo.'

He gave me another warm – *very* warm smile, blue eyes crinkling at the corners, and I could see what Annie meant, a bit, because there was just something about his expression that made you feel hot under the collar. Or the smock, in her case.

'Great, I can see she will be in good hands. Well, better get back to the gang, I suppose – not my sort of music, really, but it's good to keep my hand in!'

Another one hundred and fifty watt smile and he was gone. I sighed involuntarily, watching his retreating, blue-jeaned posterior until it vanished into the workshop. Ophelia might think he was old, but I bet that was before she saw him in the flesh.

'Well, you do seem to be managing everything very well without *my* help,' Nick said, abruptly getting up and banging his head on the ceiling light which swayed alarmingly. 'Bloody hell!'

'Jasper's started doing that too, now he's over six foot. Must shorten the chain or something. Thanks for coming though, Nick – Jasper will be sorry to have missed you.'

'He's at the dig?'

'Yes, and then his friend was going to pick him up and they were going over to talk to the owner of the student house his friend's brother rents with a couple of others. Jasper's taking that dog that Annie dumped on us, and thinks he can sweet-talk the landlady into letting him keep it in the house, even though it is supposed to be no pets. He can be very charming when he likes, so he might manage it. He'll be home late, but hopefully not *too* late, because I might want him to print out a couple of fresh pages of my new manuscript – if I can bring myself to concentrate on them for long enough to spot any mistakes!'

He gestured at the dog-eared heap at the end of the table. 'Is that what all this stuff is? Yet another glorious Perseverance Chronicle?'

'Yes – and possibly the last, I'm not sure I'll be able to write another. And I keep trying to read through it but my brain gets stuck and I read the same page over and over,' I said despairingly. 'My agent will kill me if it isn't in the post tomorrow.'

'I'll read it for you,' he offered, to my surprise.

'What – *you*?'

'Why not? I'm literate and I've nothing particularly to do for the rest of the afternoon. It's not that big a manuscript – won't take me long. I'll red pen any mistakes and drop it back later.'

It was amazingly kind of Nick and, since he obviously wanted to do something to help, I pushed it all into a manila folder and handed it to him thankfully. 'That is *such* a weight off my mind! I'll be out around seven to see to Mr Rafferty's dog, but you know where the key is if I'm out, don't you?'

'Raspberries,' he said.

'What?'

'I left you a message earlier. *Do* you have any?'

'Oh – yes, all the soft fruit up at the end of the polytunnel seemed to be going on indefinitely, but I think these may be the last and there aren't an awful lot of them. I put them aside for you in the small barn.'

'That's OK, I bought some supermarket ones just in case, though they don't have the same flavour. I can mix them together.'

'What are you making?'

'A variation on liquorice ice cream, with a raspberry coulis.'

I looked at him doubtfully, but he seemed to be serious. Then he stunned me by stooping and swiftly kissing me, which he absolutely *never* does, and left with my manuscript under his arm.

My lips tingled. I suppose we *are* now officially kissing cousins, if only by marriage . . . but I would not describe that as an affectionate peck on the cheek. Also, since he is the dark sort of man who gets a five o'clock shadow five minutes after he has shaved, I got a free exfoliation into the bargain.

Staring after his car as he drove off (and it was very nearly pressed duck for dinner), I realized what I hadn't admitted to myself before: that for the last couple of years I had really, really missed our occasional, invigorating exchanges of opinion. Every life, especially one so literally down to earth as mine, needs just a *little* spice.

Rob Rafferty did not strike me as spicy in the least . . . more of a sweet treat.

Going back in, I slightly loosened all the caps on the ginger beer bottles, just in case, then looked out the Honeycomb Crunch recipe which I put in Book Six of the Perseverance Chronicles. It is much the same as cinder toffee, really – sugar, white vinegar, water and bicarbonate of soda – only with added butter and golden syrup. It's the mixture of bicarb and vinegar that makes them go all bubbly.

It occurred to me that, crumbled up, it would make a wonderful topping for homemade vanilla ice cream. You could wrap a chunk in cling film and hit it with a rolling pin – that should do the trick.

Fourteen
Slightly Curdled

Jasper phoned: his new landlady has agreed that Ginny can take up residence in the rented house with him and his friends at the end of the month, so that is sorted. I would have preferred him to live in a student hall of residence for the first year at least, but the whole point of your children going away to university is so they can live their lives, not yours, so I would just have to go along with his decision.

The thought of my little boy exposed to all the temptations of drugs, unprotected sex and being knifed in the street . . . I had to swallow hard before I could say brightly: 'Oh, good, I'm so glad, darling. That will be great, won't it, living with your friends and having Ginny with you? What time will you be back tonight?'

'Not until pretty late. Chris's mum is going to drop me off, probably about eleven. She doesn't like him driving late at night – she's nearly as bad as you for fussing.'

'Jasper, I don't fuss! How can you say I fuss?' I demanded indignantly, then added after a moment's pause, 'What are you doing tonight?'

'Sex, drugs, tattooing our arms with old syringes off the street, that kind of thing,' he said good-naturedly.

'*Jasper!*'

'Watching DVDs, making popcorn, drinking beer,' he amended.

'I'm going into the village in a minute, to pet-sit an actor's dog – Rob Rafferty. He used to be some kind of pop star in the eighties.'

'Never heard of him,' he said, unimpressed. Had it been a

bosomy model from one of the boys' magazines I expect he would have been much keener, but the only creature with artificially inflated breasts in the Mosses is Polly Darke.

How *can* silicone be sexy? Isn't it peculiar that many men find artificial breasts just as much of a turn on as real ones? Another one of life's strange mysteries to ponder when you are examining your marrows.

I ate a generous portion of my own version of Lancashire hotpot before going out – good and peppery, with rich gravy and a shortcrust topping – and read the latest issue of the Mosses parish magazine, which must have been pushed through my door when I was out the back mending the greenhouse with gaffer tape.

According to the Verger's Village Round-up, Caz Naylor '*kindly volunteered to resolve the goose situation in Middlemoss. Children and the elderly were being terrorized, and the mess they left was proving a danger to life and limb. Caz therefore caught and re-homed them to somewhere more suitable, a solution we know will be acceptable to all interested parties.*'

There was also a notice that rehearsals for the Mystery Play would be starting in the village hall, every Tuesday for acts 1–9, and Thursdays for acts 10–22. We've filled the vacancies for Moses and Lazarus, and Miss Pym, who is a dab hand with papier mâché, is making a new Thou Shalt Not Commit Adultery commandments tablet.

I set off for the old vicarage just before seven, since it is only a short walk, but first I changed into a pair of decent, clean jeans and a pale green T-shirt with pretty old buttons sewn in a border all round the neck, an idea I got from one of Annie's magazines. I sewed them on my best Indian leather toe-post sandals too, though they keep getting ripped off.

Then I rigorously brushed all the knots out of my hair, which was probably a mistake since it went into a ripply chestnut mass round my head, like something Burne-Jones would have painted, though thankfully *sans* the sulky Pre-Raphaelite trout-pout.

Then I scrutinized my face, which looked glowingly healthy for a recent widow, in the mirror, wondering about make-up. I often *think* about make-up, but rarely do anything about it.

Then suddenly I thought, what the hell am I doing, getting

all duded up to walk Rob Rafferty's dog? Am I crackers? Do I think Flo is going to give her master my marks out of ten for effort and appearance when he staggers home from his party?

It was a bit late to change, though, so I set off and, as I passed the vicarage bungalow, I wondered how Annie and George were getting on. It seemed very daring of him to invite a single lady to dine with him alone . . . Well, I *assume* they are alone (apart from Trinny), unless he has invited half the village round for support?

I unlocked the front door of the old vicarage, now sporting its new name of Vicar's End, with the key Annie had given me, and stepped inside. It was always unlocked when Annie's father was vicar, so that seemed odd in itself. And somehow I still expected the cool, tiled hall to smell of lavender, floor polish and beeswax, just like it used to; but it didn't, just of exotic artificial household fragrance mixed with slightly acrid cigarette smoke.

The old hatstand had been replaced by a glass-topped console table bearing a rather indecent bronze sculpture and a severely tailored arrangement of decayed-looking black orchids among spiky foliage. I was just touching them to see if they were real and still alive (they were), when, with a clatter of claws, Flo hurtled down the hall to meet me, velvet coat rippling and tail thrashing about. Annie said she would be delighted to see me, even though I was a total stranger. Had I been a burglar, I expect she would have been equally pleased.

'Good girl, Flo!' I said, patting her. 'Good girl!'

My instructions were to let her into the garden and feed her, then hand her a chewy rawhide bone and shut her in the kitchen on departing. I thought I would feed her first, since she didn't seem particularly interested in going out.

What happy, smiley faces white bull terriers have!

'Come on then, Flo, din-dins,' I said, and had just started towards the door at the back of the hall that led into the kitchen, when a deep, instantly recognizable masculine voice from above called out: 'Tobe, is that you? I'm on my way!'

He was, too: leaping athletically down the stairs two steps at a time, Rob Rafferty landed in the hall almost at my feet, though an advance wave of aftershave just beat him to it.

'Yark!' I squawked inelegantly.

He looked equally startled for a moment, then smiled.

'Sorry – thought you were my lift! Did I startle you . . . ? Lizzie, isn't it?'

'Well – yes,' I said, swallowing. 'I thought you'd have been long gone.' Despite myself I was answering that effulgent smile, drowning dizzily in the depths of his cerulean blue eyes . . .

'I'm *so* glad I wasn't,' he said, to which I couldn't think of a thing to say.

Was he flirting? *My* flirting abilities were not great even in my youth and are atrophied now to the point of no return. I looked at him doubtfully, but decided it was just his usual manner and got a grip on myself. I even started breathing again: in, out – quite easy now I'd remembered how to do it.

'No . . . well, since you *are* still here, you won't need me to see to Flo, will you? You can do it before you go,' I suggested.

A horn sounded: 'No time – that's Toby. You know Tobe Little, plays Rufus Grace in *Cotton Common*?'

'No – I'm afraid not, I haven't seen it,' I confessed. 'I don't watch much TV. I quite like gardening and cookery programmes, but anything else just doesn't seem to hold my concentration. Probably because it isn't real. Life is much more interesting, isn't it?'

'Is it?' he said, looking at me curiously. The horn hooted again, impatiently. 'Look, Lizzie, why don't I tell Tobe to hang on a couple of minutes while we sort Flo, and then you could come with me, meet some of the cast, come on to the party?'

'What – *me*?' I said, startled. 'Oh, no, thanks, I couldn't! Jasper – my son – is coming home later . . .' I began automatically to stammer out excuses, though I was horrified to find that a little bit of me was rather tempted by the idea, in a fascinated-by-a-snake kind of way.

'Isn't he grown up? I don't suppose he needs his mum on the doorstep,' he said, with another dangerously beguiling smile.

How does he know that? Does he know all about me? Though I suppose that isn't hard: he only has to tune in to the village gossip, since I am sure the Mosses are still buzzing with the goings-on at the funeral.

He turned serious again, blue eyes concerned and sincere:

'But I'm sorry – you were very recently widowed, what *am* I thinking of? Of course you don't want to go to parties yet!'

'No,' I agreed, having *entirely* forgotten about Tom until that point. 'And his cousin, Nick – you met him earlier – is coming round this evening, because he kindly offered to correct the manuscript of my next book, which needs to be posted off tomorrow. It would be very rude of me not to be there. Sorry.'

'Your book? Are you another novelist, like Polly Darke?'

Ah, yes, our Trollope of the North. 'No, I write sort of autobiographical books with recipes. You know Polly?'

'Met her around a few times,' he said vaguely. 'She had a fling with a friend of mine. Apparently she's pretty fit – does some weird yoga stuff. "Muscles like knots on string," he said.'

'Really? I've never seen her arms, she always wears long sleeves. Thought she might be on drugs or something.'

He shrugged, then his eyes flicked over me and he gave me a slow, sexy smile. 'I prefer natural, curvy women to skinny ones with monster boob jobs, every time.'

'That must make you fairly unique,' I said slightly tartly, and he grinned.

The front door was thrust open and a voice bellowed: 'Rob, what the hell are you doing, you bastard? Are you coming or what?'

'On my way out!' Rob called back. Then he turned to me. 'Well, see you later, then. Be good, Flo.'

And off he went. *Was* he actually flirting with me, Lizzie Pharamond, middle-aged Middlemoss tomboy, or like that with all women? I could quite see why he had disconcerted Annie, though, because I felt slightly and interestingly singed around the edges. The words 'moth' and 'flame' came vividly to mind.

Sizzle, sizzle.

If he comes across on the TV like that, then the reason why *Cotton Common*'s ratings have risen drastically since he joined the cast was understandable.

He's trouble at t'mill.

I spent almost an hour with Flo, who is a delightful dog and will fetch a thrown rubber ball indefinitely, though she seemed quite sanguine about swapping my company for a chewy bone when I left.

* * *

Halfway home, while sauntering past the eerily quiet, goose-free green, I suddenly remembered about Nick and broke into a guilty run.

He'd obviously been at the cottage for some time – he'd let himself in and there was an empty coffee cup on the kitchen table.

'Oh, sorry, Nick. Have you been here long?' I said, panting slightly. 'I was playing with the dog, and didn't notice the time.'

He rose to his feet, heavy brows practically meeting across his impressive nose, and snapped: 'You look pretty smart for dog-sitting. Going somewhere?'

'No,' I snapped right back, flushing. 'I don't spend all day, every day, in gardening clothes, you know!'

He took me in with his slatey, sardonic eyes, from gold sandals to waving, if now dishevelled, hair. 'You always did scrub up well. Hope your *client* appreciated it.'

'How did you know Rob was still there?' I gasped, startled, then felt myself going pink again.

'You just told me!'

'Well, he was, though on his way out. And don't call him a *client* in that tone of voice, like I was a hooker!'

'Sorry!' he said, but didn't sound it. 'I'll be on my way. Didn't find too much wrong with your manuscript except a bit of tailoring of the truth.'

'I have to, nobody would believe the real things that happen: they are much too incredible. And anyway, it would be too depressing. My misfortunes are supposed to be funny.'

'Yes, your formula for success with your readers *does* seem to be a series of pratfalls linked with nursery-food suggestions,' he said unkindly.

'You offered to read through it, I didn't make you!'

'I wanted to help.' He ran a hand through his black hair, which stood up like an angry eagle's crest. 'Look, seeing you're all gussied up, why don't you come out somewhere quiet with me for a drink? I'll even give you some pudding ideas for your new recipe book.'

Men *are* like bloody buses, as the poet Wendy Cope puts it so well: there isn't one for ages and then two come along at once, flashing their signals. Not that that necessarily means they are going to stop. And I don't even want to catch one!

'That's kind of you, Nick, but I really don't feel like going out tonight, and I need to make those alterations to the manuscript and pack it up. Anyway, we'd just fight like we usually do.'

'Please yourself,' he said, and walked out. I stared after him. Which is well worthwhile – his rear view is just as good, if not better, than Rob's.

I *think* he is just trying to be kind to me in his way, like he was when Tom was unconscious in hospital. But Nick's kindness moves in mysterious ways, its wonders to perform.

Clive Potter cycled up for some tomatoes, and to tell me that Adam (as played by a local farmer) has given himself a hernia while lifting bales, and dropped out of the Mystery Play.

'We'll have to audition for a new one I'm afraid, Lizzie, unless anyone comes forward before that.'

I had a sudden mental vision of playing my Eve to Rob Rafferty's Adam, but firmly suppressed it: an innocent in the Garden of Eden he certainly was not.

Then, like a snake, the man himself phoned me up later from somewhere noisy and invited me to his housewarming party at Vicar's End on Friday night. 'Just a few people – you could come to that, couldn't you?' he said persuasively, and I won't say I wasn't tempted for a minute there, before common sense reasserted itself and I politely declined.

It got me thinking about Honeycomb Crunch again, though, and I decided to try using it in a variant of Eton Mess. I would call it Cinder Cream. I think I'm on to a winner.

Fifteen

Drink Me

Another summons to Rob's house, this time to take Flo to the Mossedge canine beautician for nail clipping and a bit of pampering.

Annie was right about the Posh Pet-sitters taking off, because I also have to feed, talk to and change the litter trays of two cats in a converted barn over at Mossrow for the next two days, plus a couple more one-off jobs. Weeds will soon outnumber vegetables in my garden.

I managed to fit in a visit to the cats while Flo was being done, and then returned her to Vicar's End, where Rob was flirting with his cleaning lady, Dora Tombs, whom he called Dorable. 'Get away with you!' was her standard response to each sally.

'Morning, our Lizzie!' she said as I went in. 'Keep that dog off my clean floor until it's dried – and the same goes for you,' she added, jabbing at Rob's feet with her mop.

Rob took a step back and gave me a lazy, glinting smile that took me in from top to bottom and lingered a bit on the way.

'Flo's clean as a whistle, Mrs T,' I assured her. Flo skittered and slid over to her bowl and started wolfing biscuits as though she was famished.

'They said at Doggy Heaven that she was good as gold,' I told Rob, adding severely, 'and you could have taken her yourself if you're not going to work and saved some money!'

'Ah, but then I wouldn't have had two beautiful women at my beck and call, would I?'

'Get away with you, you daft bugger!' Dora said. 'Yer all mouth and no trousers, you are!'

'Don't you *ever* work?' I asked, unimpressed.

'Actually yes – and I'm on my way. Just waiting for the car.'

'You don't drive?'

'Lost my licence – I've got another twelve months before I get it back again,' he said ruefully, but I didn't feel sympathetic because I expect it was drink driving, which in my opinion is a criminally stupid thing to do.

'Tough luck,' I said, but when he smiled at me I found myself smiling back. He is clearly as self-centred as most of the male race, besides being unable to resist flirting with any female who comes within range, but I must admit he *is* extremely attractive.

'I could use a part-time chauffeur?' he suggested, raising a questioning eyebrow.

'I've got enough to do – my garden will be an impenetrable jungle if I don't spend more time at home.'

A horn beeped outside. 'Pity – and there's my car. See you later, girls!'

After he had gone (and he is the type who seems to take the sun with him when he goes out of a room) Mrs T put the kettle on and we had tea, toast and gossip.

She is also Polly Darke's cleaner, which is fascinating: I didn't know she had a whole room devoted to some weird kind of yoga, and worked out in there twice a day.

'Fit as a flea and strong as an ox,' Mrs T averred, crunching toast. 'Wouldn't think it to look at her, would you? And I'm that sorry about your troubles,' she added after a pause, which is as close as anyone's got to mentioning the major revelations at the funeral feast. 'I could tell sometimes she'd had a man in the house, but if I'd of known who it was, I'd have told you.'

'Oh, thanks,' I said. 'Well, it's all water under the bridge now – I'm trying to move on and put all that behind me.'

'That's right – and I'm sure Mr Nick will help you sort everything out. He's a proper man.'

'A proper man as compared to *what*?' I asked curiously.

She gave me a Mona Lisa smile. 'Eva Gumball says he's divorcing that foreign woman and going to be living up there at the hall most of the time, now. His granddad's that made up about it!'

Information in the Mosses travels almost as fast as thought. 'I'm glad for Uncle Roly's sake that Nick will be spending more time in Middlemoss, but I certainly don't need *anyone* to help me sort things out,' I said firmly.

'That Polly Darke's turned a whole bedroom into a walk-in wardrobe, too,' Mrs T said, changing the subject.

I felt quite restless on Friday night. I'd popped into Delphine Lake's earlier to walk her dogs, and she'd said she was going to Rob's party.

'For cocktails at eight, dear. But us old ones will clear off early and then I expect it will go on until the small hours!'

I don't actually like parties, except family ones, so I can't imagine why I felt left out.

All right – I do. My mind keeps presenting me with scenarios involving Rob which are quite unbecoming to a widow of recent date.

When I went downstairs early on Saturday morning, Mimi was asleep on the sofa in the sitting room.

I don't know why I ever bother locking my front door: absolutely everyone seems to know where I hide the spare key.

Juno, who is now allowed on her feet again, arrived in search almost immediately, limping gamely. 'I wish you'd stay in your bed at nights!' she scolded Mimi, who simply gazed blandly at her like a comfortable cat.

'Stay to breakfast?' I invited. 'Jasper's getting up – he's going to the dig.' Thuds and yapping from above were evidence that Ginny was doing her best to help. The ceiling light swayed gently and small flakes of plaster drifted down, like the grey-white feathers Nick had been brushing off his sleeve when he came out of the small barn the other day. Suspiciously large feathers, too . . . and suddenly I wondered exactly *where* Caz had re-homed the gaggle of vicious geese from the village stream? But he wouldn't . . . would he?

If Caz hadn't fitted a padlock to his freezer, I'd have had a quick snoop by now.

'No, thanks – must get back, Mrs Gumball always cooks enough for twelve, and think of the waste!' Juno said, propelling the reluctant Mimi away.

I didn't think Mimi would be terribly hungry, though, since I discovered when I opened the fridge that half a bowl of Strawberry Froth had been eaten. It is surprisingly filling.

'Come up to the hall later – around eleven!' Mimi said, clinging to the doorframe with both hands and smiling at me. 'Nick's invited us all to try out some ice cream he's making – yummy!'

'He invited *me* too?' I asked doubtfully.

'*Especially*,' Mimi confirmed, still beaming but losing her grip on the gloss paint, and was borne away until her cracked soprano singing, 'Hokey pokey, a penny a lump!' faded away into the distance.

'You've just missed Mimi and Juno,' I told Jasper when he came down. Ginny shot past my ankles and scattered the chickens in the yard, but unintentionally, I think. She probably couldn't see them for all the hair in her eyes.

'I know, I heard. Mimi sounded happy.'

'She mostly does. Oh – there's the phone.'

I should have said, rather, *where's* the phone, since I couldn't find it until I traced the long flex from the kitchen into the sitting room. Mimi seemed to have built a nest for it with all the cushions, though it hadn't laid anything, not even a wrong number.

By the time I got to it, it had stopped ringing, but the caller had left a message: Rob, sounding very gin-and-cigarettes gravelly. 'Lizzie? If you get this, come round and sort Flo out right away, will you? I'm feeling a bit rough this morning and she keeps yapping . . . Don't think Dora's coming until this afternoon . . . just let yourself in.'

I could hear faint barking, and then Rob groaned (rather sexily, it has to be said) and put the phone down.

Well, he might at least have let the poor dog out, even if he *did* have a hangover! It would be nearly an hour until I could get there, since I had to drop Jasper off at the dig first, so by that time he would probably have given in and done it himself. And didn't he have to go to work every day? I know nothing about these things; perhaps they record the shows in batches or something?

The phone rang again almost immediately while I was carrying it back into the kitchen. But it was just a man who had seen the advert for the polytunnel and wanted to come and look at it later today.

'You're very popular this morning, Mum,' Jasper commented. 'And a bit pink,' he added, but I ignored that. I'd already let the hens out and fed them, watered the garden and greenhouse, put a load of washing in the machine, made an especially nice packed lunch for Jasper and cooked bacon and eggs. Who wouldn't look flushed?

When I cautiously let myself into Vicar's End, there was no sign of life other than a muffled barking from the kitchen.

Poor Flo had been unable to keep all four legs crossed and left a puddle by the door, about which she seemed to feel apologetic, though it was not *her* fault, as I told her while I let her out before finding the mop and disinfectant and cleaning it up.

Then I filled her bowl with fresh water and put a few

crunchy dog biscuits down to keep her going for a while. I didn't know what Rob wanted me to do, but I was quite sure he could afford the Posh Pet-sitters prices, so after that I took Flo for a nice long walk. It had rained in the night, so she wasn't such a clean, white and glossy creature on our return, though she was a much happier one.

I hadn't even started out clean and glossy, being back to gardening jeans and old T-shirts, Nick's remarks having rankled slightly.

While I was still rubbing Flo with a tartan towel helpfully inscribed 'DOG' that I found hanging in the scullery next to her lead, Rob wandered into the kitchen obviously fresh from the shower, in gilt-edged designer stubble and a *very* short towelling robe. Clearly he is a natural blond, because the hair on his legs was golden right up to the hem. He was carrying a glass beaker of straw coloured liquid, which he set down on the counter.

'Morning. I could do with a rub down too,' he said with a wicked if rueful smile and, opening the fridge, bent over and rummaged around. I looked away hastily.

'Thanks for coming,' he said, emerging with an opened carton of milk. 'Don't know what we were drinking last night – that's the trouble with cocktails and after a couple you don't care any more. But today I feel like shit.' He picked up the glass beaker again. 'I'll just finish this, and then make some coffee: want some?'

'What is it?' I asked cautiously.

He grinned: 'I meant, do you want some *coffee*! I don't think you would want any of this – though I could be wrong – it's pee.'

He drained the last drops and put the glass in the dishwasher. Did he say *pee*? Eeeugh!

'Er, no,' I said, backing away slightly. 'Did you say you were drinking—?'

'My own urine? Yeah, every morning – everyone's doing it. It's good for you.'

After last night I should think his was at least forty per cent proof. 'I hadn't heard about that,' I said, wondering if he was quite mad. 'How interesting!'

He gave me a wicked smile, but it wasn't working any more. 'Cures anything – that and frequent sex are all a man needs to keep healthy.'

'Really?' I felt as if some miraculously attractive bubble had burst and taken all the rainbows with it, but managed with an effort to gather my wits together: 'I've taken Flo for a walk and changed her water, so she is OK now. I'd better go – I've got things to do.'

'Sure you can't stay awhile?' He switched on one of those espresso machines that look as if you need a whole generator and a degree in engineering to make them work.

'No, really.' I wasn't drinking coffee out of any of *his* cups.

'Well, shall I settle up with you now, or do you want to send me a bill?'

'Oh, Annie will send you one at the end of the month, if that's OK. I put it all down on her chart and she does the bookwork. Bye, Flo.'

I bent to fondle her smooth, velvety head and, when I rose to go, Rob followed close behind me up the hall and reached out a long arm to open the front door, brushing casually against me as he did so.

'Oh – thanks,' I said, unnerved by the proximity of all that naked male flesh, and shuffled past into the sunlight just as Annie, towed by four large hounds, was passing the end of the drive. Unable to wave she began to smile, then caught sight of Rob lounging in the doorway in his mini-robe. The smile wavered; she went pink and hurried on.

I dashed after her, calling out: 'Hey, Annie, wait for me!'

She turned reluctantly. '*Lizzie!*'

'That was *not* what it looked like,' I said severely. 'Really, you should know me better by now! He phoned me this morning and asked me to go and sort Flo out, because he had a hangover.'

Actually, in that bathrobe it was almost a hang*under.* It's just as well it was only Annie who spotted us, because she is probably the only one who would have believed me. I took two of the dog leads.

'He simply couldn't be bothered to let Flo out this morning, which is terribly selfish and has put me right off him.'

'I should think so too,' she said indignantly. 'The dog must have been desperate!'

'She'd made a puddle, but as close to the back door as she could, poor thing. But speaking of pee, Annie, you'll *never* believe what Rob does with his!'

I was right: she didn't believe me and insisted he must have been joking, but I am sure he wasn't. It is not a fad likely to catch on in Middlemoss.

'So, how did you and George get on last night?' I asked, changing the subject.

She blushed under her freckles. 'Fine . . . he is so nice – but he can't cook, so it was just reheated ready-meals. I was telling him about the French cookery course we did after we left school and I'm going to get him a slow cooker like mine and show him how to use it.'

'You should invite him back to dinner at your place, only early enough so he can help you cook it,' I suggested. Cooking together is, I think, a *very* intimate thing to do.

'That's a good idea. Something simple but nice, like that chicken in white wine thing, or a risotto.'

'And a stodgy pud. Bet he likes those – most men do.' Even Nick, though he pretends he doesn't just to wind me up.

'Well, he had bought a chocolate gateau,' she agreed. 'And he ate quite a bit of it. Oh, well, must go and take these dogs back. I'll put the extra Rob pet-sitting on the chart for you when I get home . . . and Lizzie,' she added anxiously, 'you aren't falling for him, are you?'

'No, though he is very attractive – or was, until I got grossed out by his habits! And even were I looking for another man, one who thinks pee and hot, casual sex will cure anything is obviously operating on a different wavelength to me.'

'Gosh, yes,' she said, innocent grey eyes open wide. Rob is not the only one in Middlemoss operating on a different wavelength to me, but I love her anyway.

'No, Annie, I've served my time in the prison of love, though I might get another dog later, once Jasper's taken Ginny off to university with him.'

'Tell me when, and I'll find you a nice stray,' she promised, beaming. 'Is Ginny going to university with Jasper?'

'Yes, he's persuaded the landlady of a student house to let him keep her with him, but don't ask me how.'

'Oh, he can be just as charming as Tom when he wants to be,' she said. 'Only of course, he is much more solid, reliable and kind.'

The church clock struck eleven, galvanizing my memory. 'Oh – must fly, Annie! I'm supposed to be up at the hall tasting some ice cream Nick's made, and Mimi said he invited me especially, so he will be cross if I don't go.'

Thrusting the dog leads back into her hands, I rushed off.

In fact Nick seemed totally surprised, but not displeased, to see me. He was wearing a blue-striped apron, a smudge of sugar and a streak of raspberry, and looked good enough to eat . . . if you liked that kind of thing, of course.

I looked at Mimi suspiciously and she waved her spoon at me and called gaily: 'Just in time!'

'Hello, my dear,' Unks said. 'I didn't know you were coming. This is going to be a treat, isn't it?'

He, Mimi, Juno, Mrs Gumball and even Caz Naylor, half-concealed by the shadow of the inglenook, were all sitting round the kitchen table, spoons poised.

'Here, have mine Lizzie, and I'll get some more,' Nick said, and I took the proffered bowl and sat down, looking at it dubiously. The ice cream was sort of grey, like town snow turned to slush, and the blood red raspberry coulis swirling over it contrasted strangely.

'It tastes better than it looks,' Mimi remarked. 'I love liquorice! Yum!'

She was right. Nick sat down again next to me, long legs brushing mine. 'What do you think?'

'It looks horrible in a sophisticated sort of way, but tastes great.' I turned to see what Caz was making of it, but he had quietly stolen away leaving only an empty dish behind, which was tribute enough, I suppose. 'It's the opposite of coffee granita, which I always *expect* to be delicious, but never quite comes up to expectations.'

'Oh? I'll have to see what *I* can do.' His eyes gleamed.

'Nothing I haven't already tried!' I snapped.

'You want to take a bet on that?'

I might have been tempted to rub ice cream into that superior smile, if I hadn't already eaten it all.

Mrs Gumball was still spooning hers in with dubious daintiness. 'What that boy will think of next!' she said, shaking her head so that all the silvery-grey curls, tied up on top of her head in a skittish whale spout effect, quivered.

'Great,' Juno said, laying down her spoon. 'Mimi, don't lick the bowl!'

'Why not, when we're just family?' she demanded indignantly.

'It's still not polite.'

'Roly eats roast duck with his fingers and then licks them.'

'Would you like to go for a drive?' Juno asked, in an attempted diversion. 'I think my leg's up to it now, if we don't go too far.'

Mimi clapped her hands. 'St Martin's Mere to feed the ducks!'

'Oh, good, good,' Unks said. 'Bit of fresh air will do you both good.' He got up. 'Must go and study the form a bit – got a horse racing on Saturday. Snowy Sunday.'

'Not in September, surely?' I said, puzzled.

'Name of the horse. Snowy Sunday out of Weekend Blizzard.'

Unks has shares in three racehorses, but they usually seem to fall over, or go backwards, or do something that doesn't involve getting past the post.

'Cold lunch in the dining room at one,' Mrs Gumball said, heaving herself to her feet. 'I'm just off to see to my Joe's dinner. Mind my kitchen's clean and tidy again when I get back, Nick Pharamond!'

'Don't I always clear up after my cooking?' he demanded indignantly.

'I'll load the dishwasher myself,' I promised her.

One by one they went, and Nick and I quickly sorted out the kitchen in fairly amiable silence.

'That's that,' I said finally, looking round to see if we had missed anything. Nick is a very messy cook, and it was surprising how many pots and pans he had used just to produce ice cream and sauce. 'I'll have to go, I've got someone coming to look at the polytunnel and he said around lunchtime.'

'You have? Someone you know?'

'No, a stranger – he saw the ad in the parish magazine.'

He frowned. 'I'd better come and deal with him for you. You should let me do this sort of thing – anyone might turn up on your doorstep,'

'I can handle it – I mean, I'm only selling a plastic greenhouse, not the crown jewels,' I said firmly. I am used to doing everything myself – why would I suddenly need a man to do it for me?

'I'll walk down with you anyway, just make sure . . .' he began to insist, as though I was some frail little flower; then his mobile phone went off and while he answered it I slid quietly off home.

The man was waiting for me in the yard outside the cottage, leaning against an old pick-up truck smoking a roll-up and I rather regretted refusing Nick's offer so hastily, because there was just *something* about him I didn't like, even dismissing the aroma of stale alcohol.

'Had a bit of trouble finding you,' he said, straightening with a leer and running bloodshot eyes over me as though I were a dubious filly. 'Lonely down here, ain't it?'

'Not really, people go past on the main road all the time and my family live up the drive,' I said briskly. 'So, Mr—'

'Roach,' he slurred.

'So, you are interested in buying the polytunnel?'

'Well I was, but I took the liberty of having a look at it while I was waiting, and it's in pretty poor condition.'

'The supports are fine. Anyway, what were you expecting for fifty quid?'

'Cost you more than that to get someone to take it away for you,' he said. 'But I don't suppose a lady like you would know about that. Recent widow, aren't you? Bet you miss having a man about the place.'

He came a bit closer, flicking his cigarette on to the cobbles.

'Perhaps you'd like to make me an offer, then?' I said, ignoring the innuendo but backing off slightly. The yard brush was leaning against the wall behind me and I reckoned that, if desperate, I could always beat him into submission with it: it was a good, sturdy one.

'Perhaps I would,' he said, with what was *definitely* a leer. 'Maybe you'd like to discuss it somewhere more comfortable? I wouldn't say no – if you invited me in.'

'I don't— oh, *Nick*!' I said with relief, as his tall, broad-shouldered figure appeared round the end of the barn. He looked from one to the other of us from under dark brows, and I took his arm and squeezed it meaningfully. 'This is Mr Roach. He – he might make me an offer for the polytunnel, but he thinks it's too dear.'

'*Loach*,' the man said, straightening up and backing off

warily. 'But on second thoughts, it's not quite what I wanted. Doubt it's what *anyone* wants,' he added. 'Well, see you!'

He climbed back into the cab of his pickup and drove off with a bit of unnecessarily macho revving and tyre screeching.

Nick looked at me with one raised eyebrow, but refrained from saying 'I told you so'.

Realizing I was still clinging to his arm in a very wet way I hastily let go and moved away. 'Do you want to come in?' I said. 'Or go back for lunch? I'm going to have soup and home-made bread, if you want to stay.'

'Only if you promise to let me handle anything else you want to sell off. I am sure Roly will back me on this one – and the cottage *is* part of the estate.'

'Oh, all right!' I said. 'But don't think I couldn't handle that horrible man without you, because I could. I've already had people ringing me up and saying Tom owed them money, when they don't seem to have the least bit of proof.'

'You haven't *paid* them, have you?'

'Despite what you think, I am not *entirely* stupid,' I said with dignity. 'I asked Unks advice, and he told me to pass them all on to his solicitor, Smithers, and he would deal with them for me and let me know which were genuine ones that had to be settled.'

'I don't think you're stupid,' he said, following me into the cottage. 'You just take independence a little too far sometimes, that's all.'

'Did you come down just to lecture me, or did you want something?' I asked pointedly, and he smiled innocently and said: 'I just wanted to know what recipe you had already tried for the coffee granita?'

'One *you* sent me from Italy on a postcard of the Leaning Tower of Pisa,' I said with satisfaction. I hauled out the postcard album to look for it, and he seemed amazed that I had not only kept them all, but also carefully put them into a book. However, show me anyone interested in cooking who *wouldn't* have hoarded the recipes.

We ended up looking through the album for almost a whole hour without arguing, which must be a record. Maybe he is mellowing?

'I'll see you at the Mystery Play rehearsal tonight,' were

his parting words before striding off whistling, the sun glinting on his blue-black hair.

Tonight? Has he volunteered to help Clive?

Rob just phoned me up and invited me for a quiet drink at the café-bar in the former Pharamond's Biscuit factory tonight, so he could 'get to know me better'! I have looked long and hard in the mirror, and am at a loss to understand why, unless he is currently desperately short of another woman for his frequent, healthy sex rota.

I told him I couldn't because I had a Mystery Play meeting and we always all went to the village pub afterwards, but he said that was OK, he would meet me and come along too, and I simply couldn't think of a way of telling him not to, on the spot.

He probably won't bother after all, but if he does I will just have to hide behind the crowd and hope avid *Cotton Common* fans mob him, which seems quite likely.

Sixteen
Dipped Berries

Tonight's Mystery Play rehearsal was for Acts One to Nine, which were to be supervised by me, the vicar, Miss Pym and Marianne Potter, whose husband Clive was, as usual, overall director.

Roly, the Voice of God, never put in an appearance until the final performance, for having played the role for so many years he could do it in his sleep. On the actual day he sits in a corner of the courtyard in a little striped canvas pavilion like something from a jousting field, well wrapped up and with a warm brazier, and speaks his lines into a mike connected to the speaker just inside the barn door.

When I got to the village hall the actors were standing about in groups, chatting. Marianne was filling the boiler in the kitchen area behind the hatch, ready for its long slow journey towards the tea break, and Clive was putting cardboard signs up in the four corners of the room where the acts were to gather.

I was just handing Marianne my offering of peanut butter biscuits when Nick loomed up beside me. 'Hi, Lizzie: should I have brought something, too?'

I jumped, and nearly dropped the box: he moves disconcertingly quietly for such a big man. 'Oh, hi, Nick! No – there's usually plenty.'

'And I always bring a tin of Rover Assortment with me, just in case, but the current one's down to them pink wafer things, which no one seems to go for,' Marianne said. 'Nice of you to offer to help, Nick – and that lamb recipe of yours in last month's *Sunday Times* was a right cracker! I'd never have thought of doing that with olives.'

'Oh, thanks, Mrs Potter,' Nick said modestly, with one of his most charming smiles, and she blushed. I am quite sure he knows the devastating effect these have, like sunshine breaking out from behind lowering, purplish storm clouds.

Clive, clipboard in hand, bustled up. 'Ah, Nick – you've told Lizzie you've volunteered?' he beamed.

'To help out?'

'To be Adam to your Eve,' Nick told me blandly. 'Delving while you spin. Giving in to your temptations. Eating the apple from your hand.' He looked down at me quite seriously. 'Passing you the fig leaves.'

'*You?*'

'I'm sure we're all delighted,' Clive said. 'I hadn't thought to ask him before, because he has been here so infrequently in recent years, but Nick says he will be able to make most of the rehearsals, so that's all right. And it's only one fairly short scene, isn't it?'

'Er – yes,' I agreed.

'If I do miss any rehearsals, Lizzie can put me through my paces at home,' Nick suggested. 'I'll be living mainly up at the hall from now on.'

'I'm sure we're all very glad to hear that,' Marianne said warmly.

'Oh, there's Annie,' I said, surprised, as I spotted her

walking in. 'I thought she'd be going to the Acts Ten to Twenty-Two rehearsals on Thursdays?'

'Yes, but she is also very kindly going to assist the vicar, since he hasn't done it before,' Clive said, then clapped his hands and announced into the resultant silence: 'To your places, please!'

Everyone separated to his or her group. Mine was small enough, since I was only in charge of the *Fall of Satan*, the *Creation* and my own scene in the Garden of Eden, and I gathered them together in my designated corner.

The *Fall of Satan* scene is just the Voice of God and Lucifer, plus nine entirely silent angels. As always, God has the last word: '*I am reet disappointed in thee, Lucifer, thou art too sharp for thine own good. I loved thee like a son, yet thou art nought but a foul fiend, fit only for t' pit of damnation. Get thee gone!*'

After this, Lucifer vanishes in a puff of yellow smoke signifying the sulphurous fumes of Hell, with a receding wail – or in some years a shriek, depending on the interpretation of the role. At any rate, he vanishes. We ran through it a couple of times, and then I released the angels to go over to the vicar's corner: they have a walk on, walk off part in my scene, but in the *Nativity* they join in with the shepherds and the Three Wise Men for a stirring rendition of *Silent Neet, 'Oly Neet* around the manger.

I read the Voice of God for that scene, and also for the *Creation*, which is basically a monologue, with sound effects off. Then Lucifer took over while I put Nick through his paces as Adam. I tried to hand him a script, but he refused: he'd evidently been mugging up the Joe Wheelright version, and you couldn't fault his Lancashire accent.

It went smoothly right up to the point where he said: 'What art thou eating, Eve?' and I replied: 'Tis a fruit the snake told me was reet tasty – and see, yonder birds peck at it and come to no ill. Dost thou want a bite, flower?'

I offered him an imaginary apple and he said warmly: 'From you, darling, *anything*!'

'That's not in the script,' Lucifer objected.

'I thought we could change the script if we liked?' objected Nick innocently.

'Only if it's an improvement – this is *serious*,' I said severely. 'Stop messing about.'

'I *was* serious,' he protested, and Lucifer grinned. I was just glad I'd sent the angels away.

'And don't think me coy, but on the night, how do we preserve our modesty, Lizzie? I've forgotten.'

'In my case, with a very long wig and a body stocking. The last Adam wore a pair of beige swimming trunks and carried a strategically placed leather bucket. Apparently, in the old days Adam and Eve used to stand behind boards painted to look like bushes, to speak their lines.'

'I'll see what I can do,' he said gravely. 'Is it a *big* bucket?'

I gave him a look: we seemed to be rapidly reverting to the innuendo and sparring of our teenage years, and this was a Nick I had pretty well forgotten ever existed. Perhaps the euphoria of pending divorce has brought it out in him again?

'Thou hath tasted t'fruit of knowledge that wor forbidden thee and found it sweet – yet shall it be bitter henceforth on thy tongue!' read Lucifer, still grinning, in his role as Voice of God. That finished the scene and we stopped for refreshments before running through our lines again: I would work on the movements and check the props and costumes later.

'That'll do for tonight,' I said finally, and went to see how Annie and George were getting on with the whole *Nativity* cycle.

Dave Naylor from the garage, as Joseph, was wheeling Mary to Bethlehem on the back of an old-fashioned butcher's boy bike. On the night of the performance a star lantern is hauled across the stage on a wire, a very pretty effect.

'Not far to go now, luv. Bethlehem's on t'horizon, ower yonder.'

Mary, who was inspecting her fingernails, replied absently: 'The sooner the better, chuck, for my time's close – but will we find a place t'lay our heads?'

'I'll find thee a roof over thy head this night, flower,' Joseph promised, 'no matter what, don't thee worry thi'sen.'

'So,' the vicar was saying to Annie, 'the bike represents the donkey. But there *is* a real donkey on the night, is there?'

'Not any more, we stick to the bike for the performance, too.'

George looked baffled.

'We used to have a donkey,' I chipped in, 'but it was more trouble than it was worth, and when it died of old age and cussedness someone suggested the bike. The rack on the front is really handy for carrying baby Jesus on the flight into Egypt, too.'

'Er . . . yes,' he agreed. 'I suppose it would be.'

I looked critically at Mary, who worked at the hairdresser's in Mossedge. 'I hope Kylie's going to lose the scarlet fingernails and not chew gum on the actual night.'

'Oh, no – she's really taking it very seriously,' Annie assured me. 'She said she was going to put that cushion up her T-shirt tonight even though it's not a costume rehearsal, so she would get the right posture for sitting on the bike.'

'That's the spirit,' Nick said, having followed me over.

Clive clapped his hands again, thanked everyone for coming and said he would see them, he hoped, every Tuesday until Christmas.

'Now we all go and unwind in the pub,' Annie informed George.

'Oh, *do* we?' He was looking a little dazed, as well he might, but his eyes when they rested on Annie were almost dog-like in their devotion, which was bound to appeal to her.

'Where's Jasper tonight?' Nick asked as we left.

'At home – one of his friends is staying over, and I've left them pizza ready to heat up and some strawberries dipped in chocolate as a treat.'

'You are a good – if weird – mother,' he commented, as we all trooped out of the door on to the green, where Rob Rafferty stood leaning against a tree, smoking.

Marlborough man.

Until that moment I'd entirely forgotten what he'd said about turning up – not that I'd really thought he'd *meant* it in the first place. I stopped dead and Nick practically fell over me.

Rob ground the cigarette out under his heel and walked over, rather beautifully, as if the cameras were on him. 'Hi, Lizzie, good rehearsal?'

He looked around smiling generally, like warm sunshine. 'Lizzie said she thought you wouldn't mind if I tagged on tonight to the pub?'

'No, I didn't!' I muttered half under my breath, and Annie squeezed my arm meaningfully.

'I'm Rob Rafferty, you know – just moved into the village?'

Fortunately most of them did know who he was, and swept him along with us without my actually having to say anything, though clearly Nick thought it was an assignation and gave me a dirty look. I don't see what it has got to do with him, though, even if I *had* been making assignations with Rob – except, I suppose, that it is a bit early for his cousin's widow to be involved with another man.

But I'm not. Or not intentionally. And I can't believe Rob is seriously interested in me, so perhaps he just wanted to get out and meet the locals?

Some of the locals were certainly glad to meet him: Kylie was pretty well hanging on to his every word, and she is terribly pretty despite two nose rings and shocking pink hair, so I might well be worrying needlessly.

At the pub, which was rather full, I managed to slide on to a bench seat next to Annie. She had George on her other side and he was looking about him as if he had never been in such a place before, which for all I know he hadn't, an innocent abroad. But he was in safe hands.

Rob caused a minor sensation and even if he'd wanted to sit by me, which I daresay he didn't, by the time he disentangled himself from his admirers Nick had got there first.

He rang the bell on the wall behind my head. 'This has got to be one of the few pubs left where you can ring for service and have your drinks brought over,' he said with satisfaction. 'That way, you don't lose your seat when you get up.'

Rob pulled up a chair opposite and, leaning over, said in his warm, intimate, liquid-milk-chocolate voice: 'So, rehearsals go well, Lizzie? What part are you playing?'

'Eve,' I said. 'Yes, we made a good start.'

'And Nick is playing Adam, Annie tells me, now the original player has had to drop out,' George said. 'Keeping it in the Pharamond family!' He smiled around genially.

'Really? I wish I'd known about it – *I'd* have liked to play Adam to Lizzie's Eve!' Rob said.

'I'm sure you would have been brilliant, but the actors need to be local people, because of the commitment,' Annie explained diplomatically. 'I expect you're much too busy to give up all that time!'

When our drinks came, the barmaid also apologetically handed me a folded paper. 'Landlord says he's sorry to bother you, Mrs Pharamond, but if you could see your way to settling up this bill, he'd be very grateful.'

I unfolded it and glanced at the total, which was pretty huge. Nick leaned over and took it from my hand, though I tried to snatch it back. 'Tom's bar tab? I'll take it back with me to add to the rest, for Roly to settle.'

'It is very kind of Roly, but I don't see why he should have to settle all Tom's bills – and for goodness sake, how many more are there?'

'Oh, I should think that's about the last,' he said, tucking it into his jeans pocket from where *I* certainly wasn't going to try and retrieve it.

I glowered at him, but he smiled blandly and turned to talk to Marianne Potter, who was on his other side. Kylie had cornered Rob's attention again – he was either giving her his autograph or his phone number – or possibly both. On my other side, Annie and George were totally engrossed in their own conversation.

Suddenly I felt a total gooseberry and before I knew what I was doing, I had peeled the cardboard beer mat down to three separate layers.

The noise level in the packed bar was now so high it was hard to hear what anyone who wasn't right next to you was saying, though I nodded and smiled at anyone who seemed to be mouthing in my direction. After a while, feeling I'd had enough, I nudged Nick in the ribs with my elbow.

He grunted and turned.

'Do you think you could let me out? I'd like to go home.'

Rob caught my eye and, leaning forward until his golden head practically touched mine, said, 'Are you going, Lizzie? Wait a minute and I'll walk you home.'

'No need,' Nick said, draining his pint and slamming down the empty tankard, 'I'm going the same way.'

'But I'd *like* to,' Rob said stubbornly, and half-rose to his feet.

'Do stay, Rob!' I said hastily. 'Nick has to walk right past my cottage to get to the hall, so we might as well go together.'

Better the devil you know, after all.

Rob looked at me, eyes bluer than cornflowers and, I am sure, as sincere as a quagmire. 'Right . . . well, I'll ring you, then.'

'Ring you about what?' Nick demanded as soon as we were outside in the blessedly cool, quiet evening.

'Pet-sitting Flo, his bull terrier – and I'm so sorry to drag you away from your long and clearly *engrossing* conversation with Marianne.'

'I want the secret ingredient in her Lancashire hotpot recipe,' he said simply.

'Oh.'

There was a silence as we walked up the quiet village street and along the lane then, as we turned through the stone gates of the hall I said, following my somewhat tortuous train of thought: 'What do you think about drinking your own pee?'

He stopped dead. '*What?* You do say the damnedest things! Do you mean like on the *Bounty*, when they ran out of water and there was nothing else? At least, I think it was the *Bounty*.'

'No, it's some health thing – supposed to be good for you.'

He frowned. 'I do vaguely remember reading about it, but I don't think it's likely to take off, Lizzie! *You* aren't thinking of trying it, are you?'

'God no!' I shuddered. 'Horrible thought.'

'Why are we talking about it then?' he asked reasonably.

'I know someone who does it and I just wondered. It seemed very odd to me.'

'It seems very odd to me, too,' he agreed. 'Lizzie—'

'What?'

'Nothing!' he snapped abruptly, and abandoning me outside the cottage turned and strode off into the darkness.

'Hi, Mum. Nice night?' Jasper asked as I staggered wearily in. He was collecting cokes and an indigestible assortment of snacks out of the fridge.

'Don't ask!'

He grinned. 'We're playing computer games in my room. OK if we drop Stu home on the way to the dig in the morning? It's not far out of the way.'

'If you can get him out of bed that early,' I agreed. '*And* me – I'm off to bed, I'm shattered!'

I did look for the chocolate strawberries first, though – but they'd all gone. I had to eat cold cheese and onion pizza instead, followed by a frozen banana dipped in maple syrup and chopped nuts.

It's no wonder I had bad dreams.

Seventeen
Apple Tart

As always, the first Saturday in September brought the village fête, run with military precision by the ubiquitous Marianne and Clive Potter. I am sure if they did not have the entire management of every activity that goes on in Middlemoss, they would both spontaneously combust from sheer, pent-up nervous energy.

One or two of the minor celebrities who now lived among us had probably been half expecting to be asked to open the fête, but Mimi always does it, having assumed the role as of right on the death of Unk's wife years ago. It would certainly be more than the organizers' lives were worth to attempt to change something so fixed in her head.

Wearing a drab cotton safari skirt suit sporting many pockets, slightly muddy Gertrude Jekyll boots and incongruously lacy cotton gloves, she briskly admonished the gathered throng to spend lots of money, because the church roof had seen better days and the Sunday school room needed refurbishing and, with no more ado, declared the fête open.

Then she leapt from the podium with surprising agility and trotted over to the plant stall, which she appears to think is a kind of free lucky dip for gardeners, snatching up anything that took her fancy and leaving poor Juno to pay for (and carry) everything, like a royal lady in waiting.

Ted, the old gardener who helps her up at the hall, hovered at her elbow, offering unwanted advice in an agonized bleat: 'You don't want that, Miss Mimi! *That* won't do well, Miss

Mimi, not in our soil it won't – and who's going t' plant all of 'em, that's wor *I'd* like t' know?'

He gloomed away unheeded until Juno suggested he help carry everything to the Daimler, when he switched to the subject of his bad back and melted away into the crowd, so I helped instead.

I might as well, since I felt rather at a loose end: Jasper's dig didn't deign to stop work for Saturdays, which meant that this was the first year I'd come here alone. It felt odd . . . but it was something I was quickly going to have to get used to. In fact, he'd probably just been good-naturedly humouring me by coming the last year or two anyway.

No, life wasn't going to be the Lizzie and Jasper Show any more and I wouldn't ever again see life reflected through his fresh, young, excited eyes: the sudden realization was almost unbearably poignant.

But how thin the folds of time are! I felt I could almost step through into another dimension and there the child Jasper would be, his hot, sticky hand in mine, dragging me towards the swingboats, or riding his favourite giraffe on the little roundabout . . . dipping into the bran tub, sicking up one toffee apple too many behind a bush . . . clutching some cheap, hideous, furry toy I'd spent pounds winning for him.

I'm a sentimental idiot. Even the smell of candyfloss the night before had made the tears come to my eyes, when I was making bags of it in various colours to use as prizes on the hoop-la stall. (I had given the borrowed candyfloss maker back to Annie, but then decided to splash out and buy one of my own.)

Annie usually gets roped into organizing the children's races, where she is very popular, since she can always be guaranteed to have pockets bulging with little prizes for any disconsolate losers – sherbet dabs, jelly worms and flying saucers.

When I'd helped load Mimi's haul into the Daimler I did a stint behind the counter of the hoop-la stall, which gave me a good view of most of what was going on.

There was no sign of Nick, who is so tall that his dark head can usually be spotted above any crowd, and for once Rob must have been working, for otherwise I'm sure he wouldn't have been able to resist spreading his golden effulgence among the peasantry.

But Polly was there, brazen as ever, with a group of rather

noisy friends, though I notice she avoided me – *and* Caz, when he emerged from the shadows of the beer tent to perform his part, with silent and ferocious concentration, in the Morris dancing. Then he applied his skills to the coconut shy, awarding the resultant pink teddy bear to Ophelia, who seemed to be constantly near him while looking as if she didn't know quite why. She also, suddenly, looked *very* pregnant, even under the bunny smock.

Between their various duties I noticed the way Annie and the vicar gravitated together like those magnetic ladybirds – so it must be love, love, love! But it is a strange, old-fashioned, Jane Austen-ish love with, so far as I can see, no declarations or physical contact whatsoever.

While I am sure they think their mutual passion is a big secret – and it certainly seems to be a secret from each other, I expect the whole parish is indulgently observing the progress of their romance with almost the same avidity they watch the twice weekly episodes of *Cotton Common.*

Annie's cookery lessons now seem to take place most evenings when the vicar is not otherwise engaged, and they have been seen together walking rescue dogs up near the RSPCA kennels. But they have *not* been observed holding hands or doing any other lover-like activities.

In the absence of her parents, I can see I will soon have to ask him if his intentions are honourable, or this state of affairs could go on indefinitely. And if they marry, that will be yet another change: for though of course we will always be best friends, now she has fallen in love with George I already see much less of her than I used to.

Ever felt totally isolated in a crowd? But then I was distracted from my mood of self-pitying introspection by spotting something that made me doubt the evidence of my own eyes. When Jojo and Mick came to try their hands at the hoop-la (they were useless, but I gave them a bag of candyfloss each eventually, anyway), I said curiously: 'I didn't just see Caz and Ophelia sharing a *hot dog*, did I?'

'Caz told her there wasn't any meat in hot dogs,' Jojo said, 'and the stupid bat believed him. God knows what she thinks they make them out of. ARG! has thrown her out. I shopped her – living with a gamekeeper on the hit list.' He looked around furtively to see if anyone could overhear.

'Your secrets are safe with me, Jojo. And not only am I glad ARG! has thrown Ophelia out, but I hope you two aren't going to do any more silly things. Can't you just join the Green Party or Friends of the Earth or that kind of thing, and lobby peacefully for what you want?'

Mick gave me a pitying look. 'I expect it's just the pregnancy that's made her go weird,' he suggested. 'She might be all right afterwards.'

'Doesn't that depend on how you define "weird"?'

'Nah,' Jojo said, 'she'll be shacked up with him by then – he's already got her twisted round his little finger. He even hangs around your cottage on the nights when we're practising, so he can take her home.'

I could see there was a bit of jealousy going on, but you could hardly blame Caz for keeping tabs on a girl who so notoriously found it difficult to say no to other men. Somebody needed to.

'He hangs around my cottage anyway,' I said pacifically. 'He has the use of the freezer in one of the outbuildings, and also it's part of the estate, so he keeps an eye on things.'

'He's certainly keeping an eye on Ophelia,' Mick said.

I couldn't think this was a bad thing – if ever a girl needed looking after, it was her. 'Are they really living together?'

'Pretty near – matter of time,' said Jojo disgustedly.

'Mum's the word about ARG!' Mick said tapping his nose as they moved away.

'*Mummers* the word,' I amended, watching them shamble off. At least, unlike Tom's avaricious surfer friends, they were mostly harmless. I didn't feel any need to shop them to anyone, including Nick – I'm sure they have given up targeting the estate for the moment, and targeting *me* was all Ophelia's doing.

'We're going home,' Juno said, suddenly bobbing up next to me out of the throng, Mimi in tow carrying bags of popcorn, candyfloss and a half-eaten hotdog. 'Forgot to mention – Nick said to tell you he was coming, but he'd be late.'

'If he doesn't come soon it'll all be over. Anyway, I can't see why he thought it mattered to *me* whether he was coming or not. I don't care.'

'Don't care was *made* to care,' Mimi chanted. 'My governess used to say that.'

'Well, come along – you're overexcited,' Juno said firmly. 'Tears before bedtime!'

'She used to say *that*, too,' Mimi said, being borne away in the direction of the car. I would have said *sick* before bedtime was more likely than tears.

The flaps of the exhibits tents had been firmly closed while the vicar and two other local worthies judged the produce, but were now thrown back. I felt fairly complacent about the outcome – after several years of walking off with several Golds for my chutneys and preserves, not to mention my light pastry, I was already counting my book tokens and debating whether to give them to Jasper or blow them on myself for a change.

So, when I was relieved of duty on the stall, I strolled over, prepared to be gracious and modest as I collected my cards. And I *had* won best Strawberry Conserve, Best Green Tomato Chutney and several other preserve classes . . . but when I got to Baked Goods, I discovered that Nick, a surprise late entry, had beaten me into second place for Best Plate Apple Pie.

I stared at the gold-edged card, surprisingly infuriated by this, as though he had performed a mean and underhand trick. Several local ladies were looking secretly pleased to see me pipped for gold this time, and there was some nudging and whispering as Nick, doing his silently materializing trick, reached past me and collected his prize.

'Congratulations,' I said through gritted teeth while fanning myself slightly ostentatiously with a fistful of gold prize cards. 'Was that Mrs Gumball's recipe?'

'No, a variation of my own,' he said, smiling modestly, and was engulfed in a tide of congratulatory and admiring women. I stalked out of the tent.

Next year he won't find it so easy, I can tell you – which I told him when he walked home with me. Not that I *wanted* him to walk home with me: I pretended not to hear him when he called out: 'Wait for me!'

'Are you sulking?' he demanded, catching up.

'Why on *earth* should I sulk? And anyway, I never sulk!'

'Oh, no? Isn't this the cold shoulder because I won the pie prize? Do you have to be the queen of *all* the puddings?'

'Don't be silly,' I said, striding briskly off.

'You show me yours and I'll show you mine?' he said suggestively.

'*What?*' I exclaimed, coming to a stop and turning to stare at him.

'Apple pie recipe,' he explained innocently.

'*No way!*'

When I asked Unks to get his solicitor, Smithers, to tell me how much Tom's debts came to once he has wound his affairs up, he said it would be a while yet, and not to worry about it.

Tom really didn't have any affairs to wind up, so I suspect Roly is going to take care of it and not tell me at all, but he is horribly vague about it and it is hard to pin him down.

Still, after many delays, the insurance company has disbursed a paltry sum to compensate me for my lost 2CV – barely enough to buy a decent bicycle, let alone another car. Just as well I had had Tom's van to swap for the Morris.

I used some of the money to order knitted silk skiing long johns and vest at off-season prices – quite a bargain. They are white, so I will have to tint them flesh pink when they arrive, then they will not look too obvious from a distance under my Eve body stocking, wig and fig leaves. I will be a *very* well padded Eve.

I expect they will be useful afterwards in winter for gardening, though not sexy. But since I am not about to show my underwear to *anyone*, sexy is entirely irrelevant.

Meanwhile, we are well into the season of mellow fruitfulness and I am jamming, freezing, salting, chutneying, bottling and cordial making as though famine were just outside waiting to knock on the door. Dried apple rings hang in festoons above the Rayburn; wine bubbles in every corner and bunches of herbs dangle from the wooden rack above the kitchen table.

I always feel much happier – sort of safer – once the cottage is full to bursting with a huge store of food and drink. I think I just naturally have a siege mentality.

In-between these bouts I dashed about pet-sitting – including Rob's dog, though I haven't seen quite so much of the man himself lately, except on the evenings when he turns up to jam with the Mummers in Tom's old workshop. He's taken to calling into the cottage kitchen afterwards, where I ply him with food and drink while I work, just like everyone else who drops by.

I rather like the company – Jasper is out much more in the evenings these days, another foretaste of my solitary existence soon to come – and I don't mind the flirting now I know it's just his manner, nothing personal. Besides, he's decorative to have around *and* he says it would be impossible to make a better apple pie than mine, it is *perfect.*

According to Dora Tombs, Kylie's been seen sneaking out of his house at the crack of dawn, and she says he'd better watch out when her fiancé, who is in the army, comes home on leave.

'And she's not the only one!' she added darkly. 'A regular harem, he seems to be running. He's a charmer – like honey to humming birds, he is.'

'That's terribly poetic, Mrs T!'

'Saw them when I went over to Canada to see our Sara,' she explained. 'Vancouver Island – wings whizzing round like bike wheels.'

'Rob reminded me of honeycomb crunch the very first time I saw him – you know, a bit like cinder toffee?'

She gave me a sharp look. 'And what does Mr Nick remind you of, then?'

'Nick?' I said, surprised. 'Oh, brimstone and treacle!'

'Better for you than toffee,' she remarked cryptically. 'Honey or not.'

Eventually Clive and Marianne Potter got to hear the rumour about Kylie, and confided to me at a Tuesday night rehearsal that they thought it conduct unbecoming in their Mary.

But when Rob, who was waiting for us outside again, swooped down and kissed me a smacker right on the lips, they exchanged a meaningful glance as if to say: 'What, you too, Eve?'

Actually, I thought the way he and Kylie avoided each other in public was much more obvious than if they had been entwined for the whole evening. I am sure they had an assignation set up for later, because although Rob sat next to me and flirted outrageously, when I got up to go he didn't offer to walk me home – I went alone.

Nick had already left, much earlier.

Maybe he'd got the Lancashire hotpot recipe out of Marianne? Mission accomplished.

* * *

Jasper was home when I got there, eating cheese on toast with Ginny snuffling hopefully round his feet for crumbs. He said Nick had phoned to say he had found a buyer for the polytunnel greenhouse, and it was to be dismantled tomorrow morning and removed.

'I don't see why he didn't tell me that earlier!'

'He said he found you so distracting as Eve, even with your clothes on, that he forgot, and he'd probably go totally blank at the actual performance.'

'He *did*? What kind of thing is that to say to my son!'

Jasper grinned.

'And he doesn't mean it either,' I said snappily. 'He's just being sarcastic and horrible.'

'No he's not: he likes you, Mum.'

'I think I know your Uncle Nick by now – and *all* his little ways,' I said firmly.

I dropped Jasper and Ginny off at the dig next morning bright and early, then went home and changed into my oldest jeans, ready to help dismantle the polytunnel.

But the new owner proved to be one of those men who does not recognize any woman's existence in a business deal and so addressed himself totally to Nick, who was hanging around looking taciturn. Still, at least I could trust him to hand the proceeds over.

Without the big and rather ugly polytunnel the shape of my little domain seemed totally changed, with the last plants that had been inside it pathetically huddling together in the open, as if for warmth.

Another thing sorted out, though – and the huge TV has already gone, after I put a card in the post office window. Jasper is going to choose a little portable one on the proceeds to take to university with him, preferably with an integral DVD player, he says. I hope he is going to work and not spend his entire student loan on films, drink and stuff.

I've begun to notice that if Jasper is home when Rob calls in, he seems to constantly be in and out of the kitchen, and having six foot of sardonic teenage youth critically observing him rather cramps Rob's flirting. I don't know why Jasper doesn't like him – unless he has joined this matchmaking set that seems to have suddenly sprung up – mainly wishful thinking on Juno and Mimi's part, I think – and wishes to pair me off with Nick?

I could tell them right now that this is a horse that is never going to run.

But clearly everyone sees poor Rob as some kind of threat, either to my heart or my virtue (or both), for when Jasper isn't there, Caz seems to be hanging about the yard until Rob leaves.

And I'm forever finding Nick wandering about the place, as if he owned it . . . which I suppose he sort of does, though he doesn't own *me*.

My cottage seems to have become one of the most popular spots in the Mosses.

I've just tried out a recipe for potato and nut biscuits, which came out so well I tried making chocolate flapjacks with mash, too.

However, Jasper said they were more like *mudflaps*, so a little more experimentation is clearly in order.

Eighteen

Fruit Basket

The skiing underwear I'd ordered was sitting in a neat brown parcel on my doorstep when I got back from dropping Jasper at the dig this morning, so I went straight upstairs to try it on.

It fitted tightly, but I had quite a job getting the old, rather tea-coloured body stocking on over it (one of us is losing our stretch with age – or maybe both of us?).

When I looked in the mirror I discovered that I presented a strangely padded and seamed appearance, rather like an unsuccessful home-made Cabbage Patch doll, especially once I got the long and totally unrealistic flaxen wig out of its storage box and completed the ensemble.

Sexy it was not, and when I heard someone walk into the hall downstairs I nearly died: my heart certainly stopped and I went still as a mouse.

'Lizzie?'

'Oh, thank God!' I muttered devoutly. I'd quite forgotten I'd arranged for Annie to come over and help me finally sort out Tom's clothes and personal stuff.

'Come up – I'm in the bedroom,' I called.

She clumped upstairs and I turned to face the door, striking a soulful pose.

'Have you already started?' she was saying as she walked in. 'I'm a bit late, I—'

Her stunned expression sent me into near hysteria and after a dumbstruck minute she started to giggle too. Soon we were both entirely incoherent.

'So,' I said finally, wiping tears from my face with a long, golden tress, 'you *don't* think I should play the Eve part for laughs?'

'Oh, Lizzie – can you *imagine* Nick's face if he walked on and saw you like that?' she said, sitting, limp with laughter, on the bed.

'I *could* – but I'd rather freeze to death first!'

'Well, you can't possibly, anyway. But perhaps if you bought a new Lycra body stocking it might be warmer than that old one?'

'It hardly seems worth the expense, since this is the last year I'll play Eve.'

'Never mind, you looked stunning in the old outfit last year,' she said loyally. 'But quite indecent from a distance!'

'Speaking of indecent, I don't know what Nick intends wearing – if anything. Do you?'

'I asked him,' Annie said innocently, 'in case he hadn't given it any thought. And he said he'd ordered footless tights from a ballet-clothing place and would wear his cricket box under them to protect his modesty.'

That conjured up quite a vision . . . which I hastily dispelled, though not without some difficulty. 'He'll freeze,' I said with conviction. 'We both will!'

'I expect he'll be all right – it's only a few minutes, the Garden scene, isn't it? Then you can rush into one of the loose boxes and put your warm clothes back on.'

'Well, that does it – if *he's* going to be half-naked, then *I'm* not going out there padded up like Michelin woman! A new Lycra outfit it is. I have still got some car insurance money.'

I might even go completely mad and get myself a pretty frock, too, for Christmas dinner, which we always have up at Pharamond Hall. I can't remember when I last bought myself something new to wear that wasn't vital, like jeans. Too long.

I changed back into ordinary clothes and then we got down to sorting out Tom's stuff, which is something I've been putting off – anything of his around the house has been pushed into his wardrobe or drawers out of sight.

'Jasper's taken a couple of things – cufflinks mostly, but the rest can go to the charity shop, or in the recycling bin.'

'I'll take it all down to the Animal Shelter shop,' she offered. 'I brought the car up rather than walk, in case.'

Tom didn't have a huge wardrobe of clothes, so it didn't take long. I was so glad I wasn't doing it alone, though, because memories tended to tumble out of every open door and drawer.

'So, how are you and George getting on, Annie? You're seen almost everywhere together, like Siamese twins,' I teased, once we'd loaded her car and retired to the kitchen for a well-earned sit down and coffee. *And* a restorative plate of chocolate slab cake. 'How are the cookery lessons doing? Is he teaching you anything in return?'

'No,' she said, her face clouding over. 'Lizzie, I do enjoy being with him, but I think he's just being *friendly*. I'm that type of girl, aren't I? Men don't think of me romantically at all – I expect I'm exactly like a sister to him!'

'You daft bat!' I said, regarding her incredulously. 'He's absolutely dotty about you – when he looks at you he has that soppy sheep expression in his eyes, and every time he speaks to you he goes red as a beetroot. *And* he told me he thought you were very pretty!'

'He didn't!' Annie went pink with pleasure.

'He did.'

She looked at me doubtfully. 'Then why . . . ? I mean, you must be wrong, Lizzie!'

'No, I think he's just shy. Encourage him a bit.'

'Oh, no, I couldn't *possibly*! What if he only wants to be

friends? Think how embarrassing it would be if I'd made a fool of myself and we had to go on meeting.'

'But you do fancy him, don't you, Annie? I mean, this *is* love's young dream and all that?'

'More love's middle-aged dream,' she said ruefully.

'Rubbish, forty is a very good age for love.'

'Forty-one – and it might be, but I daren't risk destroying my friendship with George to find out.'

'You won't. You wait and see.'

'You aren't going to do anything, are you?' She looked at me anxiously.

'No of course not,' I reassured her quite untruthfully. 'I'll await events to prove me right. And then I expect to be matron of honour at the wedding, in a mid-calf length puce taffeta dress with those puffed shoulders that make you look five feet wide.'

'Not puce,' she said seriously. 'The church carpet and hassocks are scarlet, it wouldn't go.' Then she sighed, her eyes focusing again as though abandoning a beautiful dream. 'Anyway, enough of *my* boring affairs, Lizzie – what about you? The whole village is talking about the way Rob Rafferty flirts with you!'

'Oh, come on, you must have realized I'm just a smoke-screen for the women he *is* having affairs with, Kylie among others. But I do like him, and I enjoy flirting with him – at least he makes me feel I'm still attractive.'

'Yes, but it's making Nick jealous, haven't you noticed?'

I stared at her. 'Well, yes, but he's not jealous of me *personally* – he simply doesn't like Rob paying attentions to his cousin's widow. Come to that, he just doesn't seem to like Rob. But I suspect his attitude's mainly a territorial thing.'

'No, I think he's fond of you,' she said earnestly.

'Annie! It's bad enough Unks and Mimi – and now even Jasper – trying to match-make, without *you* joining in!'

'Do they? I hadn't realized. But there, you see – even the family think it would be a good thing if you got together!'

'Annie, it's not going to happen – and it would certainly be a marriage made in hell, not heaven.'

'I don't think Nick would agree with you,' she said stubbornly.

I thought about it for a minute, remembering the way he'd kissed me once or twice in a most uncousinly manner, and how he'd referred back to our short-lived romance as if he couldn't understand why it hadn't worked out . . . But apart from that, there wasn't *anything* to suggest he was harbouring an undying passion for me.

'No,' I said firmly, 'we bicker more than we agree and drive each other mad: too many cooks again. He might still *fancy* me, I don't know . . . but he isn't in *love* with me.'

'So you're just friends – like George and me?'

'Well, not quite – more sparring partners. The family – and probably the whole village, going by the hints Dora Tombs has been letting fall – just wants a neat and tidy ending: you in the parsonage, me in the hall, all's well that ends well. Only life isn't like that.'

'I suppose not,' she sighed sadly.

But I was determined that *her* romance would turn out right, at least. All George needed was a bit of encouragement.

That evening Ophelia came round, driven by Caz in his ancient Landrover (painted with camouflage, just like him) and to my astonishment asked me if she could buy the quail!

'You haven't anywhere to keep them,' I pointed out, 'and anyway, what would you do with them? You won't eat them or the eggs, and you'll be overrun with male quail in no time.'

'No she won't, then,' Caz drawled, leaning against the bonnet, his khaki hat tipped over his nose.

Really, he's getting almost loquacious! It must be love. Anyone would think it was spring, the way Cupid's fiery darts are firing in all directions.

'There's the old piggery behind my cottage – I can keep them in that for now,' Ophelia said, then rabbited at her lower lip a bit before adding, 'I've decided to become vegetarian while I'm pregnant, *and* eat fish and eggs.'

'Good idea!'

She gave Caz a half-defiant look: 'But not venison, or flesh of *any* kind!'

What does she think fish are made of?

'Right, I'll start including eggs in your basket of fruit and vegetables.'

'No, no, no, you shouldn't! It's too kind and . . . and I don't see why you *should* be kind,' she muttered, her bulging eyes taking on that sainted martyr look. 'I don't deserve it.'

'*You* may not, but we have to think of the baby – it needs good wholesome food to grow properly.'

'But you carry it all the way up to my cottage, and it must be really heavy!' She wrung her hands in an anguished sort of way. Let us hope she is never holding a quail – or, indeed, the baby – when she is in one of these states. 'Don't – please don't do it any more. Caz says he'll fetch it.'

'OK – that will be good. I'll leave the basket near the eggs in the outbuilding on Monday mornings, how about that?' I couldn't really see Caz in the Little Red Riding Hood role with a basket, but that was his problem. Maybe he'll bring a backpack.

She nodded like a car mascot and then added, after another of her lip chewing ruminations, 'Thank you for the bottled tomatoes.'

I stared at her. 'I didn't give you any bottled tomatoes!'

She blinked slowly. 'Yes you did, they were on the doorstep last night – with that yellow checked material tied over the lid, like all your jars of stuff.'

'Gingham – I bought a whole roll of it years ago, and never got to the end of it. But I didn't leave any jars of anything on your doorstep.'

'But . . . it must be you, I don't know anyone else who bottles tomatoes.'

I had a sudden horrible thought: 'I know someone who *tried* to,' I said grimly. 'Polly Darke – and gave me botulism, or something equally ghastly, when I ate them!'

'But she's not – she isn't . . . she wouldn't . . .' Ophelia trailed off and wrung her skinny hands together again distractedly, her eyelids frantically fluttering.

'Oh, I guessed she was the one who made you do the ARG! stuff to me, out of sheer spiteful jealousy – there was no one else it could have been.'

'But Caz made her stop, so perhaps she's sorry now, and this is a present?' Ophelia suggested 'But I don't want her peace offering!'

'If it *is* a peace offering – we know she is spiteful enough to do something nasty. I'd throw it away, just in case.'

'I'll do it,' Caz said, a stony expression on his face that

boded ill for Polly – though *would* she have tried something that might have harmed Ophelia's baby? I thought back to what I knew of her, which due to my avoiding her as much as possible, was not a lot.

'I could be quite wrong about her, but thinking about it now, it *is* odd that I was the only one who got the dodgy jar of tomatoes, when she was handing them out to half the village that time,' I said slowly. 'And another thing – although I've only been to her house once, for a book launch party, I was horribly sick afterwards, though I didn't hear of anyone else being taken ill.'

'Toadstool,' Caz said meaningfully.

'*Toadstool?*' For a minute I thought he'd run mad, then I remembered: 'You mean that poisonous one you showed me – was it in the basket of field mushrooms Polly brought me to swap for eggs?'

He nodded grimly.

'And wasn't it the kind you only get in woods, not open fields?'

He nodded again.

'*Could* she be that jealous and vindictive? It's all so petty and downright nasty!'

Caz shrugged.

I sighed. 'Well, if it is true, let's hope she doesn't present any more little gifts to other people disguised as my offerings! I'd better go down and tell Marianne Potter tomorrow that someone is maliciously leaving tainted jars of food on doorsteps, using yellow cotton covers just like mine, and she will spread the rumour about. And I'll stop covering the jars with anything except cellophane from now on, even if they don't look as pretty!'

Ophelia had lost interest and wandered off to commune with the quail by means of little cheeping noises. She seemed to be frighteningly at one with them mentally, which didn't bode well for the intellect of her future offspring.

I followed over. 'So, what *are* you going to do with the quail?'

'Give them a happy life. And I can sell the eggs, I think that's all right,' she said earnestly.

'OK, they're yours,' I agreed.

She is totally impractical, but I expect Caz will just quietly go in and do what has to be done with the birds when she isn't looking. Such is life.

They seem to be more and more settling down as a pair, though a rather odd couple they make. Maybe, since they know secrets about each other – he knows she was in ARG! and she knows what he does with the grey squirrels he catches – that makes a bond? And Ophelia, apart from a bit of occasional stubbornness, seems terribly malleable, so I expect he will slowly bend her into the shape he wants over time.

Why does that make me think of brandy snaps?

Caz loaded the quail up then and there, dismantling the pens and taking those, too, since I would have no further use for them.

What with the big bare space where the polytunnel was, and the lack of cheeping, moving feathers in the barn, things were looking quite deserted – apart from the hens and ducks. They'd all sheered off while Caz and Ophelia were here, but now came back looking for any pickings.

With a sigh, I went back into the cottage and looked for my brandy snaps recipe, even though trying to wind them round the handle of a wooden spoon is such a pain that I can't usually be bothered.

Later, when Jasper was home, I went for a walk in the woods and saw Caz and Nick in earnest discussion, though I don't think they saw me.

Caz seemed to be talking, or at least, replying: amazing. Then they shook hands!

What was that all about? Has some kind of deal been done?

On Sunday, we were invited up to lunch at the hall. Nick was cooking, as he often does because it gives Mrs Gumball a rest, and though she protests at having her kitchen taken over, I think she is quite pleased really.

He was in and out of the kitchen when I got there and spurned my offer of help, though accepting Jasper's, who knows only the theory of cooking and not the practicalities. So I left him to stew in his own *jus* and sat down at the dining table with the others.

Unks smiled at me vaguely and went back to reading the sports section of the Sunday paper.

'We're going on a garden tour by coach,' Mimi informed me chattily.

I stared at Juno. 'Is that a good idea?'

'Don't see why not – I'm fully fit again. I'll frisk her for knives, scissors and plastic bags before we set off, and I won't take my eyes off her for a minute within fifty paces of plant life. It's a late-booking bargain.'

Mimi smiled innocently.

'I don't think *you* will get a lot out of it, Juno,' I said. 'You could do with a more restful holiday after your accident.'

'There are entertainments in the evenings at the various hotels,' Mimi said. 'It'll be fun. But Juno and I have got to share a room – people will think we're an odd couple, heh, heh, heh!'

'Pity, I was hoping to pick up a toy boy,' Juno said. 'Preferably a rich one who could whisk me away from this madhouse.'

'She doesn't mean it,' Mimi confided to me. 'Her heart belongs to Sean Connery.'

'I've never been one of those romantics,' agreed Juno, 'but I like a man to be a man.'

'Do you think *Nick* is a macho man, Lizzie?' Mimi asked, with one of her disconcertingly clear looks, just as the man himself strode into the room carrying the soup tureen, with Jasper following up behind with a silver basket of bread.

'If macho is big, male and overbearingly bossy, yes,' I said sweetly.

Nick gave me one of his looks, the purple-edged sort.

It was good soup, followed by roast beef and perfect Yorkshire puddings – and he'd made one of his apple pies for dessert, which I have to admit was delicious, though I certainly wasn't going to tell *him* so. Instead, I said the pastry was a little dry and asked for more cream.

Jasper and Nick were talking quietly in the kitchen when I went in with the dessert plates, and I hoped it was serious male stuff, because *my* attempt to discuss safe sex and STDs with Jasper certainly hadn't gone down too well.

Nick seems to be Confidante of the Moment – but not mine. Been there, done that, and once was enough.

I was full to bursting point after the coffee, but Nick practically dragged me back into the kitchen and made me taste three different coffee granitas before I left. When I said I didn't think any of them had that extra *something* he went very sulky, even though (unlike what I said about the apple pie) it was quite true.

On the way home Jasper said I had hurt Nick's feelings and I should have pretended one of the granitas was great, and I said, astonished: 'Why should I, when he's always so rude about *my* cooking?'

'Yes, but you know he doesn't mean it, he's just joking – it's affectionate.'

'I'm not so sure about that,' I said darkly.

Anyway, I'm never again going to tell a man something is wonderful when it's not. It's my un-New-Year resolution.

Nineteen
Bottled Out

Having passed on the warning about gifts of possibly tainted bottled goods by mentioning it to Marianne Potter, who is permanently plugged into the local grapevine, I didn't give the matter much further thought. In fact, I was half inclined to think Ophelia's jar of tomatoes had been a gift from some well-meaning village lady who had simply rescued a gingham circle from something of mine. Goodness knows, I have supplied enough to village fairs, fêtes and bazaars over the years.

Then out of the blue Leila phoned me and, to my complete astonishment, apologized for what she had said at the funeral. 'Of course, much of it was true: but it was not the time or place. I had come simply to pay my last respects.'

'Quite . . . and . . . thank you,' I said cautiously, though I am not sure quite what I was thanking her for.

'I see clearly now I was deceived by Tom – but also perhaps by Nick. But that is life, and now I am resolved to stay single. Nick says he will still review my restaurant in his articles, it will not make a difference, our divorce,' she added, sounding surprised and slightly scornful of his magnanimity. 'So, we should all bury the hatchet and move on, yes?'

'Er, yes . . . and it's nice of you to phone me,' I said doubtfully, wondering if there was a catch as to exactly *where* she meant to bury the hatchet.

'You sent me the peace offering – though a pot of strawberry jam, that is not sensible to put in the post, even packed so well.'

'*Jam?* Did it have a yellow material cover over the metal lid?'

'Yes, that is how I knew it was from you. And also it says "Middlemoss Fête" on the label.'

My winning entry, that I let them raffle off with other prizewinners, for charity! 'You haven't eaten any, have you?' I demanded urgently.

'No – I do not eat jam, it is not on the South Beach diet.'

'Then don't: I did make it, but I haven't seen that jar since it was sold off after the fête and I certainly didn't send it to you. I'm afraid it might be . . . tainted.'

'Tainted? You mean *poisoned*? Someone is trying to *kill* me? But that is ridiculous!' she said scornfully.

'No, not kill you, just make you sick, I expect, while pinning the blame on me. She's tried the same thing with Ophelia Locke but I wasn't sure—' I broke off. 'Oh, you don't know Ophelia, do you?'

'I know *of* her. I have been told she claims to be carrying Tom's child, but she sounds a type most hysterical and neurotic.'

'I suppose she is a bit,' I agreed, wondering who Leila's spies in the village were. 'But she *is* pregnant and there's a possibility it could be Tom's – about one in four, if you want the odds. But anyway, she found some bottled tomatoes on her doorstep the other day and assumed they were from me, and they weren't. And then I remembered once having a bad experience with bottled tomatoes someone gave me and got suspicious. Only it seemed so incredible that I thought I must be imagining it.'

'But you are confusing me with all this talk of bottled tomatoes! Who and why . . . and . . .' There was a pause. 'It is Tom's other woman doing this, that weird person, Polly something?'

'I think so – I can't imagine who else it could be, and there are a few too many coincidences. I discovered recently that she blackmailed the local animal rights campaigners into targeting me, too, from sheer spite and jealousy, so I wouldn't put it past her.'

'I will set the police on to her!'

'There isn't any proof – but I'm going to let her know that she is found out, so that should make her think twice before trying anything else!'

Leila still thought the police should be involved, but I was wary: what if they thought I'd done it myself as a sort of double-blind? Or maybe it's all in my imagination, and I should stop reading crime novels from the mobile library?

Anyway, she said she would do nothing for the present, and rang off after adding that if I was ever in the vicinity of her restaurant there would always be a table free for me, an offer I thanked her for but am unlikely to take up.

'Poor, poor woman!' Annie said sadly, when I related this conversation to her and updated her on my suspicions.

'There's nothing poor about Leila!'

'No, I meant Polly, to do such dreadful things, and all from jealousy!'

'Well, that's one way of looking at it,' I agreed. 'Trust you to feel sorry for her! And it's all very well playing these pranks on me and Leila, but Ophelia's pregnant and it might have made her really ill or harmed the baby – goodness knows what she put in those tomatoes.'

'That's true. What are you going to do? After all, she might do something else! Perhaps I ought to tell George so he could go and reason with her?' she suggested doubtfully.

'Absolutely not – there is no way she is going to cast herself upon his bosom and weep tears of repentance, and it would be like sending Daniel into the lioness's den.'

'What, then?'

'I've already got Marianne to spread a general warning out about a malicious prankster leaving jars of jam and stuff on doorsteps – I'm surprised it didn't reach you.'

'I'm so busy – she *might* have said something about it . . .' She frowned.

Preoccupied, more like – I really must get round to having

that chat with George. 'I'm going to speak to Polly – preferably in a public spot with other people about – and tell her I know about her tricks, and if she does anything else I'll report her to the police. That should stop her.'

'Oh, I hope so,' Annie said earnestly. 'Perhaps it will shock her into realizing how badly she is behaving, so that she can move on?'

'I wish she would move *away*,' I said, getting up. 'Well, must go and see to Flo on my way home – Rob isn't going to be back until late and she's probably got all four paws crossed by now.'

'You really *aren't* falling for him, are you, Lizzie?' she asked anxiously.

'No, of course not – but if celibate widowhood ever palls on me, it's nice to know my options are still open.'

'Lizzie! You wouldn't!'

'Probably not – specially if he continues with *all* his rather dubious habits.'

In the afternoon Nick rang and *demanded* I go up and taste his newest version of coffee granita, but I declined, since I was in the middle of a huge quince jelly making operation and could hardly down tools at his bidding.

He slammed the phone down, but strode into my kitchen ten minutes later carrying an insulated box cradled in his arms like a baby.

'This one's perfect!' he said, the light of battle in his eyes and his dark hair sticking up in an angry crest, a rather fetching, if unintentional, *Last of the Mohicans* effect. 'I defy you to find fault with it!'

'Look, I'm up to the elbows in this, I can't sit down and eat,' I protested, but he followed after me around the room feeding me teaspoons as though I was a stubborn toddler.

And, much though I would have liked to find fault, I couldn't. Colour, taste, texture – perfection.

When I said as much he tossed the spoon away, grabbed me and planted a triumphantly emphatic kiss on my lips before I could fend him off with the ladle.

'Mmm . . . you taste of the perfect coffee granita!'

'I don't know what else you would expect, when you have been force-feeding me the stuff for the last ten minutes,' I snapped, taking a step back. We unpeeled rather stickily.

'You are a *very* messy jam maker,' he said severely.

'And *you* are a very messy cook, full stop. I've never seen anyone use so much equipment to make even the simplest dish.'

'Like my apple pie?' he said, a gleam in his eyes. 'Come on, Lizzie, you know there was nothing wrong with it last Sunday.'

'It wasn't bad,' I conceded, then I smiled at him innocently and said: 'That granita . . . just what did you add to make it taste like that?'

'Wouldn't you like to know!' he said tantalizingly and then, picking up his cold box, walked out.

Jasper finished at the dig, gaining some kind of excavation certificate with which he was highly pleased.

Then he immediately went off to stay for a week with one of his friends in Ormskirk and, although I would have liked to have spent every precious moment with him before the start of his first university term, I didn't try and persuade him not to go. Instead, I drove him there and dropped him off myself. I only hoped Jasper's friend's mum was expecting Ginny, too – and thank heavens she came ready housetrained.

I hope he behaves himself, though frankly there are not many dens of iniquity in the lovely old market town of Ormskirk; but before he left home Unks gave him a *huge* amount of holiday money – he must have had a win on the horses, to have so much cash about him.

'You'll be sensible, won't you, Jasper?' I said, hugging him, which he suffered me to do in a resigned sort of way.

'It's not *me* who needs to be sensible,' he protested, 'when that Rafferty man's forever dropping in and hanging out with my mother, or chatting her up in pubs – not to mention phoning you up and asking you to go round to his house all the time!'

'Yes, but he's just being *friendly*, Jasper, and I only go round to his house to look after the dog.'

'I don't see why he can't look after his own dog.'

'Well, neither do I, really. Or get one of this constant stream of girlfriends to do it.'

'So you do know about all the girls he takes back there, then?'

'I'd have to be deaf, dumb and blind not to, even if Dora

Tombs, who cleans for him, didn't tell me. The whole village is talking about him – which at least means they have moved on from going over what your Dad got up to with Leila and Polly, or taking bets on who the father of Ophelia's baby is,' I said tartly. 'Now, you stop worrying about me – anyone would think I was some naive innocent out of a Victorian melodrama, about to be taken advantage of by the villain of the piece!'

'He does it all the time in *Cotton Common.*'

'But not in real life,' I said firmly. 'And I'm not interested in Rob that way – or any other man. I just want to be left alone with my hens and my garden and my recipes.'

Especially the search for the perfect apple pie.

'Try not to fall out with Uncle Nick while I'm away,' was his final admonishment. He must have been reading my mind – and bossiness seems to run in the Pharamond blood, just like cooking.

I didn't get a chance to fall out with Nick, since he went down to London while Jasper was away, and then on to Cornwall in search of fish recipes for some forthcoming article.

I had sort of got used to having him around again, annoying though he is – someone to bounce food ideas off and argue with. Annie's interested in food, but I wouldn't call her a creative cook, and she is so even tempered I couldn't pick a quarrel with her even if I tried.

Mind you, since every second word she utters these days is 'George', exasperation might lead me to smother her to death, probably with a hassock.

Rob was off in London too, shooting some cameo role for a film, so Dora Tombs and I were taking care of Flo between us. Mimi and Juno were full of talk of their holiday and deep in planning the installation of a water feature in the walled garden; and Unks, as always, was happily doing his own thing. Although I was still terribly busy, it gave me a foretaste of what it was going to be like once Jasper went off to university.

I expect Nick won't give up his flat in London at all, and go back to dividing his time between there and the hall. Eventually, once the divorce is through, he'll marry someone young and beautiful and start a family. I am sure it will happen – even I have to admit he is wildly attractive, except when he is annoying me – so it is just as well he annoys me most of the time, isn't it?

I've made that mistake once and I wouldn't want to go down that road again, even if he was willing. Which, since he can't even be bothered sending me postcards any more, clearly he is not.

I like being on my own. I can't imagine why I am depressed.

The most *dreadful* thing happened today: I had a call from George, telling me that Tom's mother and stepfather were on their way down, to pay their respects at Tom's grave!

'What? But why didn't they call me?' I said, stunned. 'I haven't heard a word since the funeral – and it's *years* since they saw Jasper. If only they had let me know they were coming!'

'I don't know, but I thought I would mention it to you and see if you knew about it. Certainly you ought to be there. They are coming by car, and I gave Mr Barillos directions to the graveyard – they were only about an hour away when he rang.'

I ran a distracted hand through my tangled hair. 'They are such odd people, I suppose it shouldn't surprise me, them behaving like this – but yes, I'd better meet you at the graveyard.'

Not that there is much to see yet – the stone has been ordered, but not yet erected. I quickly changed into something marginally more suitable and dashed up, collecting Annie on the way for support.

George was standing by the grave, which looked forlorn: a grassy mound in the Pharamond corner. I intended planting spring bulbs around it once it had its stone, and possibly a bit of lavender. I don't much like cut flowers left dying on graves, or in those little stone urns.

I wasn't sure I would have recognized the Barillos if I met them in the street, but on a gravel path in an old country graveyard, they stood out like sore thumbs. For a start, there was something glossily expensive about their clothes and, although it was not a particularly sunny day, they both wore huge, wrap-around reflective sunglasses.

The skin visible on Tom's mother's face looked stretched

and smooth and her hair was a rich golden blonde – yet she must be in her late sixties, if not more. Her husband looked positively withered and prune-like in comparison, except for having a head of hair like black Astroturf.

George stepped forward, clasped their hands in turn, and murmured a few earnest words. Then he gestured to me and said: 'And here is your daughter-in-law, Lizzie, and Annie Vane, whom I don't think you have met . . .'

'Well, Elizabeth, I didn't expect to see *you* here,' Jacqueline Barillos said coolly.

'My wife did not wish to see her – you should not have told her we were coming,' agreed her husband.

'But Tom's widow . . .' began poor George, baffled. 'Who better to offer comfort and—'

'But we know she did not care about him,' interrupted Jaime Barillos. 'We have had many beautiful letters from the woman he *did* love, whom he wanted to marry. We know how he was grieved when he found out about his wife's affairs . . . that even his own son was fathered by his cousin and—'

'Now, just a minute!' I broke in angrily. 'I can guess who has been telling you this pack of lies and it most definitely is *not* true!'

'Certainly not!' Annie defended me stoutly. 'It was Tom who was the unfaithful one, not Lizzie, and Jasper *is* Tom's son.'

'And you, of all people, must know why my son looks so like a Pharamond!' I added pointedly.

Mrs Barillos gave me a dirty look, and threw a dramatic hand towards the grassy mound: 'Here is the proof – does *this* look like the tomb of a loved husband?' she cried. Clearly, she should have been on the stage.

'The stone is ordered – these things take time.'

'Not even any flowers . . .' she sobbed, turning to her husband, who put his arm around her and glared.

'Please,' began George. 'Please don't distress yourself! Why don't you come back to the vicarage with me now, and we can talk this through? I fear you are letting the natural grief of a mother lead you to unwarranted conclusions—'

'No!' she declared, lifting her head and turning her dark lenses in my direction like an inimical ant. 'I would like you all to go and let me pay my respects to my son – alone.'

'Then afterwards, perhaps . . .' suggested George tentatively.

'No. Please leave us in peace,' she said implacably.

I turned and walked off before I could say something I would regret, and Annie followed me, though I heard George say something to them before catching us up.

'This has been a bit of a shock, Lizzie. Why don't you come back to the vicarage for a cup of tea?' George suggested kindly, but I insisted I was fine and despite their protests, set off for home. I didn't even want Annie's company just then, only to be alone.

The ugly little scene had seemed too melodramatic to be true at the time, especially with the Barillos resembling nothing so much as a pair of *Thunderbirds* puppets, but now, suddenly, my legs began to feel a bit trembly and I realized that it had affected me more than I thought.

So when a sleek sports car pulled up by me and Rob offered to run me home, it was a relief to get in. I didn't have to talk either – he was full of what he had been doing.

It is sometimes pleasantly relaxing being with a man who notices nothing much other than himself, and it was kind of him to take me home when he had just driven all the way up from London. When we got there I pulled myself together and thanked him for the lift, then added firmly that I knew he wouldn't mind if I didn't ask him in, since I had lots to do before the Mystery Play rehearsals tonight.

'No, I'll see you later, then,' he said, and I managed to smile at him before climbing out of the car and waving him off.

Through the open barn door I could see Caz doing chin-ups on a cross-beam, like a very strange clockwork toy. Hasn't he got a beam of his own to swing from?

Without Nick, that night's rehearsals were a bit . . . *flat,* I suppose is the only word.

The only highlight was when I overheard the new Moses, in answer to God's telling him that he'd written down ten commandments on tablets of stone, reply testily: '*Could thee not find something lighter? I'm no spring chicken, tha knows! Just as well I hadn't t'carry 'em up t'mountain as well as down.*'

For some reason I also felt hugely tired and depressed,

which was probably reaction from that horrible scene in the graveyard, and I might have just gone home rather than on to the pub with the others, except that home was empty without Jasper.

There wasn't any sign of Rob after the rehearsals either – but he was already in the pub, the centre of an admiring circle. I expect he was telling *them* all about his cameo film role, too. I sat quietly in the corner with George and Annie for a while, then left early and fairly abruptly when I spotted Polly coming in, wearing a wrap-over dress that made her breasts look like a giant pair of loosely packaged white puddings.

I pounced on her near the door, grabbing her arm. 'I want to talk to you,' I said angrily, 'because I know what you've done!'

She went the colour of clotted cream and stared at me through a spidery inch of clogged mascara.

'Yes, I know all about the tricks you've been playing, Polly Darke! The jars of jam and tomatoes made to look like mine, the ARG! harassment, the poisonous fungi in the mushrooms – even the lies you've been telling the Barillos! And I'm warning you, if there are any more, I'll go to the police.'

Her colour came back in a rush. 'Tell them and see if they believe you!' she hissed, then wrenched her arm away with surprising strength and shoved her way through the crowd.

'Wait for me!' Rob called, catching me up outside. 'I said I'd run you home tonight – you look exhausted.'

'It's been quite a day,' I agreed wearily, though it just goes to show that you shouldn't misjudge people: he might have seemed totally self-absorbed in the pub, but he had still noticed I wasn't exactly a sparkling little star in the firmament tonight.

When we pulled up outside Perseverance Cottage I didn't resist when he put his arm around me and kissed me: apart from suddenly feeling too exhausted to move, I needed comfort.

He tasted, not unpleasantly, of minty mouthwash. Now, that was a relief.

After a couple of minutes he detected a certain lack of enthusiasm and sat back again. 'OK, I know when I'm flogging a dead horse. You don't really fancy me, do you?'

'I wouldn't exactly say that,' I said honestly. 'But it's pointless – I'm simply not harem material.'

'You can be chief concubine,' he offered, grinning.

'Thanks – but no thanks. And you'd better watch your step with Kylie, too. Did you know she has a very tough boyfriend – in the army?'

'In the army *and* in another country,' he said. 'Anyway, she's not serious and neither am I – it's just a bit of fun. But you and I could be serious . . .'

'No, we couldn't, don't be daft – there isn't a serious bone in your body,' I said severely, fending him off – then gasped as a pale face appeared at the window with spectral suddenness.

'What the hell—?' began Rob explosively, letting me go just as the door on my side was pulled open.

'*Hens*,' Caz Naylor said succinctly, with a jerk of his head.

'Oh God!' I scrambled hastily out. 'I entirely forgot to lock them up for the night before I left, and there's been a fox about. Goodnight Rob – thanks for the lift!'

'But Lizzie!' he began to protest, then gave up and drove off as I started across the yard towards the henhouse.

'I've done 'em,' Caz said, stopping me in my tracks and then turned and loped silently off into the darkness.

Men.

Twenty
Stewed

'I thought you might like to know that Polly Darke and I have parted company,' Sally told me crisply. 'She rang me up hysterically demanding I drop you as my client, or she would leave me. So I told her to take her business elsewhere.'

I nearly dropped the telephone. 'But Sally, she earns *much* more than I do!'

'Yes, but she's ten times the trouble. Besides, I'm not having one of my authors telling me who else I can, or can't, represent. Anyway, if she carries on like she's doing, pestering her publishers and doing her prima donna act, *they* will drop her too.'

While I was grateful that Sally decided to keep me and ditch Polly, it does give her one more thing to hate me for. But now *she* knows that *I* know she did all those spiteful things, surely she won't try anything else?

'Crange and Snicket want to know how *Just Desserts* is coming along,' Sally said. 'And so do I.'

'I'm collecting recipes,' I assured her hastily. 'I've only had five minutes to think about it.'

'Don't forget that you can use old stuff from all the Chronicles, though you need at least fifty per cent new material or your readers will feel cheated.'

'I will. I'm picking Nick Pharamond's brains, only his recipes tend to be pretty sophisticated and I have to dumb them down to my level.'

'I'd forgotten he was some kind of relation of your husband's – that's lucky. And he's really attractive too, isn't he?'

'Umm,' I said half heartedly. 'He's in the middle of getting divorced – shall I put in a good word for you?'

'God, yes!' she said enthusiastically.

Nick is *still* away, but a postcard of Penzance arrived, with a recipe scrawled on the back for a dessert that seemed to consist mostly of Cornish clotted cream.

The card appeared to have travelled the length of the country before coming home to roost, possibly because it was stuck to some other mail – the front was tacky and I had to sponge and dry it before adding it to the album. I expect he wrote it in a restaurant over a lush dinner, probably in the company of some Poldarkian Cornish beauty.

I needn't have worried about what Jasper was going to spend Unks holiday money on, because he came back laden with stuff to take to university with him: his own kettle, mugs and crockery, plus tons of archaeology books – he'd struck a rich vein in a second-hand bookshop.

He also sported a strange haircut and lots of new clothes, including several oddly-worded T-shirts that probably meant something a mother shouldn't know about: I didn't ask for a translation.

In between all my usual larder-filling, gardening and pet-sitting activities – not to mention giving the *Just Desserts* book a bit of thought – we had day-trips out to all the places he used to love when he was little, like the Knowsley Safari Park, and the museum and botanical gardens at Southport. He seemed to enjoy them as much as me, though I expect he was just humouring his old mum again. I did let him do most of the driving, so that might have had something to do with it.

A couple of days later I got back from cleaning out the cage of a rather vicious African Grey parrot, to find that Nick had phoned in my absence.

'He wanted to wish me good luck for university,' Jasper said.

'That was kind . . . where is he?'

'Back in London, but he's coming home soon. I think he has to do something about the divorce first – go to the solicitors, maybe, and sign something? He said he and Leila were getting on better now they were divorcing than they ever had while they were married,' he added.

'How lovely. I'm *so* happy for them.'

Jasper grinned. 'He said to tell you he was sorry to miss you, and had you managed to make a decent apple pie yet?'

The days slid by until there came that moment that a mother dreads, when she has to leave her beloved offspring, bag and baggage, marooned in a strange place to start a part of his life that she can only peripherally be involved in. And indeed, had *much* better not even speculate about.

Not that Jasper was entirely among strangers, since not only was Ginny present, but also his friend and his friend's elder brother were among the other students sharing the terraced house.

Jasper's bedroom was on the ground floor in what had once been the morning room, but which had been divided by a partition wall, making a long hallway from the shared living room to the kitchen.

At least if there was a fire he could get out fast.

We had arrived half an hour ago, but I was still sitting

quivering on the bed from the effect of having driven through the Liverpool traffic system trying to find the place.

And quite how Jasper managed to fit quite so much into my Morris was a trick needing magic, but now it seemed to have exploded to four times the original bulk, like popcorn in a microwave, all round his new room.

'When I went to London to do my cookery course with Annie we had—'

'Just one rucksack and a sleeping bag each,' he finished for me, ripping the tape off a cardboard box and delving inside for coffee and mugs. He had his own little sink in the corner of the room, which was handy. 'I know.'

'And I had a guitar.'

He frowned. 'I don't think you ever mentioned the guitar. And you can't *play* a guitar.'

'No, it was a fashion accessory,' I agreed. 'I swapped it in the first week with another girl, for that glass pig with the three little pigs inside it.'

'Oh, yeah, cannibal pig.' He plugged in his brand new kettle and switched it on. I could do with a cup of coffee, at that.

He looked up. 'You don't have to stay any longer, you know, Mum,' he said kindly. 'It'll be dark before you get home if you don't get off soon. Besides, no one's going to come in here while my mother is hanging about. I can hear them talking in the kitchen, so I'll go and take my food and stuff through in a minute when you've gone.'

'It'll be dark anyway by the time I get home,' I pointed out, slightly hurt. 'But perhaps I *had* better go and leave you to get on with it. I only hope I can find my way back out of Liverpool again.'

'It'll be easier finding your way home than getting here, because you'll know where you are once you are out of the city. Come on, I'll see you off.'

'I'll phone you tonight, just to make sure everything is all right, shall I?'

'Well, I might be out,' he said dubiously. 'But you could leave a message.'

Out on the pavement I gave him a hug, which he suffered with saintly resignation, then got into my now empty car, which I had squeezed into rather a small space slightly up the road.

He leaned in at the open passenger door and said: 'Now, Mum, remember what I said: don't try changing any plugs!'

'I only melted one once,' I said indignantly.

'And switch the light off *before* you change a light bulb. Don't try and change the timer on the boiler and, if the flame goes out again, don't try and fix it yourself – I don't trust you near gas with a naked flame. Ask Unks to send Joe down to do it, or if Uncle Nick is about, he can.'

'Now look here, Jasper, I'm not completely helpless, you know! I may not have an affinity with anything electric but—'

'You're the kiss of death to anything electric,' he said. 'Anyway, I expect I'll come home for the odd weekend before Christmas, so you can save anything that wants doing until then, if you like.'

Hold on, I thought, shouldn't this be *me* giving out the instructions – and not about electricity, either, but drugs, safe sex, and eating properly? Though the eating bit wasn't so pressing: I'd packed enough food and drink to last him for about ten years. Just when did my son take over the role of Keeper of the Mother?

'I expect I'll survive,' I said, then looked at him – tall, skinny, his dark hair whipping about in the brisk breeze – and swallowed hard.

'Bye then, darling. Hope you settle in quickly,' I said slightly huskily, though I did manage a smile, then pulled out and headed in the direction (hopefully) of home.

The sun was sinking in a clear sky, but just like the song it was raining in my heart.

Annie had kindly been up to see to the hens and left me a nice note telling me to ring her if I wanted to, though ten to one George is there, or she is out doing something godly or good with him.

The cottage looked desolate and empty, and that was exactly how I felt. Jasper has been the whole centre of my universe for over eighteen years: what was I going to revolve around now?

He's trying out his wings and will still return to the nest from time to time, but soon he will take off permanently and I'll be alone forever.

That's the way it should be, but it doesn't mean it isn't painful.

Unks called to ask me how Jasper had settled in, and I told him how he had turned the tables on me in the good advice stakes, which made him laugh.

Then, as usual, I turned to food and drink for comfort until I took myself to bed, where I fell into a state of comatose indigestion.

I wasn't feeling much happier in the morning, especially since I also had a hangover, and it was lucky I didn't have any pet-sitting jobs to do since I kept bursting into tears, which is quite unlike me.

I stripped Jasper's bed so that it would be made up all nice and fresh if he was homesick and popped back for a night or two. But I didn't linger in there with the bare surfaces where his computer had been and the gaps on the bookshelves – it was too poignant.

Then, while the bedding was going through the wash and dry cycle, I gave the cottage the sort of thorough cleaning it only gets when I am trying to distract myself. It didn't quite work, though, because I kept finding things of Jasper's that set me off again.

Nick walked in on me just before lunch and found me slumped in a sobbing heap in the old wicker basket chair in the kitchen, clutching a large black Snoopy sock with a hole in the heel, which I had found down the back of the radiator.

'Lizzie? What on earth's the matter?' he demanded, coming to a sudden startled stop and staring at me. 'I don't think I've *ever* seen you cry, except that once at the hospital!'

I snuffled back the tears and held out the sock. 'It's J-Jasper's!' I wailed.

He bent down and pulled me relentlessly up, looking relieved, and gave me a little shake. 'Oh, is *that* it? Come on, Lizzie, stop wallowing in it! He's only a few miles away at university, not the other side of the world. You can go and see him any time you want!'

I sniffled and tried to pull away, but he didn't let go. 'No, I can't! He's got to make his own life there – I couldn't possibly keep popping in and fussing. And it's such a long time until Christmas.'

'I expect he'll come back and visit you before then. Look,

there's no point in sitting here moping like a wet weekday: get your jacket and let's go.'

'Go? Go *where*?' I said, though he had at least made me stop feeling weepy. I was now indignant.

'I'll take you out for lunch. You look quite decent – no need to change. Come on.'

Considering I was still dressed in the old jeans and sweatshirt I'd done the housework in and my hair was a snarl, he had to be joking. I dug my heels in. 'I don't think I want to go out, thank you, Nick . . .' I began, but he wasn't taking no for an answer.

In the end it was easier to give in, but I insisted on changing, bathing my face in cold water and brushing my hair first, though.

Lunch was fish and chips, well laced with salt and vinegar, eaten out of newspaper on the seafront at Southport, with the expanse of beach stretching away under a cold blue sky scudding with clouds.

But that was *after* he'd made me walk for miles, so by then I was starving and, I admit, feeling much more optimistic.

After he dropped me back at the empty nest, Annie came around with someone else's Maltese terrier, so I didn't really have time to mope. Anyway, all that fresh air and exercise seemed to have numbed the pain a little.

I am proud of the fact that I managed to resist the urge to call Jasper and see what he was doing, but later I got hot and sweaty stuffing his duvet back in its clean cover, which is a task somewhat like giving birth in reverse, but without the excruciating agony or the person trying out their embroidery skills on your private parts.

The *good* thing about being pregnant – possibly the *only* good thing – is that at least you know where your child is and have a pretty good idea what it is doing.

Now we are only joined by the frail umbilical cord of his mobile phone.

Mimi and Juno's Glorious Autumn Garden Colour luxury coach tour set off just after seven in the morning, and since I am always up early I volunteered to drive them to the pick-up point outside the New Mystery.

Mimi was highly excited, but I was sure Juno had thoroughly searched both her luggage and her person for any sharp implements with which she might attempt to steal cuttings from the various stately homes they were to visit, so provided she kept her eye on her I was hopeful they would have an enjoyable holiday.

While Juno was seeing to the luggage being stowed away, Mimi dashed into the corner newsagent's shop to buy cough candy and Uncle Joe's mint balls for the journey and came back carrying several little paper bags, her cheeks bulging like a hamster's.

As the bus pulled away Mimi was seated in the window, a sweetly angelic little old lady in a pink velvet Alice-band and matching pearly beads. She waved benignly at me and I could have *sworn* something glinted in her hand.

Must have imagined it, or she was wearing a ring . . . though I've never know her to wear them, they get in the way of her gardening.

The coach vanished down the high street and I turned the car for home, calling at Annie's cottage on the way, as much from the hope of hot croissants as to see if any more pet-sitting jobs had come up.

It was a Danish pastry day, which was nearly as good, and she was bubbling with suppressed gossip.

'Gosh, Lizzie,' she said excitedly, 'ructions last night in the village! Kylie's boyfriend got leave from the army and came home a couple of days ago, and of course someone told him all about what Kylie's been up to with Rob. And he went round to Rob's and there were loud voices and then they had a fight! Or Kylie's boyfriend hit Rob, at any rate, and the police got called.'

'Well, I did *warn* Rob about the boyfriend – it's entirely his own fault.'

'And Kylie's,' Annie pointed out fairly.

'That's true, but I bet she put all the blame on Rob.'

'Rob's just phoned me up – he tried you first, but there was no answer. He wants one of us to go round and take Flo out, because he isn't feeling well.'

'Meaning battered and bruised? I'd better go on my way home, but I'll ring you later and tell you what he says – if I can catch you,' I added. 'You're always out these days.'

Mainly with George . . . who I still haven't had that quiet

word with. What *is* holding him back? Perhaps I ought to give him the birds and bees talk I gave Jasper before he went to university . . . ?

Except that wasn't such a great success, come to think of it.

Rob took his sunglasses off to show me his black eye, but he seemed to have escaped relatively unscathed otherwise. He certainly hadn't lost any of his bounce.

'Kiss it better?' he suggested hopefully.

'No chance!' I told him severely. 'And I did warn you.'

He shrugged. 'It was just a bit of fun on both sides, nothing serious. I don't know what Kylie told him, but he swung a punch at me as soon as I opened the door and took me by surprise, and then we had a bit of a scuffle until the police came and broke us up. I didn't press charges.'

'Magnanimous of you!'

'It is really – make-up are going to have their work cut out disguising this shiner for a couple of weeks, unless they can work it into the storyline . . . That's an idea,' he added thoughtfully, and headed for the phone.

At the Mystery Play rehearsals that evening I noticed that Kylie was much subdued, though strangely triumphant: I expect that's the glow from having two men fighting over your charms. In the *Annunciation*, after the Angel Gabriel had broken the news of the treat in store for her, she didn't look a bit embarrassed when she had to speak the line, '*By heck, then, thee'd better have words with my Joseph smartish and explain t'matter, or t'wedding's off!*'

I'd have curled up and died.

Afterwards, a stocky and pugnacious-looking young man collected her and whisked her away, though he didn't have to worry about Rob tonight, because he wasn't anywhere to be seen.

Nick, who seemed to be in a foul mood, said sourly: 'Looking for Casanova? I hear Kylie's boyfriend's sorted him out big-time.'

'Actually, there's hardly a mark on him except a black eye and I think he only got that because he was taken by surprise,' I said coldly.

'Oh? And did you kiss it better?' he asked sarcastically, so clearly his mind runs along similar lines to Rob's. Must be a man thing.

'No,' I said shortly, going slightly pink. 'We're not on kissing terms.'

'That's not what Caz says.'

'Caz? You've been discussing me with *Caz*? And I haven't—' I broke off, recalling that, actually, I *had* shared a kiss with Rob.

'Slipped your memory?'

'Not that it is any of your business, but Rob did kiss me – once – for comfort. Tom's parents showed up while you were away without telling me they were coming, though George let me know, and I went to meet them at the churchyard. It turned out that Polly's been writing lies to them and turned them against me and there was a horrible scene – it really upset me. Rob was kind.'

'I bet he was,' he said nastily.

Up to this point I had been automatically ambling in the direction of the pub, but I stopped dead and demanded: 'What is the matter with you tonight? *You* were really nice to me the other day too, when I was upset about Jasper leaving home, and now you're horrible!'

'I hadn't had a chance to speak to Caz then.'

I glared at him. 'Have you told Caz to spy on me?'

'To watch over you, after he told me about the mysterious jar of tomatoes and the mushrooms – which, by the way, you might have mentioned to me yourself!'

'I dealt with it,' I said shortly. 'And it did sound a bit unlikely, when you thought about it – The Case of the Poisonous Mushroom.'

'No, I can't say it really convinced *me* – until Leila got that pot of jam in the post and had a friend run some tests on it.'

'She did? And was it poisoned?'

'A strong emetic.'

'Well, I didn't send it.'

'You needn't glare at me like that: I didn't think you did. But there doesn't seem to be any proof that Polly did either, does there? Still, I wasn't taking any chances, so I asked Caz to watch out for you while I was away.'

'There's no need, I can look after myself. And what's more, whatever I get up to is my own private business!'

'Pardon me for caring,' he snapped.

'Look, Nick, I don't know why you are needling me like this tonight, but I've had enough: good*night*!'

I felt his eyes boring between my shoulder blades as I walked off, but he didn't follow me: he probably had other fish to fry.

This morning I found an old envelope on the doormat, with Marianne Potter's secret Lancashire hotpot recipe scribbled on it.

I suppose that is an apology of sorts for his foul mood.

Then when I opened the front door a parcel fell on my feet: the cover and copy edits of the Perseverance Chronicles, Volume Seven, had arrived.

The cover picture is too twee for words: why do they always turn my solid northern sandstone cottage into something thatched, gabled and timbered to within an inch of its Anne Hathaway life?

Twenty-One
Given the Bird

'George found three large frozen geese on the vicarage doorstep this morning,' Annie said.

'*Geese?*' I questioned, putting a mug of tea and a plate containing wedges of apple pie in front of her, each marked with differently coloured cocktail stick flags.

'Oven ready, with an anonymous note saying they were for the Senior Citizens' Christmas dinner. He called me right away, to ask my advice.'

'That was a pretty generous donation,' I said thoughtfully. 'Frozen, did you say?'

'Yes, they were in those big, see-through roasting bags, but no supermarket labels on them or anything like that.' She looked down at her plate. '*Three* pieces of pie?'

'Small pieces – I want you to taste them and tell me which one you think is best. Here, have some cream.'

'All your apple pies taste wonderful.'

'But Nick's obviously taste better, or he wouldn't have won the gold at the fête.'

'Yes, but you won practically everything else, Lizzie – you might let him have that one small triumph.'

'Not if I can help it. So, what did you and George do with the frozen geese?'

'We took them up to the hall. I thought we might as well, since Mrs Gumball always cooks the Senior Citizens' dinner anyway – with your help, of course – and they have huge freezers in the cellar they could store them in.'

She tried another forkful of pie and chewed thoughtfully. 'Nick was there, and he said this year he was going to help Mrs Gumball cook the dinner.'

'He *is*? Then Mrs Gumball won't need me as well, will she?'

'Oh, yes, Nick told George that you would *both* be doing it,' Annie said. 'And we ran in to Clive Potter on the way back, so George told him about Nick offering to help, too, and about the geese, so I expect it will be in the parish magazine in no time.'

'Then it can come out again,' I said sourly. 'I have no intention of being the Demon Chef's whipping boy, he can find another one.'

'Whipping girl – and you're very crabby today,' she said, then looked down at her empty plate as if surprised that she'd cleared it down to the last pastry flake. The coloured sticks lay round the edge like the hours on a clock.

'Which pie did you like best?'

'To be honest, I couldn't really taste much difference,' she confessed. 'They were all delicious!'

I sighed. 'Maybe he uses dark arts? Says a spell over his cooking pots?'

'You'll be able to watch him cooking the Christmas dinner and find out,' she teased. 'Has he done something to annoy you?'

'When does he *not* do anything to annoy me? But yes, he has excelled himself – he set Caz on to watch me while he was away!'

'But Caz already *does* watch you. I mean, he keeps an eye on the place because it's part of the estate – and probably also because he thinks of you as family, however remote the connection.'

'Yes, I know that, but Rob kissed me the other night when he drove me home, and Caz not only interrupted us, but he reported it to Nick!' And I repeated to her what Nick had said, about not being sure it was Polly playing the nasty tricks, and even thinking I'd imagined them at first.

'Of course, I haven't told him about Ophelia being in ARG! – and I don't suppose Caz has either. After all, it would be a bit awkward, wouldn't it, since she was campaigning against him in a way? I'm not sure how he would take it, and he might feel he has to tell Unks.'

'He'd probably find it funny,' she said.

'I wouldn't put it past him. He seems to find most things I do funny – except the bits involving Rob. And that was a *perfectly* innocent kiss, even if it was any of his business who I kiss, which it isn't.'

'It was?' she said, wide-eyed.

I grinned. 'Well, it was a perfectly *enjoyable* one, but just between friends. Rob knows I don't want a relationship with him – or anyone else,' I added firmly. 'I'm getting quite tired of Unks, Mimi, Juno and now even Jasper trying to throw Nick and me together, when it must be clear it's a complete non-starter.'

'But Lizzie, he's obviously concerned about you – *and* jealous!'

I considered. 'He *does* seem a bit jealous, but I'm sure it's not of me personally. It's some dog-in-the-mangerish male thing to do with property: I'm part of his family and living on his land, as it were . . . except it's still Unk's land, of course.'

'No, I'm sure you're wrong, Lizzie: you think I don't notice these things, but I've seen the way he looks at you and I'm sure he's in love with you.'

'No *way*,' I said positively. 'Just because *you* are in love, you think everyone else should be!'

She went slightly pink under the freckles, but carried on doggedly: '*And* you missed him when he was away.'

'Not really – and just as well, because that's just what he always does, isn't it? He goes *away.* When I was mad enough to fall for him, if you recall, he didn't let a little thing like our romance come between him and another globe-trotting, recipe-collecting expedition. I'm only surprised he's stayed around Middlemoss so long this time, but he's obviously getting itchy feet.'

'No, Lizzie, I think if it weren't for Tom, he'd probably have spent more time here in the past, he's quite sincere about loving the place.'

'He may love the place, but he's only *passionate* about his cooking.'

'And he's trying to impress you with it,' she said stubbornly. 'He knows the way to your heart is through food.'

'Well, he's not going to do it by snatching my gold prizes away . . . but if he *has* got any designs on my virtue, I'd probably do almost anything he asked for that coffee granita recipe.'

'Lizzie!' she exclaimed, shocked.

'Just joking,' I said hastily. 'You're wrong – *I'm* not interested and *he's* not interested. After all, if he cared about me that way, what's to stop him from telling me?'

Annie said quietly: 'But you were only widowed in August and his divorce isn't through yet. That might be holding him back, don't you think?'

I blinked. 'Yes . . . I suppose it might *if* he felt about me like that, which he doesn't. And I don't really feel newly widowed now I'm over the shock, since I got all the grief bit over with before Tom actually died.'

'If Nick was a dog, he'd be a big, dark Irish wolfhound,' she said inconsequentially. 'Rob is a tomcat.'

'I don't like the way your mind is working,' I said severely. 'George has been a demoralizing influence on you. And, speaking of demoralizing experiences, I'm afraid poor Juno has had one on holiday: she had to explain precisely what Mimi was doing to someone's stately garden with nail scissors. You know, I *thought* I saw her holding something metal up when the coach pulled away the morning they left – she must have got them in the corner shop when she was buying sweets.'

After she'd gone I got out the copy edits of my book and went through them for errors a second time, before parcelling them up and taking them down to the post office. The cover I pinned to the kitchen notice board in the hope it would grow on me, but it hasn't yet. Nor do all the flowers depicted in the cottage garden bloom at the same time anywhere other than in the artist's demented imagination, or not in this hemisphere, anyway.

'*The Vicar is delighted to announce that, due to an anonymous benefactor, this year's Senior Citizens' Christmas dinner will be roast goose with all the trimmings! As usual, Mrs Eva Gumball will cook it up at the hall, most kindly assisted by Mrs Lizzie Pharamond – but also, adding that touch of* Cordon Bleu, *Mr Nick Pharamond! It will be delivered piping hot to the village hall, courtesy of our friendly local Meals on Wheels volunteers*,' proclaimed the latest Mosses parish magazine, so I suppose there is no getting out of it.

The dankness of November has set in and the children are starting to collect firewood for the bonfire on the green. I thought Jasper might come home for that, but he says he is too busy, though busy with *what*, he didn't say.

Still, he seems to have settled down very happily at university and is enjoying his lectures. He told me, at more length than I really wanted to know, what had been discovered about the Viking's dietary habits from excavating their cess pits at York.

It is quite amazing what passes through the digestive system more or less whole, isn't it?

A policeman – it sounded like that boy who favours finger food – called me to say that one of the 2CV's wheel nuts had been handed in by a metal detecting member of the public and added, in a seemingly casual aside, that it had seemed in a perfectly good state of repair.

Then he told me the inquest was set for the end of January, and rang off.

The light was fading fast. I put on a warm coat and went to lock up the hens and, as I did so, Caz emerged slowly from the shadow of the barn. Since my slight contretemps with Nick I have entirely ignored Caz when he has been around, which did not seem to bother him in the least – I wonder if he has even noticed.

Now I ran my hand distractedly through my tangled hair and said: 'Oh, Caz – the police have found one of the missing wheel nuts – or rather, I think someone found it and handed it in – and the thread on it looks fine. I'm sure they still think I loosened them on purpose and encouraged Tom to take my car!'

Caz glanced at me in his usual obliquely wary yet not unfriendly way. Then he said: 'Don't you fret, our Lizzie, it'll all come out in t' wash.' With that he loped off towards the woods, his gun under his arm.

I stared after him: if he continues getting so garrulous, we might soon be able to hold an entire conversation.

He'll probably be back later, because the Mummers will be coming round to the workshop soon. Hope Rob comes too, and pops in as usual for coffee and chat afterwards – I feel like some company.

Rob not only stopped by, he took me out to the café-bar in the former Pharamond's Butterflake Biscuit Factory, which was very pleasant now we have established fairly firmly my unavailability for his healthy sex rota.

Of course this doesn't stop him flirting with me, but actually I find that quite enjoyable now that Nick has suddenly gone even more morose and distant than usual.

Rob dropped me home afterwards, though I avoided a goodnight kiss, not wanting to make a habit of it.

There was no sign of Caz, but that didn't mean he wasn't lurking about somewhere.

Having traded eggs and produce with one of Annie's WI friends, I found myself with about a ton of tart green apples, so the freezer is now full of pie and crumble.

The larder shelves are groaning with apple-based jams and jellies, apple sauce, apple chutney, spiced apple . . . Dried apple rings hang on strings and apples for wine are fermenting away in the kitchen corner.

I am appled out.

I have just made a batch of apple fritters with the very last and eaten them all, sifted with brown sugar, drizzled with honey and blobbed with thick cream. Now I never want to see another one again, unless it is in liquid and alcoholic form after a suitable interval.

I cede the apple pie prize to Nick in perpetuity.

Nick has been off on his travels yet again. Mimi said meaningfully that he was catching up on things he should have done before, only he didn't want to leave Middlemoss, but I expect he has just got bored and restless. I heard nothing from him for a couple of days, then had a spate of postcards at once – and all *tart* recipes of various kinds.

He was back for the next Mystery Play rehearsal but, like Rob, seems to have given up going to the pub afterwards. I still go, but I can only take playing gooseberry to George and Annie for so long, no matter how kindly they go out of their way to include me in their conversation.

When we came out of the village hall I thanked Nick for all the postcards, then asked curiously: 'But why are all the recipes for tarts?'

'I thought you deserved them,' he said shortly and then strode off into the night, looking distinctly like Heathcliffe.

I don't know what is biting him, unless he has heard about my friendly drink at Butterflake's the other night with Rob and misconstrued it?

Having said I never wanted to see another apple again was tempting fate, for Marianne Potter has asked me to make toffee apples and cinder toffee for bonfire night – she runs a little refreshment table and sells them for charity. There's usually someone doing hot chestnuts too, which I absolutely adore.

I added a variant, Treacle Toffee Apples, to my *Just Desserts* collection, then decided the bonfire night celebrations in Middlemoss would probably make a whole chapter in Book Eight of the Chronicles, if I included a few other interesting snippets of information – like the fact that we always burn an effigy of Oliver Cromwell, warts and all, and not Guy Fawkes like everyone else.

It is not that the villagers were all staunch Royalists in the Mosses, just that they knew how to enjoy themselves and deeply resented the Puritans or anyone else trying to put a damper on it, especially the Mystery Play.

I sent Jasper some slab treacle toffee (and a rawhide bone

for Ginny – might as well blunt her teeth before he brings her back for Christmas). I am missing him so much – it seems to hurt more as time goes on, though part of me is also of course happy that he is having a good time at university.

Annie never goes out on Bonfire Night, staying in to comfort Trinny, who clearly associates loud firework bangs with some unimaginable terror from her past and becomes a shivering heap. She said George would show his face at the event, then go back and join her and they were going to roast chestnuts over the fire and watch the home videos Annie's parents had sent her of their VSO work in Africa.

Unks was away, on pleasure bent as usual, and Juno never brought Mimi down for the bonfire since she got much too excited, but instead treated her to a short private display of Emerald Cascades and Glittering Fountains in their garden before cocoa and an early night.

What Nick was doing, I had *no* idea and nor was I even remotely interested. I set out on my own at seven, torch in hand, my innards warmed by a strong slug – or maybe two – of sloe gin.

The fire was well alight when I got there and the first of the fireworks were going off, under the direction of Clive Potter. There was quite a crowd about, and the refreshment table was doing a roaring trade. I didn't buy one of my own toffee apples, but I did purchase a plastic cup of hot, spicy punch.

Looking round the faces brightly lit by the fire I saw several familiar ones, including Polly Darke with a group of friends over on the other side, Jojo and Mick, and nearly the entire Mystery Play cast . . . . In fact, most of the Mosses residents had, as usual, turned out.

One or two of the more rebellious teenagers were sneaking off into the darkness outside the firelight and setting off explosive fireworks, and being yelled at for their trouble: it was all much as usual.

I expect it wasn't sophisticated enough for Rob and his crowd.

I sat on a log and ate a paper cone of hot chestnuts, then got another tumbler of punch and began to feel a bit happier. 'This is fun, isn't it? I said, finding myself standing next to Ophelia, who was swathed head to foot in a rather Tolkien woollen cloak. It looked pretty weird by firelight, but probably not as odd as the full-length knitted coat that *I* was wearing, a labour of love presented to me by Annie last Christmas. It has lots of little hanging daggy bits like a raddled sheep, and the strident colour combination means I can only wear it in the dark.

Ophelia's white face was upturned and rapt, watching a sunburst of stars. 'Oh – it's sooo beautiful!' she muttered. 'Beautiful, beautiful stars. Stars . . . '

The firework flickered and went out and she turned to me and said excitedly: '*Star!* I'm going to call the baby Star!'

'Star Locke?' I said doubtfully, though of course you never know, it might by then be a Star Naylor. 'If it's a boy, it might sound a bit odd.'

'No . . . no – beautiful!' she murmured again, and another firework shot up into the sky and exploded into a galaxy of pinprick lights. 'Better than Rambo . . .'

'That's *very* true,' I agreed, beginning to feel a bit muzzy – maybe my earlier shots of sloe gin hadn't been such a good idea? Or was the punch stronger than usual? I had the feeling the chestnuts were sloshing about in rather a lot of liquid and it was probably about time to call it a day and go home . . . especially since Nick had suddenly materialized out of the shadows nearby like the Prince of Darkness and was looking at me with what appeared to be acute disapproval.

'Must find Caz – tell him,' Ophelia said, vaguely looking around her, though you'd need ESP to find Caz if he didn't *want* to be found: our chameleon of Middlemoss.

She wandered off and I, too, turned to go, but had only taken a step or two away from the firelight when something landed with a thud just where we had been standing and immediately exploded with a horrendous bang and a shower of sparks.

I put my hands over my ears and staggered, almost falling – and then was suddenly knocked flat as something large and heavy landed on top of me, and rolled me over and over.

Even winded, shocked and with my face pressed into icy mud I knew it was Nick, but don't ask me how – *or* why. After what seemed ages his weight was removed and urgent hands ripped off my woolly coat.

I rolled over, dazed and winded, and sat up in time to watch him jumping up and down on it.

'Lizzie – are you all right?' Marianne cried, running over and trying to haul me to my feet, only my knees seemed to have given up and I was a dead weight.

'I'm fine,' I gasped, still trying to reinflate my lungs.

Clive appeared out of the darkness. 'I don't know who threw that firework, but if I find him, he'll wish he hadn't!' he declared vengefully.

'No one would be stupid enough to throw it in this direction on purpose, it must have been an accident, Clive,' Marianne said. 'Those boys just wouldn't be told!'

I looked around suddenly. 'Ophelia? Is she all right? Only we were talking together just before the firework went off.'

'Don't you worry about her, she was well out of range and that Caz's with her,' Marianne said soothingly. 'You were closest: did it burn you anywhere?'

Nick picked up my mangled coat and examined the limp and ruined remains. 'There, that's out – only just caught it, though.' Then he bent down and hauled me effortlessly to my feet, though he had to keep one arm around me to stop me falling over again. When I trembled violently from a mixture of shock and cold, he shrugged out of his leather jacket and wrapped it around me, the silk lining warm and slithery.

'I think Lizzie may have singed the back of her legs a bit, Nick,' Marianne pointed out worriedly. 'Her jeans look charred in a couple of places.'

'I can't seem to stand up,' I said weakly.

'Shock,' Marianne said. 'Stand back, everyone and let her get some air.'

Until that moment I hadn't realized that a ring of spectators was pressing close, watching avidly – including Polly Darke, a half-smile on her lips. Then her eyes shifted to Nick and she slowly took first one step back and then another, until she had vanished into the darkness.

I blinked. Maybe I imagined her?

'Drink's more likely than shock, the way she was knocking the punch back,' Nick was saying unsympathetically. 'I don't think there's much harm done, but I'll take her home.'

'Perhaps you should come to the post office first and let us see if she's burned?' suggested Clive. 'It might be bad enough for Accident and Emergency.'

'I don't think so,' Nick said, 'but if it looks worse than I think it is when I've looked at it, I'll phone the doctor.'

'You do that,' Marianne agreed.

'Your voices sound strange,' I said.

'I expect the blast deafened you a bit,' Clive said.

Things started to whirl around my head. 'No, I think I'm going to—' I began, and then the darkness closed over my head.

I woke in Perseverance Cottage, lying on my own sofa in front of the glowing fire, with Nick wiping the mud from my face with a wet flannel. A *cold* wet flannel, which is probably what brought me round.

His face, concerned and intent, was very close to mine. 'At last!' he said with relief when he saw my eyes open muzzily. 'I was starting to get worried.'

'What . . . what happened?'

'You fainted.'

'I *never* faint!'

'Then maybe my first guess was right, and you passed out from all that punch you were knocking back, then,' he said unsympathetically. 'How do you feel?'

I attempted to sit up, feeling strangely disconnected. 'All right – a bit shaky.'

'I expect it will go off. There are two small burns on your leg – I've put some antiseptic and dressings on them, but I don't think they're much to worry about.'

Actually, I was more worried by the sudden realization that he'd removed my jeans. Under a concealing blanket, all I was wearing on my lower half were my sensible cotton pants.

My face burned and I managed to sit up straighter and tuck the blanket primly around my legs. 'I think I ought to thank you for – well, for putting me out. That's why you threw yourself on top of me, wasn't it?'

'Yes – sorry about that, but I could see your coat was catching and it was the quickest way.' He got up and came back holding the sad remains of my coat. 'I'm afraid I've made rather a mess of this.'

'You certainly have – and Annie knitted it for me. Now I expect she'll make me another even more hideous one, because I told her I loved it.'

Maybe I should tell her he jumped on it because he was jealous, and then she might knit *him* one?

'You ought to go to bed. Do you want me to carry you up?'

'No, I don't,' I said firmly, shivering again. 'But I'd like you to fetch the bottle of sloe gin from the kitchen and then lock the door behind you when you go.'

'I don't think you should drink any more alcohol – you have shock, and would be better trying to go to sleep. You don't have to be nervous, because I'll stay here tonight on the sofa. Go to bed and I'll make you some cocoa.'

'I'm not nervous, I don't need you to stay here with me, and I don't want cocoa – I want gin. And if you aren't going to get it, I'll get it myself,' I said, attempting to rise from a tangle of blanket on slightly wobbly legs.

He sighed and got up. 'OK, but don't blame me if you feel terrible in the morning.'

My hand trembled so much the glass rattled against my teeth, so he had to sit down with his arm around me and hold it. But it did the trick and I began to calm down – or maybe go comatose is a better description. The warmth of the fire and the soft pink light from the table lamp were very soothing . . .

'I think Polly might have thrown the firework,' I said drowsily, relaxing against his broad chest, which was invitingly close. Anyway, it was that or fall over sideways.

He'd put the empty glass down but hadn't removed his arm from around my shoulders and now he rested his chin on top of my head. 'I was looking at *you* – I didn't see where it came from,' he said. 'She *was* there, but the chances are she wouldn't do something that stupid – it was just boys messing about, and you were unlucky.'

'Perhaps you're right – it's just she looked so . . . so pleased afterwards . . .' I yawned.

'Come on – you're all in, I'll carry you up to bed.' He gathered me up against this broad chest as though I was a loose-limbed doll but, before he could rise to his feet, I slid my arms around his neck.

He went quite still and our eyes met and held, his like unfathomably deep pools in the lamplight. Then he gave a resigned sort of sigh, tightened his grip and kissed me.

His lips tasted of inevitability: there was never anything of the minty mouthwash about Nick Pharamond.

I awoke slowly, with that languorous, totally sated and exquisitely guilty feeling you get after a really *bad* chocolate binge. Blissed out.

Then I opened my eyes to find I was lying, not on my bed, but on the sofa. It wasn't *chocolate* I'd pigged out on last night and instantly I remembered (*and* felt!) everything I'd done the previous evening. Yes, every single moment, right the way from Nick knocking me flat and battering me into the mud, to our kiss and *more* than make up, which had at least had the advantage of *not* involving icy wet earth.

For a woman with the memory span of a goldfish, this was quite something – but it was an action replay that could have done with some soft-focused editing around the edges to hide all that urgent hunger . . . which *surely* hadn't been all on my side, had it?

It was daylight – gloomy daylight, but latish – and the lights were off, though the fire was burning brightly behind the brass fire screen.

Instantly I knew the cottage was empty apart from myself – long empty. Slowly I heaved myself to my feet and, clutching my blanket, tottered into the kitchen, wincing at every step.

Propped against the kettle was a brief note:

> Lizzie, it's seven and I'm supposed to be in London at ten for the shortlist photo shoot for Cookery Writer of the Year. I'll phone you later.
> Mud brown suits you – you should always wear it.
> Nick

That was it. I read through it twice, slightly incredulously, then crumpled it into a ball and threw it with some force at the wall opposite. It bounced off and fell behind the fridge.

Then I slumped down on the chair, feeling humiliated and angry: this was worse, much, much worse than when I confided in him at the hospital. This time I gave him more than my secrets – and all he could think about was some stupid cookery award!

So be it: from now on, let him eat cake. I know what I will be eating – Humble (or should that be Humiliation?) Pie:

Mix just enough alcohol with a bad shock and
a dash of unadulterated essence of lust.
Put in a warm, dark place.
Remove any inhibitions and stir a little.
The leftovers can be bitter if eaten cold next day.

I have changed my mind about Nick being brimstone and treacle. Now I think he is more like that rich, dark chocolate you can buy that has been spiked with red-hot chillies, and one chunk is *definitely* enough.

Twenty-Two
Flambé

Annie, receiving news from the milkman at the crack of dawn about the more *public* parts of my sizzling evening, hotfooted it round the second she'd finished the first dog walking session.

She found me still slumped in the kitchen in my dressing gown, though I had roused myself enough earlier to shower off the last traces of mud (about five minutes after reading Nick's note, in fact), while singing the words of *I'm going to wash that man right out of my hair* through gritted teeth.

While she was applying some of her Girl Guide first aid skills to re-dressing my singed leg, I confessed that the most sizzling part of the evening *hadn't* been the firework-throwing incident.

She stopped heartily slapping on the Savlon, which was a relief, and stared up at me, grey eyes round and startled: 'You mean, you and *Nick* . . . ?'

'Yes, me and Nick!' I confirmed gloomily. 'I can't imagine

what got into me. The shock of nearly being blown up must have sent me temporarily insane.'

'There you are,' she said beaming, 'I knew you were in love with each other!'

'Love had *nothing* to do with it,' I said tartly. 'I don't know what it was – shock, sloe gin, propinquity, comfort, hormones, a substitute for chocolate . . . whatever.'

'Oh, no, Lizzie!' she protested. 'I'm sure Nick—'

'Nick left before I woke up, so I don't know what *his* excuse was – but he made it plain some trashy award is more important than I am. Read this!'

She pressed a huge Elastoplast into place and got up. I handed her Nick's terse little note.

'Why has it got cobwebs on it?'

'It's been behind the fridge. Read it and tell me if it sounds even remotely lover-like!'

She did, lips silently moving, then looked up uncertainly. 'Well, I suppose he *had* to go to the photo shoot if he's been shortlisted for Cookery Writer of the Year, Lizzie?'

'Big deal,' I said sourly. 'But never mind, at least it shows that food is still much more important to him than I am, just in case I was harbouring any illusions – which I wasn't.'

'Yes, but food is pretty important to you, too.'

'Maybe, but I still put relationships *first*.'

She sighed. 'Then perhaps men see things differently and he thought you'd understand.'

'He was wrong, then, wasn't he?'

She pored over the note again. 'It's *very* Nick, isn't it? You couldn't really describe it as romantic.'

'Short to the point of terse,' I agreed.

'I expect he was in a rush – but you'll be able to watch the award ceremony on the telly tomorrow!'

'No I won't, I haven't got one.'

'You can come and watch mine.'

'No, thank you, I think I'll stay home for a couple of days – my leg is very sore and I'm covered in bruises from Nick throwing himself on top of me. I had to hobble out in my dressing gown to let the hens out and I'm going stiffer by the minute.'

She blushed. '*Lizzie!*'

'When he was putting the *flames* out,' I explained. 'He rolled me in the mud.'

'How quick-witted and brave – he's a hero!'

'Don't start going all dewy eyed and romantic again: it's pointless. I only wish I never had to see him again, because it will be even worse than when I babbled my entire life history to him at the hospital, while Tom was in a coma.'

'You'll feel differently after he's talked to you,' she suggested, ever the optimist. 'And he *will* phone you up – look, he says he's going to – and then you'll see he really cares about you.'

'He'll find that difficult, since I'm not even going to answer the phone. I'll let the answering machine take the messages.'

'Yes, you will – you know you can't resist, in case it's Jasper.'

She is quite right, I do tend to snatch it up at the first ring – and it rang right then. We both stared at it.

At the sixth ring she gave in and lunged for it. 'Hello? Oh, Nick, it's you! Yes, Annie . . . No, I've just put a fresh dressing on it – it's not too bad, but it will be sore for a couple of days . . . I'll ask her.' She covered the phone and held it out towards me enquiringly.

'Tell him I've got much more important things to do than talk to him,' I said loudly, and started hobbling round the kitchen opening the cupboard doors and slamming things about.

'I'm afraid she can't come to the phone at the moment I . . . Oh, you heard?' She looked up. 'He says, what's more important than talking to him?'

'Food, of course – *he* should understand that,' I said pointedly. 'I'm making giant rum truffles to send to Jasper, they're his favourite.'

After a moment she put the phone down. 'He says he's sorry he had to dash off, but he will come and see you when he gets back, and to be careful. Careful of what?'

'I suppose he means careful in case the thrown firework wasn't some stupid adolescent prank last night, but Polly stepping up her campaign.'

'Oh, no, I'm sure she wouldn't do anything so dangerous,' she said earnestly.

'No . . . probably not. She's only done petty, spiteful things so far.'

'It is hard to believe anyone could be so nasty. I suppose it couldn't all just be coincidence?'

'The ARG! stuff was certainly her idea and besides, when I told her I knew what she was up to, she didn't deny it.'

'Then I expect she's stopped now and the firework *was* an accident.'

'Speaking of accidents, I'm afraid I was wearing that lovely coat you knitted for me last night, and by the time Nick had finished trampling it into the mud, it was beyond repair.'

'Never mind, at least *you* are OK, that's the main thing. I can always knit you another.'

'That would be lovely,' I agreed, then added evilly, 'and Nick said it was such a shame it was spoilt because it was wonderful, and he wished *he* had one just like it.'

'Did he? Then I'll make *him* one, too,' she said kindly. 'Well, I'd better be off – take it easy for a day or two, won't you? I can manage all the pet-sitting until you're fit again.'

'I'm just a bit stiff, really – there's nothing wrong with me.' To prove it I got up again to see her out.

'When I came in, Caz was in the barn doing exercises and Ophelia was sitting on a bale of straw watching him,' she said. 'But it looks like they've gone now.'

'I'm beginning to think I might as well convert all the outbuildings into accommodation, so everyone can just move in with me.'

I walked down to the village next day, thinking the exercise might help loosen me up a bit – I still felt as though I'd gone three rounds with a gorilla – and posted the box of giant rum truffles and an advent calendar with a chocolate behind every window, to Jasper. I only hope he doesn't get zits.

Everyone in the post office queue was still talking about my near roasting, but the news of Nick's TV appearance had also got out and was causing much excitement. I said I expected it would all come down to a brief glimpse of him among the also-rans, then realized how sour grapes that sounded and shut up.

Of *course* I want him to win it, since clearly it means so much to him. Of course I do.

On the way back home I noticed that George's car was parked outside the vicarage and, on impulse, paid him a visit.

He gave me tea and I got right down to brass tacks. 'Look George, Annie is my oldest friend and your dithering about is making her miserable. So I want to know whether your intentions towards her are honourable? Is Barkis willing?'

He choked on his arrowroot biscuit, but when I could get any sense out of him it was just as I thought: they are both pussy-footing around thinking the other only wants to be friends, when in reality they are mad about each other.

'She loves you, she told me so,' I said plainly, but he is so modest it took a while to convince him. When it finally did, he stared at me with dawning hope in his blue eyes.

'She'll be at home now, having lunch, I should think,' I said casually. 'I know she's got a busy afternoon, because she's covering my pet-sitting jobs as well as her own – but I'll be fit to work again tomorrow, I'm . . .'

But I was talking to myself: he'd gone. As I let myself out, I only hoped he had a key: we don't want our vicar arrested for breaking into his own home.

Annie phoned me later almost incoherent with happiness, to say that George had proposed and they were now engaged. They're trying to get through to her parents to give them the glad tidings, but communication with that remote area of Africa is a little difficult at present.

I think they'll be very happy and if anyone deserves it, I'm sure Annie does.

As for me, I have been cooking hare (or rather, rabbit) with chocolate sauce – *chilli-hot* chocolate sauce. It was definitely different.

A postcard of the Tower of London with a *Crème de Coeur* recipe on the back arrived next morning, but he can keep his heart to himself – if he's got one.

Unks absolutely insisted I go up to the hall and watch the awards ceremony on TV with him, Mimi and Juno that evening and, rather than upset him, I did.

We all crowded round the big set in his den, which is decorated with a mixture of old racing prints and early Pharamond's Butterflake Biscuit posters, so reflecting the varied strands that go to make up the family character.

The Cookery Award was just one among many, so we had

to sit through Sport's Writer and Fashion and goodness knows what, before we got to it. Just as well I'd taken up a box of rum and raisin mashed potato fudge and a slab of parkin.

I caught a brief glimpse of Nick at one of the tables. I'd seen him in a dinner jacket before, of course, but never at a distance, as though he were a stranger . . . and I had a better chance to examine the effect when he went up to collect his award: yes, he won the thing.

'I knew he would,' Mimi said complacently.

'You can't have known,' Juno said. 'He's not the only good cookery writer around.'

'He's in a league of his own,' she said loyally. 'And Lizzie, don't you think he looks handsome in his dinner jacket? He's the best-looking man in the room.'

He was certainly the tallest. And while, with those strongly marked features, you couldn't in all fairness call him handsome, he was possibly the most attractive-looking man there. I realized I was sitting forward and leaned back again casually. 'He scrubs up well,' I agreed grudgingly.

'He's coming home in a couple of days, and bringing some people with him,' Unks told me. 'He asked me if I would mind if they decorated the hall, kitchen and dining room up as if it was already Christmas, so they could photograph it for an article.'

'Don't magazines usually do that sort of thing months before? November seems very late,' I said dubiously.

'Yes, they had a celebrity footballer and his family lined up, but now it seems he's involved in some unsavoury sex scandal and his wife has filed for divorce, so the magazine's had to find a replacement, fast. Nick writes for them anyway, so I suppose he was the easy choice.'

'Yes, and it will be *such* fun, like having two Christmases,' Mimi said. 'Will we have presents too, Roly?'

'No, it's all fake, don't get your hopes up. They'll bring everything they need to decorate the place with them, and Nick will cook up a Christmas dinner. Lizzie, he said to ask you if you would come, they need extra guests for the photographs. And perhaps Annie and the Vicar, too?'

'Kind of him,' I said dryly.

'We'll all be in the magazine,' Mimi said excitedly. 'Pulling crackers and opening parcels.'

I seemed to have already pulled a cracker. Unks may have detected a certain lack of enthusiasm, because he asked anxiously: 'You will come, won't you Lizzie? And Jasper too, of course, if he's home.'

'He'll still be at university, but he'll be back for the real Christmas.'

'I'm going to wear my blue lace dress,' Mimi said.

'You'll have to, it's the only dinner dress you've got,' Juno pointed out.

'Well, you've only got that black thing. Unless we buy new ones? What about you, Lizzie?'

'I don't have anything suitable at all, so I'd better not come,' I said hastily. 'I'm sure Nick won't want me there anyway.'

'He said to ask you *especially*,' Unks said, and they all beamed at me meaningfully.

They knew about the accident, of course, for news travels, if not instantly, certainly fast round here.

'He was so brave at the bonfire, wasn't he, Lizzie? If he hadn't been so quick you might have been badly burnt,' Mimi said.

'Then he carried you back to your cottage after you fainted,' Juno sighed. She clearly has a much more romantic streak than her bluff exterior would lead you to believe.

'Yes, he's a real hero,' I agreed sourly. 'And he even spent the night on the sofa, in case I was suffering from shock and needed anything,' I added pointedly – which was quite true, except that so did I. And, unfortunately, I *had* needed something.

Mimi looked thoughtful, but before she could say anything else, I said quickly, 'Did you all know that Annie's got engaged to the vicar?' which was distraction enough to keep them going until I went home.

I have put the phone down on Nick twice. I hear his voice, and I can't think of a thing I want to say to him. He has now stopped phoning. Good.

He missed another rehearsal, too – though we are all word perfect and into sorting out the costumes and props, ready for our final dress rehearsal in Christmas week, which we do in two sessions. Though Adam and Eve are excused wearing their skimpy outfits for that, because of the cold.

Mimi and Juno came to watch, which they never usually do, and Juno kindly read Nick's part in her big, deep voice.

'Might as well come along to the pub with you afterwards for a quick snifter,' she said heartily when we had all finished.

'Actually, I'm going to the bar at the Butterflake's Factory with Rob, tonight,' I said, slightly self-consciously, though there is nothing particularly secret about our occasional friendly drinks. But I certainly don't want Nick thinking that there aren't lots of other men interested in me, even if he isn't . . . . Or *one* other man, anyway and a very undiscriminating one, at that.

'Oh, that sounds such fun!' Mimi said. 'I've never been to Butterflake's – why don't we go too, Juno?'

'Oh, we couldn't possibly intrude on Lizzie's evening,' Juno said, and Mimi's face fell.

Rob was awaiting me outside, but when I turned around to introduce Mimi and Juno they had vanished. Somehow, I wasn't completely surprised to find them already ensconced at a corner table at the café-bar when we went in. They smiled and waved.

'Friends of yours?' asked Rob.

'Roly Pharamond's sister, Mimi, is the one with curly hair. Juno is her companion – and I think they are here to keep an eye on me.'

'Do you need keeping an eye on?' he asked, brightening. 'Got anything planned for later tonight?'

'No, just a drink and chat, and then home – alone,' I said pointedly.

'Oh, well, worth a go. Dora told me Nick Pharamond was the hero of the hour at the bonfire and you and he are, as she put it, only waiting for your mourning year to elapse before naming the day.'

'*Dora* said that?' If she did, then the whole of Middlemoss probably thinks the same! How on earth do these rumours get about?

'Yes – sounds like something straight out of *Cotton Common*. So, are you and the Young Master going to get hitched, then?'

'No!' I said forcefully.

'Well, you needn't bite *my* head off, I didn't suggest it!

Though God knows he gives me jealous enough looks whenever he sees me talking to you,' he added, thoughtfully.

'That's just a sort of general disapproval,' I explained. 'He thinks of me as part of the estate's goods and chattels.'

I was not surprised when Mimi and Juno followed us out later, though they could hardly hitch a lift in Rob's sports car. Juno stooped and said to me through the window: 'Might just call in on the way home, Lizzie – Roly wanted some more of that lemon marmalade and it slipped my mind earlier.'

So I am definitely being chaperoned – but I expect it is entirely their own idea, and they can't keep it up twenty-four hours a day. It did the trick though, because Rob dropped me off and left immediately: I think he finds Juno rather alarming.

When they turned up, Mimi had a miniature paper umbrella behind one ear and was full of exotic cocktails, giggly and overexcited, but I thought she'd go out like a light once her head hit the pillow.

Annie and I have had an expedition to buy new dresses, not something we often do, since we both hate shopping. Annie usually buys hers from an outsize shop and then has to take the waist in, since hers is tiny – she's a very *curvy* hourglass.

She settled for a midnight blue velvet affair with a modest neckline, while mine is a dark, clingy, holly green with interesting draped bits, that looked like nothing on the hanger but certainly made the most of what assets I possessed when it was on.

Frankly, it was dead sexy, and not at all the sort of thing I would normally wear, but in it I felt armoured for any eventuality.

Nick came back and instantly threw the hall into a flurry of preparation for the mock-Christmas staging, though they don't have to put any decorations or a tree up or anything: everything is supplied and the house will be professionally 'dressed' for the shoot.

After a few hours he managed to tear himself away and walked into my house without a by-your-leave.

I gave him one glance, as he lounged in the doorway in dark thundercloud mode, then concentrated on beating my fruit cake mix to death: when he's wearing his Neanderthal caveman expression it's never a good sign.

'Why did you keep putting the phone down on me, Lizzie? Don't we have something to talk about?'

'We have *nothing* to talk about.'

'The other night—'

'Shouldn't have happened. As far as I'm concerned it *never* happened,' I said firmly. My arm was starting to ache, so I stopped beating and began buttering the cake tin instead.

'But Lizzie—'

'Look, I don't want to *think* about it, let alone talk about it!' I snapped, crashing the tin back down on the tiled work surface.

'Why? What was so wrong about—?'

'I'm not discussing it,' I said. 'Just forget it, OK?'

He stared at me, black eyebrows drawn together in a ferocious frown. '*Forget* it? Come on, Lizzie, it must have meant something to you!'

'Shock makes people do the strangest things, Nick, but if you like you can put it down to gratitude for saving me from serious burns,' I suggested coolly.

'I don't want your damn gratitude,' he snarled and slammed out, making everything rattle.

After putting the cake in the oven I sat down and scraped the mixing bowl clean as usual. It tasted salty – but that was probably all the angry tears dripping into it.

Cookery tip of the day: never, ever, put salt in your fruitcake.

Twenty-Three

Crackers

Annie and George collected me in her car next day for our stint as pretend-Christmas dinner guests, and it seemed very odd to be getting glammed up for a smart dinner before it was even lunch time. Mind you, I dress up smartly so infrequently that it would have felt odd at any time.

They were looking forward to it, but I would have got out of it if I could have done it without upsetting Unks: I mean, it wasn't even as if we could *eat* the damned food, since it was all going to be faked and glazed with something to make it photograph prettily, or sit under the lights for so long it would be rife with three strains of salmonella.

Mimi had already called me to tell me that Christmas had arrived at Pharamond Hall earlier that morning in a large van, along with a miscellaneous assortment of photographers, food technicians and the like, plus a rather snootily elegant grey-haired woman, whose job was to dress the rooms they were to use: deck the hall with boughs of holly.

Mrs Gumball let us in and said that they had already photographed the kitchens and the hall, with its garlanded oak banister, until she was fit to scream, and she would be glad when they were done. Then she took our coats and sent us through to the dining room.

There, although it was barely midday, the crimson curtains were shut and the only light came from thousands of candles glittering off the polished dark panelling and the swags of festive foliage and baubles draped everywhere. The colour scheme was crimson, gold and a rather rich purple: very ecclesiastical. I'm sure George felt quite at home.

There seemed to be a lot of strange people milling about with cameras and lights and things near the dining table, which gleamed with silver and cut glass, but the family were all gathered round the fire among a litter of discarded festive gift wrap.

Nick, morose in an immaculate dinner jacket, leaned on the mantelpiece with his foot on the fender, like the young lord and master.

'Come in!' Unks said jovially. 'They're nearly ready for us to do the Christmas dinner scene. Annie my dear, you look lovely,' he added, kissing her. 'Being engaged suits you! You're a very lucky man indeed, George.'

'I certainly think so,' the vicar agreed devotedly and she blushed.

'Lizzie looks pretty too,' Mimi commented. 'Don't *you* think so, Nick?'

'She certainly looks different,' he said, taking in the clinging folds of my new dress with a raised eyebrow and I suddenly began to wish I'd come in the dungarees I wear when I white-wash the henhouse.

'We've been opening presents,' Mimi said. 'They were all empty, but we're having real crackers.'

'And real wine,' Unks added. 'Need something to keep us going!'

'Can you take your places at the table, please?' someone called, and we went where we were directed, which in my case was between Juno and Nick.

People darted in to tweak, dab and twitch everything to perfection as we posed, slightly self-consciously, as directed. My dress fitted where it touched – and it touched almost everywhere – but I soon began to wonder if it might be a bit over the top in more ways than one, when the photographer kept zooming in on my cleavage. Then Nick glared at him and he backed off a bit.

'Can we pull the crackers now?' Mimi asked plaintively. 'Haven't they finished yet?'

'Yes . . . go ahead,' a man's voice said from the dark shadows. They were certainly big, expensive looking crackers and turned out to have equally pricey-looking little novelties inside. Mine, which I pulled with Nick, contained a gilded pen, a hat and a tightly rolled piece of paper.

'Does your motto make sense?' Juno asked, puzzling over hers. 'I think mine is supposed to be a joke, but I'm not sure – I mean, how *could* you cross an elephant with a mouse?'

'Read yours aloud, Lizzie!' ordered Mimi gaily. She was becoming flushed and excited.

I unrolled the long, thin strip of paper, which was entirely covered in Nick's instantly familiar spiky handwriting. 'Mine doesn't make sense either,' I said, crumpling it into my hand. 'Do you want my pen to go with your little photo frame and gold dice, Mimi? They seem to all match, don't they?'

Just as I was handing it over, there was the sound of an altercation outside the door and Mrs Gumball lumbered in, with a small, rotund and apoplectic man hard on her heels.

She jerked a thumb over her shoulder. 'It's that little twerp Lionel Cripchet from over Rivington way.'

'*Sir* Lionel,' he protested, bobbing up in front of her and glaring generally round. We must have presented a very *Night Watch* tableaux, but if so, the strangeness of it escaped him under the urgency of his anger: 'I'm here for an explanation!'

'Are you?' Unks said mildly, taking another sip of wine. 'Well, now you are here, I wouldn't mind an explanation myself – about that supposedly sound horse you sold me a couple of years back. Remember that? The one that mysteriously went permanently lame the day after I bought it?'

'I'm not here to talk about horses but *squirrels*!' He glared around at us all. 'Yes, that's taken you by surprise, hasn't it? I suppose you thought I wouldn't find out!'

'Is the man mad?' Juno asked. 'Why is he blethering on about squirrels?'

'Well, spit it out, Cripchet,' Roly said amiably. 'Why are you blethering on about squirrels?'

'You know very well!' he exclaimed slightly wildly, looking at the vicar and Annie as if he expected them to come out in support, despite their baffled expressions. 'I've been overrun with the little grey bastards these last two years, and now – last night – I caught him in the act!'

'Who?' asked Nick; then added, after a minute, 'What?'

'Your gamekeeper, Caz Naylor – his Landrover was parked up a track next to my estate at one this morning! Now, what do you say about *that*?' he demanded triumphantly.

'Is Caz still around?' Roly asked Mrs Gumball.

'In the kitchen,' she said. 'Shall I send him in?'

'Do,' he agreed. 'I am quite sure he has a perfectly innocent explanation.'

'Ha!' said Sir Lionel, moustache bristling.

Caz slid silently into the room, but no further than the dark shadows beyond the reach of the candlelight.

'Ah, Caz – Sir Lionel wants to know what your Landrover was doing parked up a track next to his estate in the early hours of the morning,' Roly said. 'Were you indeed there?'

Caz nodded, almost imperceptibly.

'And I'm sure you had a very good reason?' prompted Unks.

'Of course he had a damn good reason!' yelled Cripchet, going puce and practically dancing up and down on the spot. 'He was releasing hordes of flaming grey squirrels on to my land, that's what he was doing! There's practically standing room only and they're fighting for territory. It's like World War Three out there!'

'And what do you say to that, Caz? What *were* you doing?'

'Courtin',' he said laconically.

'Courting?' demanded the infuriated baronet. '*Courting?* You can't expect me to believe that, Caz Naylor!'

'Actually,' the vicar interjected quietly, 'Caz and his fiancée, Ophelia Locke, have just asked me to put the bans up, so I see no reason to doubt it.'

Fiancée?

'That's right,' agreed Caz and, clearly feeling that enough had been said, sidled back out of the door again.

'But the squirrels—' began Sir Lionel, baffled and furious.

'You know, Caz said he'd found a lot of the traps sprung but empty lately,' Unks said thoughtfully. 'And that animal rights group – ARG! are they called? – *they're* very active around here. I daresay they've been releasing them on to your land, that's what it is.'

Cripchet's lips worked silently and his skin, if anything, went an even more ominous shade of puce.

'A drink before you go?' suggested Nick hospitably.

Sir Lionel looked from one to the other of us and said slowly: 'It's a damned conspiracy! You're all in league together!' and slammed out.

The magazine crew, who had been watching with silent appreciation unnoticed in the background, broke into a spatter of polite applause. Roly bowed.

'Well,' he said happily, 'all's well that ends well, isn't it? And if you have finished with us, too, ladies and gentlemen, then I suggest we adjourn to the kitchen for something real to eat and leave you to pack everything up.'

I discovered I still had the curl of paper from the cracker clenched in my hand and, for want of a handbag, shoved it down the front of my dress when no one was looking.

Mrs Gumball had hot soup and sandwiches ready, and by the time we had finished those, Christmas had been dismantled, packed away and driven off again. Then Annie and George said they would give me a lift home.

As we left, Nick called out to me, showing one of his more disturbing smiles. 'Lizzie, don't forget our date in December, will you?'

'Date? December?' I echoed blankly, stopping dead and staring at him.

'The Senior Citizens' Christmas dinner, remember? Mrs Gumball is expecting you up here to help cook it.'

'That's right,' she agreed.

'But if Nick's helping, you won't want me under your feet, too?' I suggested hopefully.

'Many hands make light work,' she said firmly, 'and I've three geese to cook!'

The note in the cracker was Nick's recipe for prize-winning apple pie.

I can't see that there is any startling difference between it and my own, so if his really *is* better, then it must mean that he has a lighter hand with the pastry.

That is even more unforgivable. If he wants a motto for *his* cracker, I would suggest 'I shot myself in the foot' would do admirably.

Nick is hell on wheels in a kitchen, and takes no prisoners.

He and Mrs Gumball had divided the cooking between them and my role in the preparation of the Senior Citizens' Christmas dinner was that of a skivvy. Had it not been for such a good cause I wouldn't have stood it for a second.

Never again: the moment when it was all packed into the Meals on Wheels van and trundled down the drive was wonderful – as was the stiff drink and long soak in the bath I had as soon as I got home. Nick offered to drive me back, but by then I wasn't speaking to him – if I had been in the first place, which was a moot point.

Still, Clive reported that the dinner was a huge success, the geese were delicious, and we all got a vote of thanks for our labours at the end.

There was no Mystery Play rehearsal on the Tuesday, since it was the village Christmas show, but at least all I was expected to do for that was buy a ticket and go and watch it, along with Mimi and Juno and just about everyone who lived in the Mosses.

The display of salsa dancing was particularly memorable. Who'd have thought Mrs Gumball would have had that much energy left in her after our labours only the day before? Some of the others may have been more technically perfect, but I thought the fire and liveliness of her performance made up for any little mistakes.

After the next Mummers session in the workshop, Rob popped in and said he thought Ophelia was going to give birth to a chest of drawers.

'She has suddenly grown a big bump,' I agreed. 'She's no idea when it's due, though – you'd think she was living in the Middle Ages, the way she avoids modern medicine. Did you know she and Caz are going to get married?'

'Are they?' He looked at me over a table spread with home-made goodies and unleashed his glowingly attractive smile. He looked blondly wholesome – pity about his more dubious habits.

'Yes, and Annie's parents are delighted about *her* engagement, too – they hope to fly back in the New Year on leave and meet George.'

Annie is now sporting a modest sapphire ring and going about in a glow of happiness.

'They seem perfectly matched,' Rob said. 'Maybe *I* should try it?' He gestured at the table. 'A woman who can cook like this is worth hanging on to!'

'Don't be daft,' I said, though rather flattered. 'Monogamy isn't in you and I wouldn't settle for anything less.'

Went to Liverpool to fetch Jasper, dog and baggage home for Christmas, though I took a wrong turning at one point and circled the same part of the city twice before charging off in what luckily turned out to be the right direction.

It was lovely to see him again, but he looked indefinably different – more grown up, I suppose. Ginny was still about as attractive as a hairball and gave an experimental nip or two at my ankles as I hugged Jasper.

His belongings seemed to have doubled since I left him here in September, so that even the few 'essential' items he insisted he needed to survive a Christmas at home (including his computer, folding bike, TV and about a ton of books), made a dauntingly huge heap. We had two goes at fitting it all into the Morris. The second time I treated it like a sort of three dimensional jigsaw puzzle, which is a skill most women are good at: life *is* a three-dimensional jigsaw puzzle containing several trick two-sided pieces.

All the way home he was silently texting messages on his phone, and when I asked who to, he said his girlfriend, but did not expand on this interesting remark. I expect he'll reveal all eventually.

I had been avoiding Nick since my stint as kitchen slave, but the day after Jasper came home he slammed in through my door like a whirlwind and demanded: 'Why didn't you *tell* me Ophelia Locke was the ARG! supporter who was targeting you – *and* at Polly Darke's instigation?'

'How did you find that out?' I blurted, taken off guard.

'Caz just told me – among other things – and I might have taken the other incidents more seriously if I'd known about it.'

Jasper, who had been sitting at the table, looked up. 'Ophelia was? What, with those animal rights people?'

'You mean, *you* didn't know either?' Nick said, seeming slightly mollified.

'I didn't tell him – or about the other incidents,' I said. 'I didn't want to worry him.'

'Which other incidents?' asked Jasper.

Nick gave him a quick resume of what had been happening and then added, '*And* there was a firework thrown at her at the bonfire, did she tell you that?'

'We don't know that was Polly,' I said, going pink, as any mention of bonfire night always makes me do.

'Actually, we do: Caz spotted her doing it.'

'He did? Then why on earth didn't he say so?'

'You know how he feels about the police. It took him long enough to tell me.'

'Oh . . . You – you won't tell Unks about Ophelia being in ARG! will you? Only they've thrown her out now, and since she and Caz are getting married it would be a pity to spoil everything.'

'You are the strangest woman!' he exclaimed, looking exasperated.

'She certainly *is*,' agreed Jasper traitorously, 'I found her crying over a postcard album last night, and when I asked her why, she said there was something terribly sad about *Crème de Çoeur*!'

Nick seemed cheered by the thought of my misery. 'She did? Well, well!'

'Shouldn't we do something about this woman, if she's playing tricks on Mum?' suggested Jasper.

'Something *is* going to be done,' Nick said. 'Leave it to me.'

'Oh, right,' Jasper said, looking relieved. 'Well, come on, Ginny. Mum, can I borrow the car?'

'Why, where are you going?' I asked automatically.

'Meeting some friends, but I won't be late. And I won't drink and drive,' he added patiently.

I handed him the keys. 'Are you meeting your girlfriend?'

Jasper tapped the side of his nose but, infuriatingly, said nothing. Nick followed him out, and I saw them talking together before I closed the door against the icy wind.

When I looked out again, the yard was deserted: even the hens had retired to huddle somewhere warmer.

The garden is a sad cold winter thing, and so am I.

Twenty-Four
Haybox Cookery

It was lovely to have Jasper home, even if he did seem to be out of the house most of the time, and there was certainly nothing wrong with his appetite: food vanished practically overnight, and I was making mincemeat brownies on a daily basis.

He's still largely nocturnal, too, but when I wake up in the morning I often find little handyman jobs have been done around the house, that I've been putting off since he left.

His Christmas present wish list seemed to consist almost entirely of books and CDs, although I had already collected a few bits and pieces, including the most spectacular Swiss army knife with millions of gadgets, that I rather coveted myself. I'm sure it will come in handy.

I've made Christmas cake and puddings, but I don't need to think about Christmas dinner, because we always have it up at the hall with the family. It will be yet another goose . . . but then, it usually is.

Jasper has suddenly become even more antagonistic towards poor Rob, if that is possible, and warned me that if he became his stepfather he would leave home. I assured him that even if I had been tempted to remarry, which was the last thing on my mind, I would certainly not replace one chronic philanderer with another.

He must have heard Rob jokingly asking me to marry him again, when he caught us having a Christmas kiss under the mistletoe I'd suspended from the drying rack. I hang mistletoe up every year, but this was the first time I'd struck lucky.

Rob and I had already exchanged presents, although I hadn't expected him to buy me anything. He gave me a delightful little crystal snowman brooch and I gave him a box of home-made Turkish delight and a large rawhide bone for poor old Flo, who was about to be immured in kennels while he flies off to stay with friends in the Caribbean for Christmas.

I might have felt compelled to offer to have Flo myself if it hadn't been for Ginny: one snap of Flo's powerful jaws and she would be only a lingering memory. However, Flo is booked into the local luxury Dogtel, with heated beds and her own run, so I don't suppose she'll find it too traumatic.

Nick seems now to have accepted that I simply want to forget what happened on the night of the bonfire and continue as we were before, which I am, of course, perfectly happy about.

He's been bringing down bundles of his old notebooks, so he can suggest recipes for *Just Desserts*, though his idea of what is suitable and what isn't does not exactly coincide with mine. Still, it has inspired a whole series of yummy puds loosely based on cream and crumbly meringue with all sorts of additions.

Jasper seems perfectly happy to leave Nick and me to our own devices, even pointing out the mistletoe to him before he went out on one occasion, but I don't think Nick heard him.

I have adjusted my chocolate intake to compensate for . . . well, I don't really *know* what for, but it is very comforting. Have you ever tried hot chocolate custard?

* * *

One morning I opened the door to find Policewoman Perkins standing on the doorstep, lightly frosted with snowflakes like a rather odd Christmas card. She suggested, very politely, that we go and look in the outbuilding where I kept my gardening tools, because she had received an anonymous tip-off.

She didn't say a tip-off about what, but I said she was welcome to go and look and I would follow her over.

I shoved my feet into my wellies, pulled on a coat and ran across, to find her standing staring up at the wall rack where my tools hung fairly neatly with, hooked among them, my blue steel wheel brace.

'Is that the one you used to change your tyre, on the day your husband took your car?' she enquired.

'It certainly looks like it,' I began, reaching for it, but she stopped me.

'Please don't touch it, Mrs Pharamond.'

My hand fell to my side. 'But . . . but I'm sure it wasn't there before – I'd have noticed it! I mean, it doesn't live there, I always kept it in the car.'

'So when did you last see it?'

I frowned, trying to remember. 'I'm pretty sure that when I'd finished changing the wheel I slung it in the footwell behind the driver's seat,' I said slowly. It all seemed a long time ago now, and like a bad dream 'But then, of course, Jasper said he checked the wheel while I was in the cottage, so he probably used it, too. When he gets home, I'll ask him if he remembers what he did with it, shall I?'

'If you don't mind,' she said and, unfolding a large plastic envelope, inserted the wheel brace into it. 'And I'll just take this and check it for fingerprints, if you have no objection?'

'Not at all,' I said politely, 'but you'll only find mine and Jasper's, won't you?'

'Just routine,' she said, smiling that 'I'll get you yet, you murderess' smile at me. *Am I becoming paranoid?* 'We like to tie up all the loose ends.'

Jasper said he thought he might just have propped the wheel brace up against the barn wall when he'd finished tightening the nuts, but he couldn't be sure.

'Someone must have put it with the gardening tools recently and then told the police,' I said, puzzled. 'I would definitely have noticed it if it had been there all this time, since I'm constantly taking tools and putting them back – *and* it was on top of my favourite spade. But what's the point, when it won't tell them anything they didn't already know?'

'I wouldn't worry about it, Mum – I expect she really meant it, about tying up loose ends. And you *are* vague sometimes – you might have moved it to get at the spade, and not noticed it was there.'

'I'm not *that* vague. And who tipped them off about it – and why?'

'It's a mystery, but not one that's important, Mum – I'd forget it,' he advised. 'Or you could tell Uncle Nick about it and see what he thinks?'

'No, thanks,' I said crisply. 'He'll probably just accuse me of being senile, like you.'

On Tuesday afternoon the first of the Mystery Play dress rehearsals was held, up at Pharamond Hall.

The audience stands in the courtyard, which is bounded on one side by the kitchen wing, and on the others by stables and outbuildings. The entrance is through a large arched gateway, and directly facing it is a second arched doorway to the coach house, which forms the stage for the performance.

Various bits of scenery and old props had already been dragged out of storage, and the loose boxes on either side set up as changing rooms. The day before the real performance, Joe Gumball would hang up the stiff canvas curtains in the archway and check that the star slid easily across the wire, among other final jobs.

There was a chilly wind blowing, so we ran through our scenes briskly. Clive read the Voice of God, Lucifer was cast out of heaven, and the silent angels trooped on and off on cue.

Due to the skimpiness of our costumes, Adam and Eve are excused having to change for the rehearsals, which was a relief: I don't know about Nick's, but I am having serious doubts about the decency of my new Lycra outfit.

We stuck more or less to the Wheelright text, but when Moses came on he interjected a little acerbity into his lines: his rheumatism was clearly still playing up.

Miss Pym brought the children up in an orderly but excited crocodile, carrying their animal masks, to practise the ark scene.

'*And all the animals came into t'ark out of the rain, and by heck it were pouring down,*' Noah said, standing next to Mrs Noah, who was seated on a bucket. The children started to march past, two by two, growling, roaring, hissing and generally sounding like a zoo at feeding time. Last of all, and silently, came a solitary unicorn.

'*There's two of every darn thing – except t'unicorn. Yon's not going to breed on its own, wife.*'

'*Well,*' said Mrs Noah, reluctantly looking up from her knitting, which was probably a late Christmas present she was keen to finish. '*There's no more of 'em. Reckon that's the end o' the line for t'poor little beast. I never did see much use for it, though it's proper bonny.*'

'*It attracts virgins, so they say,*' said Noah.

'*Well, it's just thee and me now, chuck, so reckon them have died out an' all,*' said Mrs Noah. '*Knit one, purl two!*'

After the ark scene we always have a break before the *Nativity*, so all the little animals can see Father Christmas before going home. By now Annie and George, the heavenly twins, had arrived and helped Miss Pym shepherd them out through the arched gateway and line them up again, *sans* masks, outside the front door of Pharamond Hall.

The rest of us went through the kitchens the back way to the Great Hall, where Roly Pharamond was sitting in an ancient carved chair, dressed in a red, hooded suit and puffing at a cheroot. Over the years his wig and beard had yellowed with nicotine, and the scent of tobacco would, I was sure, forever remind generations of local children of Christmas.

In the shadows just behind the chair lurked Caz Naylor, the largest elf you ever did see, wearing pointed Spock ears and with his hat jammed down hard over his eyebrows, waiting to hand the presents to Father Christmas. What always surprised me was the way he could move so silently when his outfit was entirely covered in little bells.

Perhaps he'd stuffed them with something?

The fire flickered in the huge hearth, and the candle bulbs in the cartwheel of evergreen foliage that was suspended from the ceiling were dimmed. The house smelt of cinnamon and burning fir cones, hot mince pies and spiced punch from the trestle table laid out ready.

From beyond the great oak doors came the sound of a lot of reedy young voices belting out *Good King Wenceslas*.

'Here we go,' Unks said, regretfully removing the stub of cheroot from his mouth and tossing it accurately into the fire. 'Let the little buggers in.'

Nick swung the door open and a tide of children rushed forward, only to be halted in their tracks when barely inside by Miss Pym, who is a little woman, but with a presence and a voice that could command armies. 'Stop!'

'Ho, ho, ho,' Unks said benevolently. 'Come in, one and all!'

Joe Gumball activated the CD player and *White Christmas* chirruped merrily in the background.

There was a gift for every child and while Miss Pym orchestrated the queue, the adults fell on the food – and especially the drink. There were a few more children than expected, but there was an emergency gift bag for extras.

By now Jasper had arrived too, and was talking seriously to the vicar in the corner. At a rough guess, I would say they were discussing the eating habits of biblical folk and such like subjects, unless the vicar had a personal hobby horse and a stronger will than Jasper's. Annie had gravitated across to join them and Trinny, wearing a collar of tinsel, was circling Ginny in a vaguely menacing manner, probably trying to decide which end was which.

Jasper picked Ginny up and Trinny lost interest and wandered off under the table, where by now there were rich pickings in crumbs and discarded pastry. Mrs Gumball's idea of children's party food was miniature pork pies, tiny triangular sandwiches and little jellies in paper cases with a blob of cream and a diamond of angelica on top.

Eventually all the tired but happy children were collected and, as the last car vanished down the drive, Clive Potter rounded everyone up for the final part of today's rehearsal: the *Nativity*, and another song or two from the Mummers.

So out we all trooped out, warm, full and a bit reluctant, into the growing dusk. Marianne and Kylie made for the loose box changing room to adjust her costume, while our Joseph, Dave Naylor, leaned against a wall in his striped robe, smoking a cigarette.

'Where's Ophelia?' Jojo asked, looking around him vaguely.

'We're supposed to be playing *While Shepherds Watched* before the next scene starts.'

'Dunno, haven't seen her for ages,' Mick said, then cupped his hands round his mouth and bellowed: 'Ophelia!'

'That's funny,' I said. 'I don't remember seeing her in Pharamond Hall, either. Has she gone home? I hope she's all right.'

Caz appeared, without his elf ears. 'Caz,' I called, 'do you know where Ophelia is? Only no one seems to have seen—'

My words were drowned by a howl of anguish from the stables on the other side of the courtyard, the ones we use as dressing rooms. Then Marianne Potter's cropped, silvery head appeared over the half-door and she cried wildly: 'Help! Is there a doctor in the house?' before bobbing down again.

It was more Punch and Judy than Mystery Play. There was a second's breathless hush – and of course no doctor responded, for Dr Patel would be helping with the scenes that were to be rehearsed later in the week – then we all rushed across the yard.

Caz beat Annie and me to it, but it was a close-run thing and the others crowded up behind. Inside the dimly lit stable Ophelia, with no more ado than a couple of pains and an animal urge to be alone, had chosen to give birth – if not *in* the manger, certainly right next to it.

She lay pale and spent on the straw, her big eyelids closed, panting slightly, while Kylie, looking revolted, was holding a messy and screaming baby practically at arm's length.

It was amazing: I have never seen an infant that so closely resembled a fox cub and there could be absolutely no doubt that it was Caz's.

'Something to wrap him in,' Marianne ordered distractedly, but Joseph was already passing his voluminous headdress of striped towelling over. Caz slipped through the door and, removing his child from Kylie's uncertain grasp, enfolded it in the warm material and sat down on an upturned bucket. The baby, as if by magic, stopped bawling.

George, leaning over the half-door between Annie and me said, uncertainly, 'Bless you, my child!' like an aged bishop, but I don't expect this is a situation he's ever had to contend with before.

Clive, efficient as ever, had already trotted back to the hall to call an ambulance: the horse might have already bolted, but a check-up of mother and baby was clearly necessary.

There was a feeling of anticlimax about the rest of the rehearsals once Ophelia, the infant and Caz had been whisked away to hospital. Ophelia hadn't wanted to go and Caz had almost balked at the sight of the ambulance's brightly lit and clinical interior.

'I wonder if she's actually got anything ready in her cottage for the baby's arrival yet?' I mused.

'Oh, yes – Dave says all the Naylors have rallied round with baby clothes and equipment,' Annie assured me.

'I think their wedding had better be postponed until after the christening,' George remarked thoughtfully.

'If they can decide on a name. Star and Rambo seemed to be front-runners last time I talked to Ophelia,' I said, and George gave me a doubtful smile: I expect he thinks I'm joking.

Kylie was distinctly huffy during the *Annunciation*, *Nativity* and *Flight in to Egypt*, clearly feeling she had been upstaged. Joseph, bareheaded, performed his part with perfect sangfroid.

Afterwards most of the cast were still set on going down to the New Mystery as usual, and I bagged a lift with George and Annie. Nick followed us down in the estate pick-up, with nine angels crammed in the back and Lucifer sitting beside him.

When we got there I took our usual corner seat with George and Annie, but it was only when we sat down that I realized Nick hadn't followed us. Then I spotted him, smiling and talking with Polly Darke over near the bar. He's so tall he must have had a bird's eye view down her cleavage: her twin prows were jutting out like the front of a catamaran.

She noticed me watching and gave me a triumphant look as he steered her away to a darker corner, one hand under her elbow and his dark head bent towards hers.

My mouth was probably hanging open, because Annie asked anxiously: 'Are you all right, Lizzie? You look a bit odd.'

'I'm fine,' I said with an effort. 'Just a bit tired, suddenly.'

'Yes, me too. Where's Nick? I thought he followed us in.'

'He decided to go for a bit of a tramp,' I explained.

'I expect he needed some fresh air,' George said vaguely, though we had spent most of the day out in the cold.

'If you don't mind, perhaps I won't wait for a drink, I'll

just get off home,' I said. 'There's such a crowd it'll take her ages to come for our orders anyway.'

'Don't you want to wait and we'll drive you back?' asked Annie. 'We won't be long, because Trinny's in the car, and she'll get cold.'

'No, that's all right,' I said, getting up. 'It's five minutes walk and Jasper will be home when I get there. I'll let you know if I hear any more about how Ophelia and the baby are doing.'

On my way out I sneaked a glance at the corner where Nick and Polly were sitting, their heads still together.

'Come on, Mum – obviously he's doing it for a reason,' Jasper said, when I told him about Nick's betrayal – which I did about five seconds after arriving home. It was that or burst.

'I could see that,' I said shortly. Ginny, not liking the tone of my voice, was running her teeth thoughtfully up and down my ankle.

'No, Mum, I meant it must be part of some plan he has – he said he would deal with her, didn't he?'

'Then he's going about it in a strange way! And if you're right, why didn't he tell me what he was going to do?'

'You kept everything a secret from him, didn't you? He found out from Caz and Leila what was going on. I expect if he'd told you, your reaction when you saw them together wouldn't have looked half as authentic. Now she'll think she's putting one over on you.'

'Maybe she is: he wouldn't be the first man unable to see past a pair of pneumatic boobs.'

'Not Uncle Nick,' he said stoutly. 'Really, Mum, you can't possibly believe that – she's a complete dog.'

'Speaking of dogs, Jasper, do you think you could teach yours not to nip my ankles?' I snapped crossly.

'She's just being friendly,' he said fondly, bending down and giving her a pat. 'By the way, Unks rang and told me about the nativity at the *Nativity* – sorry I missed it!'

'Just don't expect a repeat performance on New Year's Day,' I warned him. 'I think we'd all better stick to the script from now on.'

* * *

On Christmas Eve Jasper and I went up to Pharamond Hall to listen to the carol singers, whose first call it traditionally always is.

I drove up in the Morris, since I had my contribution to tomorrow's Christmas dinner with me: a vat of Mulligatawny soup and a large Christmas pudding, and also the family's presents to put under the tree, most of them home-made and edible.

In the past, Mrs Gumball used to do breakfast on Christmas Day and put the goose into the oven, then I would go up and finish the cooking and serve it; but this year Nick, apart from my soup, pudding and brandy butter, was doing it solo. He would have to: after my experience as chef's assistant while cooking the Senior Citizens' dinner, I had no intention of ever becoming his second-in-command again. In fact, despite it being Christmas Eve, I avoided him altogether: every time I looked at him a nasty picture of his and Polly's heads, flirtatiously close together, slid into my mind.

Back home, full of sherry and mince pies, we watched an old film on Jasper's little TV. I wouldn't unwrap the presents we had brought back from the family until next day, because that would spoil the surprise, but I couldn't resist fingering them a bit until Jasper removed them and put them under our little tinsel-covered tree, carefully out of Ginny's reach on top of a carved chest.

We had an orgy of unwrapping next morning while Ginny disembowelled her dog stocking, and although I'm sure we both *thought* of Tom, neither of us mentioned his name.

Then Jasper retired to his room to have a long conversation on his mobile phone with his girlfriend – about whom I still know practically nothing, except that her name is Kelly – while I tidied up the discarded wrapping paper and ribbons.

Jasper always gives everyone the same present every year, and this time it was pens, the kind with liquid inside that you tilt so something moves along, changing the picture. Mine was ingenious – a sarcophagus lid that slid open to reveal a mummy's mask.

Nick's present to me was a postcard album, bound in soft blue leather. He must have noticed my old one was full up to overflowing . . . and he must also intend sending me more, so I expect I was right about him being tired of staying in one place and he will soon be off on his travels again.

Later I put on my new green over-the-top dress (why should all the honours go to Polly?), and we went up to the hall for dinner, which felt like déjà vu after the photo shoot, except we actually got to eat the food this time. Annie and George were there again, but of course Jasper was too this time . . . *and* Ginny, who was sick behind the door from too many titbits, so that was different to last time.

Unk's gift to me had been a ring – something old and valuable looking, which I was sure was a family heirloom. I was wearing it, but as soon as I got the chance for a quiet word, I asked him if he was sure I should have it?

'Yes, my dear, it's quite fitting,' he assured me. 'Don't you like it?'

'Yes, of course – it's lovely! But isn't it a family piece? I'm sure I've seen it in one of the portraits in the gallery.'

'It's the betroth—' began Mimi, suddenly popping up unobserved, but a glance from Unks silenced her, and she wandered off again with a giggle.

'I want you to have it,' he said firmly. 'And I know Nick does too.'

I thanked him, rather doubtfully. The first opportunity I get I mean to go and check the portraits in the gallery and see if I can spot it. And I *must* remember not to wear it when I'm gardening, or it will go the way of my wedding ring: into the earth, never to be seen again.

Tonight there was nothing in my cracker that shouldn't have been there.

Twenty-Five
Lightly Frosted

The sun shines on the godly, they say, and certainly a weak golden light began to spread over the courtyard of

Pharamond Hall on the morning of the Mystery Play, just as I arrived there with Jasper.

The Mosses Women's Institute was setting up the refreshment stand near the kitchen door as usual – the money raised goes to local charities. I handed over my contributions of ginger parkin, rich fruitcake and bags of natural vanilla candyfloss.

Jasper went off to help Caz and Joe Gumball with the myriad last minute jobs: setting out the charcoal braziers, testing the microphone in Unk's little striped tent, from where he would speak as Voice of God, and moving scenery. I stored my Eve costume, wig and fig leaves – which are threaded on to elastic, so they are quick and easy to put on for the *Expulsion* – in one of the loose boxes used for changing rooms: men to the left of the coach house, women to the right.

When I came out again the audience had started to arrive, bearing picnics, folding chairs and rugs, and Jojo and Mick were warming their hands at one of the charcoal braziers. I hadn't thought how depleted the Mummers would be, since Rob was still away basking in the Caribbean and Ophelia, of course, had just given birth; but when I spoke to them they told me that actually Ophelia and the baby were in the kitchen with Mrs Gumball, who would mind the infant while she popped out and performed as usual.

'Is that a good idea?' I asked doubtfully.

'Yeah, she's fine, she wants to do it,' Jojo assured me, but I imagine the poor girl's performance will be even limper than usual.

'Have they decided on a name for the baby yet?'

'Sylvester Star, according to Ophelia,' Mick said, 'but I heard Caz Naylor calling it Sly.'

'That's got to be better than Rambo?' I suggested, and they agreed.

The only toilet was previously the outside staff one behind the stable, but of late Roly has arranged for a portable toilet block to be set up as well, which saves much queuing during the breaks. I sensibly repaired there now, before putting on my Eve costume under my clothes: it would certainly be impossible to go again in that outfit. Makes you wonder how Spiderman and that ilk manage, doesn't it?

The Lycra felt odd under my jeans, but quite warm. I left

my wig hanging on the post outside the stall, together with my fig leaves, and went outside again. The courtyard was now quite full and noisy and the WI ladies were doing a roaring trade in hot drinks. The air was cold and smelled of spices and roasting chestnuts – or, if you suddenly found yourself in the vicinity of Polly Darke and her little circle of friends, as I did, civet cats.

'You've been making candyfloss again, I see,' Nick said, doing his materializing trick right next to me.

'No, it's Hoar Frost – I'm dedicating the recipe to Polly,' I said tartly. 'What is *she* doing here? And why hasn't anyone run her off the premises?'

'Because I invited her specially and told her it just wouldn't be the same without her,' he said, with an enigmatic smile. 'I suppose you feel much the same about Rafferty. Poor Lizzie – didn't he invite you to go to the Caribbean with him?'

I felt myself blush, because actually Rob *had,* though I know he was only flirting, as usual. 'Yes,' I said shortly and ambiguously. 'It's a pity he isn't here for the play,' I added, fingering my sparkling little snowman brooch rather ostentatiously. 'Several of the *Cotton Common* cast members are, though I don't know if they will have the stamina to stay for the whole thing.'

Nick's hand captured mine and he stared at the ring on my finger. 'I didn't get a good look at that last night,' he said thoughtfully. The flat red stone gleamed in the light with restrained opulence in its heavy, antique gold setting.

'I hope you don't mind Unks giving it to me? I suspect it's a family heirloom, but I did ask him if he was *sure* he wanted me to have it.'

'Well, I suppose you could say he's given you the family seal of approval,' he said. 'And look – he's arrived, so we must be about to start. Who's that with him?'

'Delphine Lake – she's in *Cotton Common*, too.'

Pretty as a picture from silver curls to tiny, pointed blue shoes, she had somehow managed to insinuate herself into Roly's royal pavilion – but then, he always did have an eye for an attractive woman. There was just enough room for another folding canvas chair and their heads were close together in earnest conversation.

Clive Potter came out and stood in front of the canvas

curtains, holding up his hands for silence, then welcomed the throng to the Middlemoss Mysteries.

'Let our Mystery Play begin!' he said dramatically, bowed and walked off.

A small silence ensued, then there was a squeak as Nick leaned in and switched on Roly's microphone. His voice could be heard, confiding to Delphine, 'And then blow me if it didn't pick itself up at the fifth, overtake the field and gallop home by a head!'

'*Voice of God!*' Nick whispered urgently.

'Ah, yes – excuse me, my dear . . . *I AM GOD, THE ALL-POWERFUL, ALL-KNOWING*,' he declaimed loudly, then lowering his voice to a more normal level continued, '*Listen to my words – take heed of the mysteries that will unfold before you.*'

The curtain was pulled back to reveal Lucifer and nine angels against a gilded cloudy backdrop and the Mysteries were well and truly up and running. Or *bicycling*, as would be the case for Mary and Joseph's journey to Bethlehem and subsequent flight into Egypt.

Various interesting noise effects accompanied God's description of creation, which I could hear as I shrugged off my clothes in the changing room and concealed as much of myself as possible with the long, blonde wig.

Then we were on.

If you have ever tried to remember your lines while inches away from a tall and attractive man dressed in little more than ballet tights, you will understand why I found it hard to keep my eyes on the apple. He was carrying a small sheaf of hay, which may have preserved his modesty from the audience, but was not much help to me. I expect ballerinas quickly get blasé about this kind of thing.

Of course, it might have helped if he'd stuck to the text, like he did at the dress rehearsal, instead of soulfully telling the audience in the most *hammy* way, when I offered him the apple, that I'd had his heart and he didn't think a piece of fruit was much of an exchange.

I was tempted to elope with the snake.

Then he took a bite, tossed it over his shoulder into the wings, and led me offstage to assume our fig leaves.

'Nice costume,' he said, casting away his sheaf of hay and

adjusting his fig leaves like a hula skirt. The effect was interesting. 'Need any help with yours?'

'No, thanks,' I said primly. Whoever plays Eve next year will need new elastic: the twang has quite gone out of mine.

We quickly took our places behind the painted bushes and the Voice of God demanded why we had eaten the forbidden fruit? I only wished I knew.

'*The woman tempted me*,' Nick said, passing the buck, just as men have done from time immemorial, and we were expelled from Eden.

The curtain came down and the Mummers began to play something lilting while the scene was changed from Eden to Noah's ark.

Nick dashed off for his changing room and I headed for my own warm outfit, shivering. I quickly changed and then went out into the courtyard through the back doorway, avoiding the scurrying animal-headed infants and a harassed-looking Miss Pym.

Nick was already in the courtyard, talking to Polly. I elected to watch *Noah's Flood* from the other side, with Annie and George.

'What's Polly doing here?' Annie whispered to me worriedly, when George had kindly gone to get me a hot drink. I was still freezing. 'And why is Nick chatting to her like that, and laughing and . . . well, *flirting*?'

'Search me,' I said shortly. 'He said he invited her, so perhaps he's fallen prey to her fatal beauty.'

'No, he was flirting with *you* in the Adam and Eve scene, Lizzie – he couldn't take his eyes off you! He must have an ulterior motive.'

'That's what Jasper says,' I agreed grudgingly. 'But I think he seems to be enjoying himself too much.'

The curtains closed on Noah's ark and the animals and there was another short break before a tetchy-looking Moses was seen on the mountain.

God ran briskly down his list of Ten Commandments while Moses hobbled about collecting the tablets of stone up in his tea towel headscarf.

'*Do thou understand my commandments?*'

'*Yea, Lord,*' Moses said obediently, though with an evil look in his rheumy blue eyes. '*I'm not deaf, tha knows! I'm going back down t'mountain as fast as me legs can carry me, and I'll be straight on t'case. Idol worshipping and other ungodly goings-on will be reet out t'window.*'

'*Good, good – for I see everything, you know, I am omnipresent*,' God added, conversationally.

Then the mike squeaked and his voice suddenly boomed: '*FOR INSTANCE, POLLY DARKE, I KNOW WHAT YOU DID LAST SUMMER! I KNOW IT WAS YOU WHO LOOSENED THE WHEEL NUTS ON LIZZIE PHARAMOND'S CAR*.'

Everyone, including me and a slightly flummoxed Moses, turned to stare at Polly Darke. Nick let go of her arm and stepped away, but I could see from his face that this was no surprise: God's accusation was prearranged.

She found herself the centre of a staring, whispering circle of shocked faces: even her friends were wide-eyed.

'*Polly* did?' I exclaimed. 'But—'

'No – no I didn't!' Polly yelped, looking from face to face for some sympathy. 'Why on earth would I do that?'

'Because you expected Lizzie to drive the car, not Tom,' Nick said clearly and coldly. 'It was just one of a series of little spiteful accidents you arranged for her, because you were eaten up with jealousy.'

'No! No I didn't – I haven't—'

'Good heavens! Surely she wouldn't do something so evil?' gasped Annie, shocked, and George put his arm around her. I wished someone would put their arm around me: I was shaking even more now, and not from the cold.

PC Perkins stepped out of the shadows and said clearly: 'Polly Darke, you are under arrest . . .' and proceeded to give her the official warning.

Polly stared around like a hunted animal, but there was no escape: I could see the flashing light of a police car beyond the archway and other officers. Then her eyes fixed on me: 'It was her – her!' she cried. 'I've said so all along . . . you've no proof!'

'*It was not!*' said God. '*And there was a witness to your wrongdoing*.'

'That's right,' Caz agreed loudly from the shadows. 'I seen her doing it.'

'*EVIL WOMAN, BEGONE!*' God added. I think the excitement of the moment had quite rushed to his head.

There was a buzz of excitement as she was escorted out and we all listened until the scrunch of gravel under tyres vanished into the distance. Nick was speaking to Caz – and suddenly I realized who had hidden and then revealed the wheel brace . . . and with Polly's fingerprints on it. My mind raced . . . surely Polly wouldn't have had the strength? But then I remembered what Rob had said about her working out – and really, anyone can change a wheel with one of those cross brace things, it's not that difficult.

A wheel on *my* car. It was *me* she wanted to hurt, not Tom. Not kill . . . none of her little tricks had been intended to kill; though I suppose she would have looked on my death as a bonus.

And in the end Caz had told Nick everything, and they had set this very public accounting up – as revenge? I wondered whether Polly would be charged with anything serious.

The courtyard was still buzzing, but then Moses suddenly awoke as if from a trance, and banged his shepherd's crook on the floor a couple of times to regain the audience's attention.

Slowly they quietened and turned back to the stage.

'*If that's all, Lord, I'll be getting off, then*,' Moses said, back to the script.

'*Aye, go with my blessing upon you*,' God said, suddenly sounding tired, and invisible hands began to draw the canvas curtains across the front of the arched doorway. 'A hot rum toddy, that's what I need,' Roly added, forgetting to switch off the microphone. 'Delphine, my dear, you'll join me, won't you? There's a short break before the *Nativity* for refreshments, and I'm sure we all need them.'

Jojo and Mick picked up their instruments and began to play and Ophelia, looking harassed and frightened, ran out of the house, fiddle in hand.

Nick forged his way through the crowd and handed me a plastic tumbler of hot toddy, which I took automatically and drained in one: I needed it. 'Well,' he said thoughtfully. 'I don't know *how* we'll be able to follow that next year.'

I turned on him accusingly. 'You *knew* that was going to happen – you, Caz and Uncle Roly set that up. How long have you known it was Polly who sabotaged the car?'

'Not long at all – I thought *that*, at least, was an accident, until Caz told me what he'd seen. He'd been watching from the woods that day and saw Polly come out of Tom's workshop and look at the car, then pick up the wheel brace (which Jasper must have left leaning against the wall, by the way) and start unscrewing the nuts – by sheer coincidence on the same wheel you'd changed earlier. Then she put the wheel brace back where she found it and left. Caz was going to go down and see what she'd been up to when the coast was clear, but Tom drove off in your car before he had a chance to. Caz wrapped the wheel brace in sacking and put it behind the freezer you let him use.'

'Why? And why didn't he say anything?'

He shrugged. 'Well, you know Caz. And he said he thought at first it was something to do with ARG! and he didn't want to get Ophelia into trouble. It was before he knew that Polly wasn't a member of the group, just forcing Ophelia to target you.'

'He's not keen on the police anyway. But he confided in *you*.'

'Yes, he finally told me the whole thing, because he was angry that Polly was prepared to harm Ophelia even when she was pregnant. I spoke to the police and they are going to forget that Ophelia was ever a member of ARG! in return for Caz's statement.'

He seemed to feel this was worthy of praise, for he paused expectantly.

'Oh, well done, Nick!' Annie exclaimed. 'You are clever!'

I gave her a withering look. 'I think you might have let me in on what was happening, Nick!'

'Why? You didn't tell *me* anything – I found it all out for myself.'

'Yes, but Lizzie was upset when you were flirting with Polly, Nick,' Annie said traitorously.

'No I was not!' I exclaimed indignantly. 'I—'

'Ssh . . . afterwards,' Nick said, a gleam in his slatey dark eyes. 'They're starting again.'

I gave him a glare and moved away, avoiding him for the rest of the entertainment, which isn't easy when you are enclosed in a courtyard. I can't say my mind was completely on the play – or even on the refreshments – which just goes to show how churned up and confused I felt.

But eventually I began to be caught up in the Mysteries again, just as I was every year.

Kylie was a subdued and modest Mary, only wisps of violently pink hair escaping from her hooded robe and her fingernails unpainted. The huge rock that sparkled in the muted light on her engagement finger was not quite in role, though: Kylie had got her soldier.

Twenty-Six
Well Stirred

'*Here is my judgement, and t'pure of heart need fear nowt,*' said Roly as the Voice of God, speeding up now the finishing post was in sight.

'*What is thy wish, Lord?*' asked an angel, the one with glistening white goose-feather wings.

'*That retribution shall visit t'wrongdoers.*'

'*Lord, it shall be done.*'

'*Let it be so, for as the old year dies, another, Lazarus-like, rises anew. Our play is played out, our Mysteries unfolded,*' said God.

The angel, who had been gazing vaguely up into the rafters, now turned to look directly at the audience and said weightily: '*Look into t'mirror of thy heart and, if thou like not what thou see, then freshly start again, fer Christ died fer thee.*'

God, as always, got the last line. '*Heed my commandments. Keep thy conscience clear. Remember, I'll see thee agin, this time next year!*'

Well, going by the wild applause it was certainly another Middlemoss Mystery success, but more than one mystery had been enacted, revealed and resolved tonight. It had been a cathartic and exhausting experience and the audience was subdued as they slowly began to leave.

I felt like a well-wrung-out dishrag.

'Me, George and everyone else involved in organizing the play has been invited in for a hot toddy before we go home,' Annie said, taking my arm and giving it a squeeze. 'You're coming too, aren't you, Lizzie? Look, there's Jasper going in. And I want to know all the details about Polly, too – did you really not know *any* of that was going to happen?'

'No, of course I didn't!' I snapped, finding myself being swept through the kitchen and along the passage to the great hall, where the steaming silver punch bowl and a tray of sandwiches were laid out before a blazing log fire.

Roly beckoned me across to where he was sitting with Delphine. 'Well, my dear,' he said, 'that seems to have worked out for the best, doesn't it? Justice has been served, and everything is sorted out satisfactorily.'

'Is it?' I said, slightly sourly.

'You were very good as Eve,' Delphine said kindly. 'Quite beautiful in that costume.'

'Yes, you're much better with Nick as Adam,' agreed Roly.

'That was Lizzie's last turn in the role, wasn't it?' Nick said, having come up behind me unobserved. 'I'm not playing Adam to anyone else's Eve.'

Roly looked from one to the other of us and, beaming, took our hands and clasped them together in his. Theatricality also runs in the Pharamond bloodline. 'Let it be a New Year, a new beginning for both of you!' he said sentimentally.

'I don't know *what* you mean, Unks,' I said, trying and failing to loosen my hand from Nick's strong grip. 'And I'm afraid I'll have to be going home now. Jasper?'

'I'm going out again, to help clear up,' Jasper said quickly. 'I'll see you later.'

'I'll walk you home, Lizzie,' Nick said, 'but first there's something I want to show you.'

I couldn't imagine *what* he'd got that I hadn't already seen. But I let him lead me upstairs to the long gallery, switching on the wall lights as we went. He came to a stop in front of the portrait of an eighteenth-century Pharamond bride, who posed with one slender hand resting on a book – and on her finger, my ring. I *knew* it was an old family piece.

'There – you see?' he said.

'Nick, I can't possibly keep a family heirloom, whatever Unks says – please take it back!' I protested, tugging it off my finger and handing it to him. He accepted it, then calmly took hold of my left hand and shoved it over the knuckle of my ring finger instead.

'What on earth are you doing?' I said, trying to pull away.

'It's the betrothal ring of the Pharamonds.'

'I daresay it is, but we're not betrothed—'

'I think we are and Unks thinks we are – so you're outnumbered. Just as well he wouldn't let Leila have the ring, because I'd never have got it back.'

I glared at him. 'This isn't the Middle Ages, so I do have a say in all this, Nick Pharamond – and I'm not engaged to you! You are an underhand, devious—'

'Yes, I know,' he said soothingly, pulling me close. 'But I do love you. I think, deep down, I always did.'

'You have a damned strange way of showing it!'

'There wasn't much point when we were both married to other people, but the postcards showed I was always thinking of you. I never wanted to quite let go of you. *And* you kept them all.'

'Only for the recipes,' I said quickly, fighting a rear-guard action, for close proximity was starting to scramble my brain cells and weaken my knees. 'Besides, we argue all the time and you despise my cooking!'

'No I don't, I just like to wind you up. You should know that by now.'

'Yes, but you think *your* cooking is more important than I am!'

He grinned. 'No, I think it's a pretty even match, actually. I don't see why I can't have my cake and eat it.'

'I do. And anyway, we're just too different – it'd never work,' I said firmly, then ruined the effect by smiling back at him.

'If mayonnaise works, I don't see why mixing the two of *us* together shouldn't – if we do it *slowly* and very carefully.' His lips moved over my face and then lingered on my mouth before I could point out that curdled mayonnaise was a lot easier to rescue than a curdled marriage.

Oh, hot chilli chocolate! I thought, but more in resignation than revolt. *He* was the one who broke that clinch: I couldn't have, even if you'd waved a giant Mars bar in front of me.

'And I've had a great idea! Once you've finished *Just Desserts*, we'll collaborate on a joint recipe book of all the postcards. We'll call it *A Feast of Romance*,' he added soulfully.

I laughed. Sally was going to absolutely *love* it – and him. 'That is a totally corny idea! And what's more, I'm not cooking anything with you, because I always end up doing all the donkey wo—'

I stopped dead as I spotted Caz silently slinking out of the dark shadows at the end of the gallery. He jerked his head back at the stairs: 'Mr Roly says t'champagne's open – you two done, yet?'

'Rising nicely,' Nick said.

'Half-baked!' I amended, giving him a quelling look. 'Caz, tell him we'll be down in a minute. And perhaps you ought to cork up the champagne again, because there are just a *few* rules of engagement I need to thrash out first, before I even *consider* this insane idea.'

'Like what?' Nick asked suspiciously.

'Separate kitchens,' I said, smiling sweetly. 'And that's just for starters!'